Kim -
Thanks ... support: Encouragement - Enjoy!
Recita

THE TRICKSTER

ALSO BY R. LANIER CLEMONS

JONELLE SWEET MYSTERY SERIES

Burial Plot

Gone Missing

Visit the author's website at www.rlanierclemons.com

The Trickster is a work of fiction. Names, characters, places and incidents are the products of the author's imagination or are used fictitiously. Any resemblance to actual events, locales, or persons, living or dead, is entirely coincidental.

ISBN: 978-0-9967554-2-9 (Ebook)
ISBN: 978-0-9967554-3-6 (Paperback)

THE TRICKSTER

BY

R. LANIER CLEMONS

CHAPTER 1

Small and disheveled, he limped along on the other side of the street. He stayed several feet behind, tracking her movements. She dodged prostitutes and drug dealers, head held high and holding something tight to her chest. Still, he followed.

From a distance, the dark face and hands might have been the product of years of living on the streets of Baltimore, rather than a testament to his race. His small, close-set eyes trailed the blond as she stopped next to an alley between a liquor store and gated carry-out. She glanced left and right, turned, and retraced her steps. A few feet farther on she stopped. He hoped she was headed back to the warehouse. Instead she squared her shoulders, reversed direction and walked back to the alley. This time, she entered.

Puzzled, he resisted the temptation to follow. She'd already yelled at him earlier when he tried telling her it wasn't safe for a woman like her to walk the streets alone; people might get the wrong idea. She'd laughed and told him to mind his own damn business.

But he couldn't.

So he waited for her to come out of the alley. And waited. Was there another way out of there? The liquor he'd consumed earlier begged for release. He glanced around, stepped between a bus kiosk and dented trash bin and sniffed. He snorted; he wasn't the first. After relieving himself he crossed the street, skirting cars along the way and flipping a few the one-fingered salute as drivers honked and yelled obscenities.

Intent on following and not paying attention to everything around him, he bumped into a prostitute.

"Hey," she yelled. "Get your smelly ass off me."

"This smelly ass don't want nuthin' to do with somethin' what look like you." In spite of the heavy makeup, massive lines and sags broke through the powder.

"Ain't you a little bit old to be doin' this? Ain't nobody gonna spend any hard earned money on the likes 'a you."

"Ooo. My, my. You must be one 'a them *uptown* bums, huh? Whatsamatter? You got extra cash in your pocket and wanna spend some?" Her bright read lips parted showing a mass of empty spaces.

He waved the woman off, ignoring her loud cackling and headed to where he last saw the blond. Not caring if she got pissed or not he ducked in the alley.

Overhead, a security light buzzed off and on. The strobe effect bothered his eyes and distorted his vision. The man walked-hopped deeper into the passageway. Rats *squeaked* all around him and the smell of rotted food assaulted his nostrils. Where the hell did she go? He looked mid-way down and got his answer.

The woman lay face up on the ground next to a Dumpster, her throat cut so deep the head nearly separated from the body. A bloody cardigan covered the top half of her torso. The dress she wore, now hiked up to her waist, was so filthy the original pattern and color were a mystery. Athletic shoes, torn and without laces, remained on her feet. The pulsating light revealed a stark white substance which stained her face from forehead to chin. Black paint smeared the area around the eyes and mouth, invoking the image of a sad panda bear. Part of a paper bill, denomination unknown, protruded from her mouth.

The homeless man wailed in agony and tried in vain to shoo the flies swarming over the body.

When the police took him into custody, they found a private investigator's business card in his possession. The next day, at the police station, Detective Thelonius Burton stood in front of Jonelle Sweet and wondered how and why.

"For the second time Burt, I have no idea," Jonelle said. "If you'd just let me see the man I might be able to answer your questions."

Burt rubbed thick hands over his dark, round face. Bloodshot eyes stared unblinking at Jonelle. "Problem is we're not having any luck calming him down. He came in two hours ago, screaming and tearing at his clothes. We finally got restraints on him, but he won't stop yelling. Since we found your card, my hope is you could tell us a little about him."

Jonelle thought back. Last year, on one of the first cases assigned to her by her uncle's agency, she came in contact with a homeless man. He'd helped save the life of the subject of her investigation. She wondered if this was that same man.

"Is his name Luther? Did you get that much out of him?"

Burt shook his head. "Didn't get anything out of him. Once we fumigate the bag we found on him we may find some kinda ID. Hell, we don't even know who the victim is at this point. All we have is part of a one hundred dollar bill found stuffed in her mouth and a piece of paper with four letters and a bunch of numbers pinned inside the dress. What they mean, well, we were hoping this guy could tell us. As it stands, he's not cooperating."

Unless Luther lost the card she gave him, which was a possibility, she was pretty sure he was the man the police had in custody. Jonelle touched the gold, mini handcuff and pistol necklace she always wore. She paced in front of Burt's cubicle, a carbon copy of all the other ones in the division, and remembered the case. The police had searched for but never found Luther who'd provided shelter for the victim. That attempted murder case, resolved to everyone's satisfaction, ended with the perpetrator behind bars. She did not believe that the man who had kept a total stranger alive then was the same one who could take another person's life now. Yet, her instincts had been wrong before.

"Tell you what," Jonelle said, stopping in front of Burt, "why don't you let me see him? If it's who I think it is, he may calm down. He knows I'll listen to whatever he has to say without judgement."

Burt frowned. "Is this that same bum—?"

"Homeless people are not *'bums'*. They are homeless for a variety of reasons. Illness, joblessness, handicap …"

Burt held up his hands. "Okay, okay. I got it." He smiled at her. "Boy, you don't give up that soapbox of yours."

Hands on her hips, Jonelle tried hard not to smile back. "Just let me see him."

Burt motioned for her to follow. He led her out of the Criminal Investigations division and down a long hallway. The corridor ended at a heavy door. "It's easier to take the steps instead of waiting for the elevator," he said.

After walking down two flights, Burt opened the door and Jonelle found herself in an area with gray walls and without windows. "You okay down here?" Burt asked. He knew about Jonelle's claustrophobia.

"Yes," she said, sounding more confident than she felt.

The basement area was where suspects were photographed, fingerprinted and placed in holding cells. Jonelle concentrated on her breathing and tried not to dwell on how close everything seemed. "Lead the way."

Burt turned right and then made a quick left down a short hall. Raised voices sounded in the distance. Her heart sank. If that was Luther, she may have more problems with him than she thought.

They faced another door where Burt punched in a code. Loud screams and obscenities filled the air as they entered. A large, red-faced policeman sat behind a desk. "Why can't we just leave this bastard alone in here? Sorry lady, but I've about had it with this dude. Plus, he stinks to high heaven."

"Let me outta here, you motherfuckers," the disheveled man screamed. "You got no right, you got no right."

"Gotta make sure he doesn't hurt himself. Go ahead and take ten, Jake. We're gonna see if he recognizes Jonelle." The cop nearly ran over her in his haste to get out.

The man in the cell sat handcuffed and shackled. He rocked back and forth on the cot, eyes closed. His matted hair, more gray than black, was twisted in front as though he tried to make dreadlocks but gave up halfway through the process. Black dirt caked the already black skin.

"Luther! Stop it! Now!"

He stopped screaming. His brow knitted. He opened one eye then shut it again.

She took a few steps toward the cell.

"Careful," Burt said, his hand ready to grab Jonelle's arm. "They've been known to spit."

Jonelle dismissed the comment with a wave of her hand. "Luther," she said quietly. "It's Jonelle. Remember me? We met last year. I gave you my card. Remember?"

Luther moaned and continued rocking.

Jonelle turned toward Burt. "Could you leave me alone with him for a few minutes? He might open up if you weren't standing there."

Hands shoved deep in his pockets, Burt looked first at Jonelle, then at Luther. With eyebrows pressed close together and mouth pursed in a tight line, Jonelle could tell Burt didn't like the idea.

"Listen," she said, gesturing at the man behind bars. "What's he gonna do? You've got more hardware on him than Dunkin's got donuts. Go. Leave us alone for a while."

Burt frowned. He pointed a finger at the man still rocking and moaning. "If he looks like he's about to try something, don't play hero. Come get me. I'll be right outside the door."

Jonelle waited until she heard the door close behind her before talking to Luther again.

"Luther, I remember how much you helped me last year. Well, now I want to return the favor. But I need you to talk to me. I know you didn't do it. The man I met couldn't do anything like what happened to that woman. Will you at least let me help you?"

Luther continued rocking. His moans quieted. A few seconds later he mumbled something.

Jonelle stepped closer to the cell. "What was that? I didn't understand."

Luther stopped swaying. He looked up with watery eyes. Tiny tracks of dried tears snaked through the dirt on his face, leading from his eyes to his chin.

It broke Jonelle's heart to see him in despair. "I'm going to get you through this, but you need to do something for me. Okay?"

Luther stared at Jonelle. His mouth opened and closed but no sound came out. He slowly nodded.

"Good. The main thing is, you need to calm down. No yelling, no screaming, and no spitting. Got that?"

Another weak nod.

"I'm going to try and convince detective Burton to take off the cuffs and shackles. Also, you need to clean yourself up a bit. They're going to take you to the courthouse. Put on the uniform they give you and don't fight them about it. You'll have to stay there until you're released."

Luther frowned and shook his head. "No, no, no," he shouted. He started rocking again.

Jonelle walked over to the desk on the opposite wall, took the notebook that was lying there and slammed it against the surface. Luther jumped. His eyes widened as he stared open-mouthed at Jonelle.

"Now that I have your attention, this is how this is going to work. First, you can stop that crazy act with me. I know you're smarter than you let on." She approached him again. "Second, my agency works with a lot of lawyers so I'll find you someone decent to get you released. Don't answer any questions or make any statements until the lawyer meets with you. I'll bring you some clean clothes to wear when they let you go. Got that?"

"Yeah. I gots it," he said. "What about my own clothes? What'll those bastards do with my clothes?" He pouted like a little child.

Jonelle hoped the police wouldn't burn them but couldn't blame them if they did. "I'll check with Burt on my way out. I'm sure they'll take care of all your possessions."

Until she could get more information about what happened, Jonelle figured jail was probably the safest place for him right now. "Third, and this is just between you and me. How well did you know the woman who was killed?"

Luther's eyes focused on a spot above Jonelle's head. She turned and looked up at a video camera bolted to the ceiling.

"Ah," Jonelle said. She'd forgotten about the automated eyes. She used her body to block Luther from the camera's lens.

"Right," Luther said. He turned sideways and lowered his voice to a whisper. "You go back where we met the firs' time. Tell who you see that you and me is frien's and you need to speak to Chester. You tell 'em about me helpin' that girl las' year. That should convince 'em. If they believe you, they'll go git Chester and he'll tell you what he knows. If they don't believe you,"—Luther shrugged—"they won't."

"What does Chester look like?"

Luther frowned at Jonelle. "Now who's suppose 'ta be smart, huh? He looks jus' like every other homeless man that walks around that's white. Raggedy. Dirty. Pitiful. You jus' go do what I tole you."

Luther winked. He shuffled over and sat on the edge of the bed. He did not sway and he did not yell. A look passed between him and Jonelle.

CHAPTER 2

On the drive over to her office at Shorter Investigative Services, Inc., Jonelle pondered how to approach her uncle and owner of the firm about Luther's predicament. Marvin Shorter was a businessman through and through. She knew he wouldn't appreciate the company taking on a case where payment was sketchy right from the beginning.

Jonelle pulled up to the booth of the small lot a block and a half beyond the low rise building where she worked. She took the ticket from the attendant who wished her a good morning, drove up two rows and made a left down the last aisle. She eased her Jeep into a spot marked "Res. Shorter Inves. Svcs." Everyone was thrilled when they learned the city agreed to build the open lot on wasted abandoned space. By pulling strings and calling in favors, Marvin managed to wrangle assigned spaces for him and the rest of the staff. She noticed two other empty spots, and if history was any judge, it meant Omar Kamal and Ben Winfield weren't in yet.

Jonelle grabbed her purse and briefcase, locked her Jeep and hurried to work. Instead of rushing, head down past the panhandler standing at his usual spot on the corner the way she normally did, she reached in her purse and gave him a dollar.

"Thanks," he said.

"Welcome." What she wanted to add but didn't was, *and you can thank Luther for my attitude change.*

Jonelle punched in the security code, opened the building's glass doors and entered a small carpeted foyer. Two large plants in maroon ceramic containers stood on opposite sides against the wall. On either side of the narrow hallway, closed office doors announced CPA's, a family practice and something else in Korean. She ignored the elevator and instead walked to the end of the hall where a closed metal door blocked her way.

She used her back against the bar, turned and hurried up the stairs, her pale yellow Mary Janes clicking on each step. She pulled open the heavy door marked "2" and entered. More office doors lined both sides of the hall. Straight ahead, a set of wooden double doors greeted her at the end of the corridor, the firm's name spelled out in raised brass letters. She let herself in.

Rainey Gottzchek looked up from her computer, now resting on a sleek mahogany desk instead of the old gray, metal one. "There you are," Rainey said. "Marvin's got a few surveillance cases he needs you to work on. I didn't see anything else on your schedule, so he went ahead and made the preliminaries. Hold on a sec and I'll print out the sheets for you." The receptionist tapped a few keys and the printer against the left wall came to life. Rainey started to rise. Jonelle waved her back down.

"I'll get it," Jonelle said, taking the papers off the printer. She scanned the words and her heart sank. "Do you know if Marvin's busy? I'd like to talk to him about something."

"Go on back. He only got here twenty minutes ago."

Jonelle walked through the open entrance behind Rainey and slipped past her former office, now reassigned to its rightful place as storage closet. The next door marked "J. Sweet," with "Investigator" directly below, still gave her chills.

The remodeling completed late last year had expanded the agency's existing space by fifty percent. Business was great and Jonelle wondered why her uncle still gave her the grunt work.

Surveillance meant sitting still all day and sometimes night, watching people and getting a sore butt. It was as boring as watching the "next number" board at the DMV.

Jonelle dropped her purse on the client chair and wandered over to the window. In consideration of her claustrophobia, Marvin gave Jonelle the option of a smaller space with a larger window, or a larger space with a small window looking out onto the alley. She chose the small space, large window office that provided a view of the city. On a clear day like today, the Johns Hopkins Hospital complex, identifiable by the curved glass façade and the glass enclosed walkway, glittered in the sunshine. The elevated walkway loomed over Orleans Street and connected the parking garage to the hospital and sprawling medical campus.

She scowled at the sheets in her hand. The only way to find out why her only assignments were two surveillance jobs was to ask why. She took a deep breath and went to find Marvin.

He still occupied the largest corner space with the same furnishings. Rainey tried to convince him to at least agree to adding an en-suite bathroom, but he objected saying he could go down the hall just like everybody else. Since Marvin believed in open door management, Jonelle knocked on the frame.

He looked up from a printout he was reading and smiled at her. "Come on in."

"Hope I'm not disturbing you," she said. Before she sat down across from him, she put the papers on his desk and circled his office, inserting an index finger in each of the three potted plants that decorated his space. She heard his theatrical sigh behind her. "In order to get me to quit doing this, you should really try to stop killing your plants. All it takes is a little water." She looked at her finger. "They feel okay, so I guess they'll survive another day." She pulled a tissue from the box on his desk and wiped her finger.

"You finished playing plant police?"

"For now." Jonelle sat, picked up the papers and took a deep breath. "See, thing is I thought that when I completed my first two cases, you'd realize I could handle investigative work."

Marvin leaned back in his chair. "Of course you can. You're a regular member of the staff now, you know that."

"Then why do I continue getting the surveillance jobs? I thought you'd give me more interesting assignments. Even background checks are more appealing than this." She fluttered the papers in the air.

Silence filled the office. Marvin's eyes bored into his nieces'. He remained quiet so long Jonelle played with her gold handcuff and pistol necklace, a gift from the man sitting on the other side of the desk.

"How long have you worked here?" he asked.

Her stomach lurched. "Um, a little over a year."

"Right. And out of the three investigators I have, which one of you has the least seniority?"

So that's where this was going. "I do. I also know that Omar and Ben get the most complicated cases. I just think that when it comes to the surveillance work, well, it would be nice to maybe spread it around a bit. Those guys may be here forever, so that means I'll always be low man on the totem pole."

Marvin raised an eyebrow. He looked at Jonelle for a few seconds, then glanced down at the printouts. "These sheets represent all the work we're doing," he said, tapping a finger on the papers spread over his desk. Marvin pressed his lips together. "The reason we're doing as well as we are, is because I assign and approve work to the agent I feel could do the best job."

"I'm not disputing that, but I just thought—"

"Let me finish," Marvin said with a sharp edge in his voice.

Jonelle sat back in her chair, hands clasped tight in her lap.

"When surveillance jobs come in, and my most experienced agents are busy doing other work, those jobs will fall to you. If you have a problem with that, then perhaps this agency isn't a good fit for you."

Jonelle's eyes widened in shock. "I love it here," she said.

"And I love having you here. But I can't have one of my employees questioning the work they're given." His voice softened. "Outside of this office, you're more than my niece; you're like a daughter to me. But in here, you're a member of the staff and you're treated as such."

Jonelle felt like a schoolgirl chastised by the principal for cheating on a test. "I understand." She picked up the papers and stood.

"Are we good?" Marvin asked. He winked at her.

Jonelle smiled. "Always." She paused a moment. "Um, maybe this isn't a good time, but remember me telling you about Luther?"

"Is that the homeless guy that helped you last year?"

"Right. He's in trouble and needs help. I thought I could, uh, handle the case for him."

The lines between Marvin's brows deepened. "Since he's not able to pay you, the agency can't afford to take him on as a client."

She sat back down, and folded her arms on his desk. "Hear me out on this. I'd like to ask one of our lawyer clients if they do pro bono work. If so, would you object if I asked them to look at Luther's case and see if they can get him out of jail? I think they're holding him because he found the body."

"I don't have a problem with that as long as it doesn't affect your work for the agency." Marvin picked up the printouts, a signal to Jonelle that the meeting was over. She ignored the gesture. As she watched him reading, an idea occurred to her. "Has the agency ever done any work, you know, *gratis*?"

"I cannot believe you," Marvin said, looking up from the sheets, a slight smile on his lips. "Maybe once or twice."

"Good. So, how do I go about assigning myself that type of case? I know I can find the time, you know, in-between my stimulating surveillance jobs."

Marvin ignored the sarcasm and studied his niece. "This is a police matter. There's not much the agency can do anyway."

"I know. I want to make sure Luther isn't railroaded into taking the rap for something he didn't do."

"How do you know he didn't?"

"Because he's not that kind of person. Burt, detective Burton that is, said he was inconsolable when they discovered him over the victim's body."

Marvin's eyes narrowed. Neither said anything for several seconds. Marvin shrugged and broke the silence first. "Tell Rainey to open a special case file. She'll know to assign a distinct number so we don't include it on the profit and loss spreadsheets." He pointed to the door. "Now go. Get outta here before I change my mind."

Jonelle grabbed her papers. "You're the best."

"Out!" he said, pointing to the doorway.

She heard him chuckle as she left his office.

After giving Rainey the information needed to open Luther's case, Jonelle sat at her desk and pulled up her contacts list. The first three lawyers she phoned said they'd already done their pro bono work for the year. The fourth firm she called agreed to look into the case. She gave them Thelonius Burton as the lead detective. Jonelle didn't know if Luther was still using the last name St. Vincent or if he told the police something different. When Jonelle first met Luther he'd taken the St. Vincent surname off of posters found in the abandoned warehouse where he camped out at night.

Jonelle grabbed her cellphone and some money out of her purse. After a quick wave and "I'll be back soon," to Rainey,

Jonelle left her office building, intent on speaking to the panhandler on the corner.

He looked up and smiled as she approached.

Jonelle smiled back. "Hi. Do you mind if I ask you a question?" She took a dollar bill out of her pocket and handed it to him.

Unfocused eyes squinted at her. "What kinda question?" He shoved the money in his pants.

"You ever hear of a guy named Luther?" Jonelle watched his reaction. She noticed a slight flicker in his eyes as she said the name.

"Not sure," he mumbled.

"What about Chester? Do you know a Chester?"

The man shrugged. "Lotsa people got that name."

Jonelle grabbed a five dollar bill from her pants pocket. "From what I understand, Luther and Chester are friends. They probably work the same area together. You look like a smart guy. This is for you if your memory changes."

He stared at the money, mouth open.

"I have to find Chester because Luther needs his help."

"I knows where he usually is about now." He snatched the money out of Jonelle's hand, turned and started walking.

Jonelle followed, hoping her investment would pay off.

CHAPTER 3

After walking a few steps behind the man for several long blocks, Jonelle wondered if he was leading her on a wild goose chase. She decided to continue on until she either got tired of following him or he got tired of her shadowing him, whichever came first.

At the intersection of Wolfe and Monument he stopped. Jonelle moved up beside him. In front of them, seemingly endless construction work left part of the street torn up. At the stop light on the next corner, two white men dressed in worn jeans and red-checkered flannel shirts stood talking. As she watched, one handed a cigarette to the other, who put his cardboard sign under his arm, nodded and walked off. Both seemed oblivious to the traffic flowing around them.

"Are either one of those men Chester?" she asked, raising her voice in order to be heard over all the noise.

"Naw. But I seen him talkin' to that one sometimes." He nodded to the man who remained on the corner. "He prob'ly could tell you where Chester is. I can't get too close. He gets funny if he thinks you want his spot." He looked at Jonelle. "You on your own here lady." With that last comment, he turned and ambled off back the way they came.

For a moment Jonelle considered calling out to the man's retreating back and asking his name, then realized it didn't matter. She knew anonymity was the norm in his world. She took a deep breath and approached the guy on the corner, now looking in her direction. On a piece of cardboard propped against a beat up cooler, a hand printed sign read, "Homeless vet. Please help." Next to it was a coffee can half full of bills.

Before she could say anything, he pointed at her. "You a cop?"

Jonelle groaned inwardly. For all her efforts made in the past to join the police force, it seemed the one thing she already had going for her was "the look."

"No, I'm not a cop. I'm a private investigator trying to help a man named Luther. He's been arrested as a person of interest in a crime. Maybe you heard about it. Woman found behind a Dumpster with her throat cut?"

He continued staring at her. A car stopped at the light caught his attention. The driver held his hand out the window, waving a paper bill in his hand. He hurried over. "Thanks, man" he said, grabbing the money.

Up until now, Jonelle hadn't felt threatened by the people who lived on the street. This guy was different. He radiated danger. The body beneath his clothes looked hard and fit, almost healthy considering his lifestyle. Tattoos covered both arms. It was as if he'd just gotten out of prison where the only thing he did was exercise all day, every day.

"What you lookin' at lady? You standin' there 'cause you think I'm hot and you want some 'a this?" He grabbed his privates and sneered at her.

Jonelle's face burned. "I'm waiting for you to answer my questions. Do you know Luther? Chester? Do you know anything about the woman killed not far from here?" She held his gaze when what she really wanted to do was run away from this Neanderthal. "Luther helped me with a case last year, so I want to do what I can to help him."

Cold, hard eyes stared back. "Yeah. Heard about ole Luther savin' some queer's life. You was involved in that huh?"

Jonelle bristled at the slur. "You know what? I don't need your help. You're an ass and you give the homeless people a bad name. Forget it. I'll find Chester another way." She turned around and started walking.

"Hey, you," he called out.

Jonelle stopped and turned around, straightening her spine against the insult she knew he was about to hurl in her direction.

"Check Pratt Street. Near the harbor." He laughed and gave her a mock salute.

"Jerk," she mumbled. She felt the money in her pocket and decided to hop a bus to the inner harbor rather than going back to the office and getting her Jeep. Trying to find a place to park near the harbor was a nightmare.

A low rumble behind her sounded as a bus came into view. She jogged the few feet to the bus stop and hopped aboard. Ten minutes later she disembarked in front of an office complex that backed onto the inner harbor. She walked along the sidewalk and down the few concrete steps. A small street band played to delighted tourists who tried to ignore the dirty, smelly people standing all around the perimeter.

Although most of the down and out were men, Jonelle was always dismayed to see women in their midst. She noticed a white woman with dark, shoulder length hair sitting on a bench a little ways from the crowd. Her arms and legs were crossed so tight it appeared as if she was trying to fold into herself. Her pinched face had deep frown lines around the eyes and mouth. The gentle rocking of her body reminded Jonelle of Luther in his jail cell.

"Mind if I sit here?" she asked in a quiet voice.

The woman scooted over to the edge of the bench.

"Thank you," Jonelle said, sitting near the other edge. Although she'd lost weight this past year, Jonelle didn't want her size to intimidate this fragile woman.

Conscious of people walking all around her, Jonelle tried to focus on how to ask the woman about Luther and Chester. Best to come out with it. "I'm looking to help an acquaintance of mine. His name's Luther. He's got a friend called Chester and I was wondering if—"

The woman made a squeaking sound, jumped up and ran off.

"Well, damn," Jonelle said to herself.

"You lookin' for Chester, you ain't gonna find him that way," said a voice behind her.

Jonelle turned around on the bench.

"I overheard you talkin' to Maxine."

A stocky man in a navy blue work shirt and pants looked down at her. His sandy hair sported a buzz cut and his hazel eyes observed her with amusement. The name "Phil" was stitched in white above his shirt pocket.

"Well, Phil, I'm open for suggestions. You got any?"

In answer, Phil came around and sat next to her. He offered her his hand. "Since you know my name, what's yours?"

She shook his hand. "My name's Jonelle. I'm trying to help a friend of mine. He told me to contact someone named Chester, and frankly I had hoped to find him somewhere out here. I think I know where he goes at night, but I have other, uh, responsibilities at that time. And before you ask, no I'm not a cop."

He nodded. "I believe you. To tell you the truth, I was wondering about Chester myself. See, I always have lunch around here, and I try to help these guys when I can. Maxine over there"—he nodded to the woman now swaying on another bench—"doesn't like anyone near her. It's taken me a while just to get her to let me hand her a few dollars." He sighed. "As for Chester. He's normally around here about this time, but I haven't seen him in a few days. Ever since they found that woman."

"What does Chester look like?"

Phil opened the brown paper sack he carried and took out a zip lock bag. "Want half my sandwich? It's meatloaf. Wife makes the best meatloaf around."

Jonelle grinned and shook her head. "No thanks."

Phil took a big bite of sandwich. After swallowing, he drank from his water bottle. "You know, I never really thought about it before, but it's hard to describe these people. I don't mean that I'm one of those folk who don't really look at them, 'cause I do. But still …" He squinted in concentration. "Guess Chester is a little taller than me. I'm five ten, so he'd be a little under six feet. Long, straggly gray hair hangs almost to his shoulders. Pale eyes. Tell you the truth, don't know if they're blue or gray." Phil took another bite of sandwich.

"White guy, right?" Jonelle asked.

Phil nodded.

Jonelle stared up at the sky. No doubt about it. She needed to go back to the warehouse.

CHAPTER 4

The unseasonable warmth of the day had vanished, replaced by a cool, but not too cold night. Crickets chirped and clicked all around. Jonelle loved this time of year when summer struggled to hang on while fall tried to take its place. She frowned at the surveillance sheet lying on the passenger seat of her Jeep. The client, a nurse named Polly Cole, wanted the agency in place no later than ten forty-five and last until three a.m., two hours before she returned home. Ms. Cole, a single mom, requested someone watch and make sure her teenage daughter didn't leave the house after she left and most importantly, didn't let anyone in. The client had given Shorter Investigative Services permission to call the cops if the investigator, in this case Jonelle, ran into any problems.

"So, this is what my life's come to," Jonelle grumbled to herself, "babysitting teenagers."

The time on her cellphone read eight thirty. She had a little over two hours to drive to the deserted warehouse, check inside for Chester and make it back to the client's house by the agreed upon start time. Along the way, she made a mental inventory of what she packed for the night. Her backpack held a flashlight, night vision goggles, camera and her Beretta .38. A thermos of coffee, large bottle of water, chips, peanut butter crackers and a chocolate bar took up the rest of the space. Good thing there was a convenience store around the corner from the Cole place in case her bladder complained.

The neighborhood around the old warehouse district hadn't changed since her first visit last year. If anything, it was even more gloomy at night. A few harsh sodium lights barely illuminated the area. The scene epitomized the hopelessness and despair of those unlucky enough to live there. Looking around at all the rubble, rusted out cars, trash and boarded up buildings depressed her. Jonelle pondered what she'd say to Chester when she found him. That is, *if* she found him.

She pulled up next to the curb of the large building, its concrete façade glowing pale orange under the streetlights. The rusting chain link fence had the same large gap she remembered from last year. Of course it was the same. Who was going to complain that lights weren't fixed and trash needed picking up? And what would be the point? Jonelle turned off the engine. Now that she was here, she hesitated about going inside. A quick glance all around through the vehicle's windows caught furtive movement behind and to her right. A human form stopped. The shadow turned toward her. As Jonelle considered whether or not to call out, the shape scurried through the fence and disappeared.

Jonelle knew what lay beyond the opening. She grasped her backpack and felt around inside. Her hand closed around cool, smooth metal. She left her Jeep and stood close to the door. She removed her pistol, placed it inside the holster she had brought with her and strapped the weapon around her waist. She shrugged into her pale blue denim jacket, which concealed the gun from view. The last thing she wanted was to upset anyone inside. Next, Jonelle removed the flashlight. She clicked it on and off and on again. Satisfied the beam was powerful enough for what she needed to do, Jonelle strode up to the fence.

"Here goes," she muttered. Jonelle slipped inside and played the light against the outside walls. She aimed the beam in front of her and followed it to the left side of the building.

After skirting around three rusted cars sans wheels, Jonelle moved over to where the large opening to the structure allowed access inside and entered. A faint yellow light shone in the darkness.

"Hello," she called out. "I'm a friend of Luther. Is there anyone called Chester in here?"

Jonelle sniffed the air. The pungent odor of something burning filled the space. She touched her weapon for reassurance, dragged her feet through the trash strewn all around the floor and aimed for the glow in the distance. A slight rustling noise brought her up short. She pointed the flashlight over to the right and detected movement in the corner. She shuddered. "Damn rats," she mumbled under her breath. Jonelle forced herself to breathe as deeply as possible to stave off the tightness she knew would grab at her chest.

Shapes hovered near an open flame. The murmur of voices floated over to her and she stopped. "My name's Jonelle Sweet," she called out to the shadows. "Luther helped me on a case last year, so I've come here to return the favor."

"You that PI lady Luther tole us about?"

Jonelle jumped at the disembodied voice that came out of the darkness behind her. "Jeeze. Give a girl a heart attack why don't you." Soft laughter bounced off the walls. A figure drifted out from the gloom.

"Chester?" Jonelle asked. She trained her flashlight on the image. The figure that faced her was that of a very thin, dark-skinned black man.

"Naw," the man said. "Chester ain't here right now."

Jonelle's heart sank. "Do you know when he'll be back? Luther wants me to find him."

"Firs' you gotta git that damn light outta my eyes," he said.

"Sorry." Jonelle lowered the beam.

"Tha's better. Tell me what you know 'bout Luther. Then, if I thinks you're on the up 'n up, I'll let you know 'bout Chester."

As a visitor to his world, Jonelle was in a no BS zone. The hairs standing up on her arms told her there were many more eyes and ears trained on her than she could actually see.

Jonelle took a deep breath and recounted her first meeting with Luther last year. "I'm sure you remember what happened if you were around. Luther took care of someone and kept her safe until I found her." Now, she explained, she planned to help him fight whatever charges the cops filed against him for the murder of the woman found behind the Dumpster. "I've already got a lawyer for him lined up," Jonelle said. "Someone who'll represent him at no charge."

The man never took his eyes off Jonelle the entire time she talked. "How you know ole Luth didn't do it?" he asked, after she'd finished.

"He's not that kind of person. Luther helps people ... he doesn't hurt them." What made her so sure about that? To her own ears she sounded like a bad cable television movie. "By the way, what's your name?"

"Ever'body calls me TJ," he said.

She nodded. "Now, about Chester ... "

TJ shrugged. "I tole you, he ain't here. Right before they pinched Luther, he, uh got into some trouble and disappeared. Don't know when, or if, he's comin' back."

"You could've told me that in the first place," she said evenly. "Would've saved us some time."

"Time is the only thing I got plenty of lady." TJ walked a few steps closer to Jonelle. She held her ground. They stood eye to eye for several seconds, with Jonelle taking quick breaths to keep from inhaling too much of TJ's rank body odor.

After a few moments, he laughed. Sour breath blew in her face. As she was about to move away from the smell, TJ stepped back. He shook his head over and over. "Luther said you was somethin' else."

"About Chester," Jonelle said again, emphasizing the name. She looked around. Her eyes had adjusted to the dim light well enough for her to make out several shapes milling about. The fire that caught her attention earlier still flared from a barrel in the distance. She realized that even in this place, there was some sort of hierarchy; that's how they protected themselves and survived.

She turned back to TJ. His eyes still studied her.

"Rumor has it Chester is hidin' out in one 'a the shelters," he said.

Finally. "Which one?"

TJ snickered again. "Hell. If I was to tell you that, then he wouldn't be hidin' no more, now would he?"

That did it. She'd had enough. "Which part of me wanting to help Luther do you not get?" she asked, raising her voice. "Obviously you think this is some kind of damn game. Well, it's not. Luther sitting in a jail cell while we play twenty questions is not funny." She pointed a finger at TJ. "You gonna be straight with me or not?"

Jonelle got the satisfaction of watching TJ back away from her as she unleashed those last words.

TJ glanced nervously around him. Jonelle wondered if with both Luther and Chester gone, he was next in line as head of the group. Her yelling wasn't helping him keep that status, but she had about one nerve left and his crappy attitude was stepping all over it.

He cleared his throat and cocked his head for her to follow. He led her to a spot against one of several thick columns that ran down the center of the immense room.

"Here's the thing," he said, voice low. "A few days before they found the body, Chester stopped showin' up so we figured he found someplace else to crash. The day the cops took

Luther away, I came back jus' before dark an' found Chester limpin' from up on the corner. He was bleedin' real bad. Said some Mex'cans beat him an' he needed to lay low for a while. So, I helped him clean up an' then he left. Some 'a the shelters got medicine, so he prob'ly went to one 'a those." He shrugged. "I don't know which one."

"Did he have any idea why they beat him? Did it have anything to do with the dead woman?"

TJ eased down to the ground, his back against the column. He reached in his shirt pocket and retrieved a pack of cigarettes and plastic lighter. He held the pack out to her. She shook her head. Jonelle rearranged her backpack and sat down next to him, the flashlight next to her hip. He lit a cigarette. After two deep pulls of smoke assaulted his lungs, TJ looked off in the distance.

"It could'a been just some shitheads lookin' to roll a bum," he said.

"You don't believe that, do you?"

TJ paused. He shook his head. "Naw. They only beat him around his head. It looked worse than it was. Those assholes usually like to try an cripple us up some. They think it's funnier that way." He snorted and puffed some more. Jonelle waited for him to continue. "Those idiots was lookin' to send him a message. An' before you ask, no, I got no idea what the message was." He looked at her. "But I guess the message was received 'cause he ain't here."

The attitude TJ displayed earlier had disappeared. "Okay," she said. "I know a few of the shelters around here so that's where I'll start." She struggled to stand up. TJ hopped up to help her. "Thanks. Sorry if I went a little too far before," she said, brushing dust off her pants.

"Most other people would'a run outta here fast as they could," he said, grinning. "Not you. You one hard-headed woman."

Jonelle took that as a compliment. "What's Chester's last name?"

"Lady don't nobody got last names around here."

She turned to go, then stopped. "Just one more thing."

TJ groaned. "You's wearin' out your welcome, Columbo."

"What about the dead woman? Do you think the attack on Chester had anything to do with her?"

TJ looked around him. "We was talkin' 'bout that before. Things was fine before she showed up. Once she got here and hooked up with Luther, weird shit started happenin'. We kept tellin' Luther, leave that white woman alone. There's somethin' wrong with her. Susanna ain't no good."

Jonelle couldn't believe what she'd just heard. "You know her name? Wait a minute. You mean she was a regular around here and she and Luther were close?"

TJ nodded.

CHAPTER 5

After TJ's revelations and an uneventful night of surveillance, Jonelle drove home exhausted and in desperate need of a bathroom. Per the contract, Jonelle was due back at the Cole place at the same time that evening.

Once inside her condo she dragged herself to the bathroom and took a shower. Afterward Jonelle wrapped herself in her long cotton robe, lay down and drifted off to sleep. The insistent buzz of her alarm clock woke her at noon. Surprised at having slept so well during the day, Jonelle dressed in tan slacks and white pullover. She searched for and found an old bag she'd wanted to give to the thrift store. She put the bag on the bed and went back to the closet where some of her late husband's clothes still remained.

After removing four pairs of pants, Jonelle put them all back. Somehow she didn't think Luther would want to wear expensive clothes. She dug through the items on one of the bottom shelves and came up with three pairs of jeans. Each pair was steam pressed, the result of Del sending them to the cleaners over Jonelle's objections. "Nobody takes their jeans to the cleaners," she'd argued. After a few moments of stroking the fabric, she folded the jeans and placed them in the duffle. Next, she found five cotton polo shirts, two long sleeved shirts and an old down vest and stuffed those in as well. The last items she added were several pairs of socks. Jonelle zipped the bag and stared down at it, shaking her head. No doubt about it. Luther was gonna be the city's best dressed homeless guy.

Jonelle thought about calling Burt to give the detective a heads-up that she had a name for his victim. Instead, she'd called the law firm representing Luther and was told his release was imminent, so she decided to drop by the courthouse. Whether or not she'd tell Burt about the closeness between Luther and Susanna as implied by TJ, Jonelle wasn't sure.

She parked her Jeep in one of the courthouse's visitor spaces and left the duffle bag on the floor in front of the passenger seat. Among all the people coming down the courthouse steps was one of the lawyers from the firm that agreed to help Luther's defense. Disappointed they had assigned one of their youngest associates, Jonelle waved to get his attention.

"Hey, it's me Jonelle Sweet from Shorter Investigative Services. I called you guys about representing Luther."

He stopped and waited for her on the bottom step.

"Sorry I don't remember your name. So, how'd it go?" she asked.

He shrugged.

Up close he looked even younger than she remembered. She wondered how many years it'd been since he graduated law school.

With his head, he motioned for her to follow around back to the parking lot. He said nothing until he stopped at a red Fiat. "Name's Brian Muir," he said opening the driver's side door and throwing his briefcase in the back. "I've got good news and bad news. Would you like the good first?"

"Sure, go ahead."

"He's lucky we got a sympathetic judge. I got her to release him without bail because right now the police don't have much to hold him on. He's a material witness to the crime's aftermath, and I got the feeling even the police don't think he killed that young woman. He stayed at the scene, had no weapon and no blood on his clothes." He peered at Jonelle through hazel eyes. "The bad news is he's a belligerent sonofabitch who won't help himself one bit unless he gets an attitude change. And quick."

Jonelle sighed. "I was afraid of that. Thing is, what you're seeing is mostly fear, not anger. I'll see what I can do about getting him to tone it down when I see him." Jonelle played with her necklace. "This might sound strange coming from me, but I don't know Luther's real last name. I only know him as Luther St. Vincent, but I suspect that last name came from a poster he saw on the wall of the warehouse where he stays at night."

Brian laughed and eased into the driver's seat. "After we got your call, I contacted detective Burton. He told me Luther had calmed down enough so they took the cuffs off and said I could see him. When we first met he tried telling me his name was Luther Vandross. Guess he figured a young white guy wouldn't know who the singer was. Thing is, I was a huge fan. Still am. Anyway, not only did they find a match on his prints, taken when he was picked up for loitering two years ago, they also found ID in his belongings when they did a thorough search."

Jonelle stared. "ID? He had ID all this time? Jeeze, Louise."

He nodded. "A lot of the shelters won't let them stay unless they have some form of identification. His real name is Luther Dukes." Brian started the car. "Sorry, but I have another appointment. I got him released so he's probably on his way out."

Jonelle stepped away from the car. "Thanks for all the info."

Ticked off that Luther kept his true name a secret from her, Jonelle rushed to the side entrance of the courthouse, looking for him in the group of smiling faces exiting the building. She found him holding tight to a paper bag, cleaner and much calmer.

"Hey, Luther," Jonelle called out. He stopped and turned, his eyes squinting in the glare of the afternoon sun. "Hold on a sec. I need to talk to you."

"Guess you expect me to thank you for what you done for me. Well, okay then, thanks." He gripped his bag tighter and didn't meet her eyes.

"You okay?"

He shrugged.

Jonelle tried a different tactic. "Sorry about Susanna. I'm going to see Burt, detective Burton that is, and let him know what I found out about her."

Luther's eyes opened wide. "What did Chester tell you? I tole him to wait for me before he gave out anything 'bout her. I promised her I'd keep her secret for as long as I could."

"What secret?"

Luther shook his head and clamped his mouth shut. Jonelle waited. When it appeared as though Luther wasn't going to say anything else, she motioned to him.

"Follow me. My Jeep's over here. I have something for you, and I need to tell you about Chester." Jonelle turned and started walking back to where her vehicle was parked.

"What you mean? What's that you say 'bout Chester?" He asked those questions behind her back. She picked up his footfalls limping along the sidewalk in an attempt to keep up with her. Jonelle wasn't about to let Luther dictate things now that she'd gotten herself involved. He'd just have to wait until she decided to reveal what she knew. She stopped at the passenger's side door and disengaged the lock.

"I've got some things for you that I'd been keeping after my husband died. If you want them, they're yours. If you don't, well maybe one of your friends could use them." She reached inside, removed the duffel bag and held it out to him.

He took the bag from her and without looking inside, opened his mouth to speak. Jonelle rushed on before he had the chance.

"Hop in and I'll give you a lift to where you want to go," she said. "That's the only way you're gonna find out what I know." She left the passenger door open and took her time going around to the driver's side. She stared at him over the hood, her eyes questioning.

He slowly nodded his head.

"Good. Put your things in the back."

Luther did as he was told without comment. Jonelle got perverse pleasure in the man's silence. For once there were no wise-ass remarks.

Once inside the Jeep, now that she had Luther where she wanted him, Jonelle wasn't sure what to do. She glanced at the clock on the dash. Almost one o'clock. "Hungry? There are several places where we can get something to eat. Anything in particular you'd like?"

"Yeah, how about a thick steak, baked potato an' a bottle 'a wine."

To help hold her anger in check, Jonelle mentally counted to ten. When she reached 'seven' Luther spoke.

"Sorry," he muttered.

She turned and glared at him. "You just made it," she said.

Jonelle drove for about ten minutes without saying a word. A fast food place appeared on the right side and she pulled around to the drive through. She placed an order for a ten piece bucket of grilled chicken, mashed potatoes with gravy and large green beans and coleslaw, plus biscuits and two iced teas. She asked for paper plates, eating utensils and napkins. After she paid for everything, Jonelle pulled over and parked. A few plastic tables and chairs ringed the small structure. Jonelle walked over with her bags to one of the tables. Luther got out of the Jeep and followed.

Without her words to give him something to use against her, he stayed silent. She waited until his mouth was full of chicken and potatoes before she told him the information TJ divulged about Chester. His eyes narrowed when she recounted the attack, but he remained silent.

"In addition to telling me her name, he also said you and Susanna were close. How close would that be?" Luther had pieces of chicken and potatoes and gravy dribbling out the sides of his mouth. Jonelle handed him several napkins.

He swiped the napkins from her hands and rubbed vigorously at his mouth. Luther stared at the people going in and out of the restaurant. It was several seconds before he replied. "I noticed her wanderin' around downtown 'bout three, four months ago," he said, not meeting Jonelle's eyes. "It's a hard life out on the streets. 'Specially for a woman. Oh, the nut cases do all right. People tend to stay away from them. But Suze was different. I could tell." He stopped, picked up a thigh and took several bites.

Jonelle held her patience in check.

After swallowing another mouthful, he sighed and let out a huge burp that seemed to originate from the bottom of his feet all the way up to his mouth. He grinned at the look on Jonelle's face. "That feels better," he said.

"Susanna?" she prompted, trying not to sound as disgusted as she felt.

"Yeah. Well the firs' day I noticed right away she didn't belong out here. She was too clean. Too neat. She looked real nervous, but not crazy nervous, just scared nervous. Know what I mean?"

Jonelle wasn't sure she did, but nodded anyway.

"So, second day I see her in the same place. She had the same clothes on, but this time she struggled with a couple large shoppin' bags. One 'a the ole timers started circlin' her like a shark circlin' a baby seal, so I kept my eye on 'em both. Sure enough, the ole fart starts to grab one 'a her bags so I yelled an' ran forward an' pushed him away. He balled his hands in a fist 'til he saw who it was an' backed down. Stupid ole' fool." Luther looked down at the chicken.

"There's plenty left. I'll package it all up for you," Jonelle said. "Go on with the story."

"I asked her if she was okay an' she says yes. Tole her she gotta be careful. Then I sat next to her and started tellin' her the right way she gotta handle herself if she's gonna survive out here." Luther's voice broke. Jonelle waited for him to finish.

"Guess I didn't do so good, huh?" Tears welled in Luther's eyes.

Jonelle patted his arm. "You did the best you could." The smell of deep fat fried meat weighed heavy in Jonelle's nostrils, but she waited quietly while Luther composed himself.

He took a deep breath. "I figured the safest place for her would be the warehouse. That's our patch. Strangers know to stay out. Took us a while but we got our own community." Luther paused again.

"How did the others take to her?" Jonelle asked.

"They didn't like it at firs'. But she stayed to herself and didn't cause no trouble, so after 'bout two weeks, she became one 'a us."

Jonelle thought of Burt and what he might want to know. "Did she ever say how she ended up on the street?"

Luther shook his head. "Naw. We don't ask stuff like that. If somebody wants to say, they'll say in good enough time. She never did."

A different line of questioning occurred to Jonelle. "So, Mister Dukes, what about her last name?" Luther turned and glared at her with such intensity that Jonelle was afraid he was about to bolt. After a few beats he looked up at the sky. "Quinley," he said to the clouds.

For a moment, Jonelle felt like jumping up and down. She had a name to give to the police. One of her mother's old sayings came to mind: *now we're cooking with gas.*

"Was she from around here?"

Luther scowled at Jonelle.

"Okay. I get you don't ask a lot of questions. Law of the street and all that. But I bet you got some sense of where she was from. Just through everyday conversations. Could you pick up an accent? Virginia maybe. Southern Maryland or DC? Anything?"

He pulled the straw out of his cup and chewed on it. "Can't say I picked up on an accent, but I got the feelin' she was from someplace else. Someplace kinda far up north."

"Why do you think that?"

"'Cause she kept complainin' 'bout the heat. How she couldn't believe how much she kept sweatin' day and night. Then she said somethin' like, 'at least where I'm from it doesn't get this hot, an' we don't have this damn humidity.' Stuff like that."

As she was about to ask another question, Luther stood. "I'm gettin' tired. I can find me a way back from here if you don't wanna go out of your way."

A quick glance at the hard set to his mouth and the fierce glow in his eyes told Jonelle Luther had said all he was going to for now. Luther grabbed the bag with the food and they both walked over to her Jeep.

Once inside the vehicle, Jonelle turned to face him. "Thanks for all your help, Luther. I mean it. I have some good information to give to detective Burton."

Luther grunted in reply.

Before Jonelle backed out of the parking space, she looked around and tried to get her bearings.

"At the street turn left, go down five lights, then make a right," Luther said.

Jonelle followed his instructions. As she drove on, the area started looking familiar. She knew where she was.

"Do you want me to take you all the way over to the side?" she asked.

"Yeah."

She pulled up to the curb and left the engine running. Luther stayed where he was.

"Would you like some help with your things? I could carry the duffle while you handle the food."

He shook his head and slowly climbed out. With one hand he grabbed the duffle and slipped the strap over his shoulder. The other hand grabbed the food and his paper bag. He started to go, then turned back around. "Thanks for puttin' up with an ole fool," he said.

"You're not a fool and I'm not through helping you. Got that?"

Luther smiled. Jonelle watched him limp to the opening in the fence. He stopped and turned to look at her. She waved. He shuffled back to the Jeep.

"I think I best tell you this part, too," he said, bending down and gazing at her through the passenger side window.

Jonelle nodded encouragement.

"Suze had a secret. A big secret. She only got a chance to tell me part of it, 'cause …" He shrugged.

Jonelle's heart skipped a beat. "What kind of secret?"

"Money," he said, just loud enough for her to hear. "She said she had a shit load of money and needed my help hidin' it."

CHAPTER 6

The day after Luther's release, Jonelle met with detective Thelonius Burton in his office at the Violent Crimes unit of the Criminal Investigations division. She sat in his cubicle, her chair positioned next to his desk, and sipped coffee from the Styrofoam cup he'd given her. She winced as the hot, bitter liquid hit her tongue. The brew was long past fresh and smelled as bad as it tasted. Voices from the other detectives echoed through the office—some angry, some pleading, all loud.

Jonelle set the cup down and picked up the Bugs Bunny figurine that sat against the fabric wall which separated Burt's space from the detective on the other side. She fiddled with the statuette while he two-finger typed the information she'd shared about the murdered woman in his so-called Murder Book. Though not technically a book but a computer file, it still carried that name as a source for all the information on every open case that involved a suspicious death.

His typing style took twice as long as it would have taken her to log in the facts about Susanna. In words drawn out to match his typing, Jonelle told Burt how Luther met the woman called Susanna Quinley and why he thought she wasn't local.

"Pretty good catch of his. Picking up on a little thing like her commenting about the weather," Burt said, a huge smile on his dark, round face. "You've saved me some time here and I appreciate it."

She returned his smile. From the moment she first met him two years ago, Burt's openness with her had always been a plus whenever she needed his help. She put Bugs down and pointed to the tie around Burt's neck. "I like that one," she said.

"This old thing?" Burt fingered his baby blue tie with Homer, Bart, Lisa and Marge prominently displayed. In her opinion, Burt's unusual taste in neckwear added to his overall charm. She also liked how his gentle demeanor disarmed most people. Those who didn't know him often made the mistake that since Burt was so easygoing, he might not be the sharpest investigator on the force. They were soon proven wrong. He often said listening was sixty percent of a detective's job. The rest was observation. As his eyes bored into hers, Jonelle's hand reached up and played with her necklace.

"What else you got for me?" he asked. The smile never left his lips.

"Listen," Jonelle said, leaning in and carefully measuring her words. She needed Burt on her side if she was going to help Luther. "For over a year, I thought Luther's last name was St. Vincent. Yesterday I found out his last name is Dukes, and not only that, he had ID on him all this time. It's hard to get Luther to open up. I don't mean to brag, but I think I can get him to tell me more about the victim than you can. It's just gonna take some time."

Burt reached over and put his hand on top of Jonelle's. "You have to promise to find out what you can from Luther, and Luther only. Don't go around town asking questions about the victim. Someone may hear about it and it could get back to the perp."

Jonelle waited a few beats before gently removing her hand from under his. "I'm a licensed private investigator, Burt." He opened his mouth to say something, but before he could she added, "And I bet I can shoot better than most people on this police force. Plus, look at me. I'm not what you'd call a delicate flower. I can handle myself."

Something flickered in Burt's eyes. "I know you can," he said, looking down at notes scattered across his desk. He scanned a piece of paper. Jonelle tried to read the note upside down, but couldn't.

"What this says," Burt said, picking it up and holding the note in one hand, "is what was on the piece of paper pinned to her clothes. The only reason I'm showing this to you is that we can't make head nor tails of what it means. Maybe you can. I doubt Luther knows, but if you want to show it to him ..." Burt shrugged.

Jonelle took the paper. "WH V M 285696? What's that mean?"

"Damn if I know. Safety deposit box number? Bank account? Bus locker? Ask your, uh, contacts. See if someone knows."

"What about the condition of the body?"

Burt's eyes narrowed. "What about it?"

"Don't play coy. That area is known for drugs and prostitution. Was she sexually assaulted?"

"She was found with her dress pulled up around her waist and her underwear pulled down, but there was no evidence she was raped. Why?"

"Curious is all." Jonelle made a note in her phone and photographed the image of the paper with the code for good measure. Afterwards, she cleared her throat and stood. Burt started up from his seat, but she motioned him back down. "I can let myself out. If I find out anything more about Susanna, I'll let you know." She started to leave but remembered something and turned back around. "Oh, and does it go without saying that you'd do the same?"

Burt covered his mouth with his hand. "Do the same about what?"

"We've agreed to share what we uncover, right? Don't play dumb. I'm interested in whatever you find out about Susanna. I'd like to keep Luther up to date about the case."

Burt's grin widened. He fumbled with some papers on his desk.

Jonelle waited. "Well?"

"Last I heard, he already had a lawyer. And that lawyer's job is to keep his client informed," Burt said, the grin still plastered on his face.

"Oh, didn't I tell you? Luther is also my client." She raised an eyebrow. "See you later." With that, she left his cubicle and didn't look back.

CHAPTER 7

The end of the week meant a Shorter Investigative Services staff meeting. Jonelle dreaded today's conference, feeling that she had little to contribute. In addition to helping Luther for free, which was bound to raise snickers from Omar and Ben, the only other cases she had were watching a nurse's teenage daughter and following an irate wife's husband on the weekends. Jonelle sat in her office and struggled with how to make the assignments interesting enough so the other two agents wouldn't make her the brunt of their jokes.

After several attempts at trying to make a little something out of a lot of nothing, Jonelle gathered notebook and pencil and walked up to the open door of the conference room. She stopped short before going all the way in, shocked to see Ben sitting there. Usually Marvin and Rainey arrived first, then Jonelle wandered in followed by Omar, with Ben last. His presence at the end of the table closest to the donuts and coffee threw off her timing.

"Did I miss something? Did you start early?" she asked looking over at Marvin.

Rainey pointed to Ben. "See? I told you, you were messing with the normal order of the universe. You gotta give us a heads-up if you're gonna start acting like a regular, respectable employee."

"Who's respectable?" Omar stood in the conference room's doorway next to Jonelle. "Hey! What's he doing here?" Omar looked at Jonelle. "Are we late?"

Jonelle shook her head. "Apparently the earth burped and this is what happened."

"Oh, hardy har har," Ben said amidst laughter from the others. He scowled at his plain donut and black coffee.

Jonelle grabbed a glazed, poured coffee and milk in her mug and sat down beside Rainey.

Everyone waited until Omar had poured hot water over a tea bag and took the other seat next to Marvin.

"Okay, Rainey," Marvin said. "You go first. Then I'd like status reports from Omar, Ben and Jonelle. In that order."

In a clear voice, Rainey provided the staff with the number of current open cases and how many were closed the past week. Much to Jonelle's chagrin, Rainey mentioned the agency was taking on a client's case for no fee.

"For free?" Ben asked. "Since when do we do charity cases?" He stared at Jonelle who looked away, somewhat embarrassed that he knew it was one of hers.

Before Jonelle could respond, Marvin answered. "It's not *cases*, it's only one case. And it has special circumstances. Jonelle is helping someone who assisted her last year, and she'll be working with the police." He moved his gaze away from Ben and looked over at this niece. "The police are in charge. Right, Jonelle?"

"I'll tell you more when it's my turn."

Omar reported the status of each of his cases in his usual no frills manner. When he paused, Jonelle assumed he'd finished and glanced at Ben. Omar coughed into his hand and raised both eyebrows at Marvin, who nodded his assent. He then told the group he was working on a "top secret" case for "a world renowned bank" and that sadly, he couldn't go into details with the group.

Ben snorted his opinion after Omar had finished. Based on the smug expression on Omar's face, Jonelle could tell her co-worker wasn't too unhappy about keeping his assignment close to his chest.

When it was his turn, Ben reported on the result of his two government background checks. "Both looked good to me, although I recommended that the security clearance on one shouldn't go any higher than what they were offering now. I didn't find anything suspicious, but my gut told me this one guy might talk a little too much. If you know what I mean." Afterwards, when he complained about being forced to start a diet by his latest wife, Marvin cut him off mid tirade.

"Enough, Ben. Sorry, but you've got to try and keep your personal life out of the staff meetings. Okay? Come see me later if you want."

Ben grumbled a reply, took a bite of donut and sat back. He crossed his arms and positioned them over his protruding belly.

Everyone looked at Jonelle. She took a deep breath. "My first surveillance case started last Wednesday night. Basically, a single mother by the name of Polly Cole works as a nurse overnight. She wants us, me that is, to keep tabs on her house to make sure her teenage daughter doesn't leave and doesn't let anyone in. The young woman has sneaked out of the house in the past, and also let boys inside against her mother's wishes."

Ben snickered. Jonelle shot him a look and continued.

"Anyway, I have permission from the mom to call the police if I need to. So far, there haven't been any problems. I don't start my other surveillance job 'til tomorrow night. In this case the wife,"—Jonelle looked down at her notes—"her name's Becky Henshaw, thinks her husband is cheating on her. He tells her he's going out in the evenings to visit friends. I asked her about these friends of his and she stated that she'd contacted a few of them and they back up her husband's story."

"So, what's the problem?" Omar asked. "Sounds straightforward to me. But, I guess if she wants to pay for her being jealous,"—he shrugged—"so be it."

Jonelle nodded. "I agree. But I also think there may be more to this. Anyway, I'll soon find out." She hesitated and looked down at her almost empty notepad.

"About the case I'm handling for no fee." She tapped her pencil on the paper. "The man's name is Luther Dukes and the police think he's a person of interest in the murder of a woman found knifed to death next to a Dumpster."

Ben whistled softly. "Why do the cops think he's involved?"

"Because he knew the victim and he was discovered next to her body. At the time, they didn't know who she was because she had no identification and he was too distraught to tell them anything."

Omar clicked the top of his ballpoint several times as he glanced first at Marvin and then Jonelle. "The guy's in jail, right? We can't do anything about that. Especially for free."

"One of our law clients agreed to take Luther's case pro bono and has already secured his release."

Ben raised his eyebrows. "The dude's out already? Remind me to contact you if I get in trouble with the law."

Pleased that the agent with the most experience had paid her a compliment, Jonelle continued on with her report with more confidence than she started with. "I've given the full name of the murdered woman to the detective assigned to the case. Thelonius Burton is his name." Jonelle didn't look at Marvin when she mentioned Burt. She knew her uncle probably had a grin on his face. In the past he'd ribbed her with his opinion that the detective was, as he put it, sweet on Mrs. Sweet.

She cleared her throat. "Luther gave me some more information, but I want to verify that before I tell the police. Sometimes he tends to stretch the truth a bit."

"I'll bet," Omar said. "So how exactly are you going to help him?"

"Try and make sure the cops don't railroad him for something he didn't do. He's more comfortable with me than with strangers. I'm hoping that whatever I find out about his relationship with the murdered woman will exonerate him and prove he had nothing to do with her death."

"Good luck with that," Omar murmured.

"Sounds like he trusts you," Marvin said. "That's a good thing. But don't forget to keep the police informed every step of the way." He leaned forward. "We don't need you withholding anything because you think you can handle it yourself. That won't look good for the agency. Understand?"

Even though her uncle's comments referred to the agency's reputation, she also knew his concern ran much deeper. Two years ago she was shot and wounded. Another attempt on her life was made last year. "I understand."

"Anyone have anything else?" Marvin asked, looking at each one of his employees. "Well, I do. Starting this month, I'm putting practicing at the shooting range on the honor system. Give Rainey the dates you go and she'll note the calendar. But if you guys let me down and I'm forced to require proof, I'll do that too." He looked at each one in turn. His eyes lingered on Omar longer. Omar squirmed in his seat, unable to meet Marvin's gaze.

No one spoke. Everyone knew of Omar's dislike of weapons.

After a few moments when no one said a word, Marvin dismissed the group and they all filed out of the conference room. Ben grabbed two donuts on his way out. Jonelle stared open-mouthed. "What about the diet?"

"Screw it," Ben said, cramming his mouth full of raspberry-filled sugar and fat.

Jonelle shook her head and followed Rainey to the reception area.

"So, what's the history with Omar and guns? Once you know how to handle them, they're no big deal."

Rainey put her finger to her lips. "Shh. I don't want anyone else to hear." She motioned for Jonelle to come closer and peered down the hall. She waited until the other agents had entered their respective offices. "About six months before Marvin hired you, Omar got mugged and was pistol whipped with his own weapon. Witnesses said once he pulled it out of the holster, he just froze. Couldn't move. From then on we knew that Omar would rather deal with white collar and computer crimes. Marvin's been real good at throwing all those cases his way, but we haven't been getting too many of them lately. It's fortunate that the bank case came in when it did, or we'd have to give Omar a surveillance job."

"Oh, what a shame," Jonelle said, her voice dripping with sarcasm. "If he doesn't like something, Marvin accommodates him. Me? I just have to deal with the leftovers." Jonelle's words hung like thick molasses in the air.

"Feel better now?" Rainey asked, sitting down at her desk.

Jonelle looked at the notepad still gripped in her hand. She shifted from one foot to the other. "Actually, I feel like a toad. Sorry about the pity party." Jonelle smiled at Rainey and turned to make her way back to her office.

"Hold it a sec," Rainey said. "Promise to keep to yourself what I'm about to tell you."

Jonelle nodded.

The words came out of Rainey in a rush. "We've always gotten lots of employment applications and have had to turn down some really good people. You and Ben, because you're both weapon savvy, are more valuable to the agency. Omar is becoming a little too specialized; we're too small for that. Marvin hasn't said much, but his insistence on everyone going to the shooting range is the first step. He wants all his investigators skilled enough to handle whatever projects come in. Or, he may have to make some hard choices."

For a moment Jonelle felt faint stirrings of hope that if Omar left it would move her up in the ranks. The fear shown on his face when Marvin told him to find his weapon had pleased her more than she wanted to admit. Now she felt uneasy for having those thoughts.

"I'll wait a couple weeks," she said, with a sigh. "If Omar doesn't mention going to the shooting range, I'll invite him to come with me."

"Atta girl," Rainey said, patting Jonelle on the arm.

If she thought about her situation she'd get bummed again so she changed the subject. "Since we're not getting paid for me handling Luther's case, how often do you want me to provide updates?"

"The format's not as strict as that with our paying clients. Let me know what's going on from time to time so I can add it to the report."

"Will do."

Jonelle ambled down the hall to her office. Once inside she noticed the message light blinking on the landline phone. She picked up the handset and punched in her code. One message was from Burt. He said he'd just learned more information about the victim. Before calling him back, Jonelle listened to the second message. It was from someone named Sophia Quinley Reyes. She wanted to find out as much as possible about her sister, Susanna.

CHAPTER 8

The sun streamed through the window in Jonelle's office, the rays jumping off the silver-framed photos of her late husband that adorned the right side of her desk. After she'd gotten the call from the murdered woman's sister, she tried doing paperwork but couldn't concentrate. The glazed donut and coffee from that morning's meeting rumbled inside her stomach. She reached inside her top desk drawer, removed two antacid tablets and popped them in her mouth. Was the stomach upset a result of the caffeine and sugar, or was she nervous about meeting the dead woman's sister?

"Most likely both," Jonelle murmured to herself.

She got up and walked over to the window. She gazed out at the buildings surrounded by the few trees the city had decided to leave in place, their leaves just starting to change colors. Excited Susanna's sister was on her way to talk to her, Jonelle speculated about what the woman could possibly want. Deciding she was getting nowhere staring out the window, Jonelle left her office and went to the break room to make sure they had fresh coffee.

On her way back, Jonelle heard voices coming from the reception area. She went to see who Rainey was talking to.

"Oh, there she is," Rainey said. "I was just getting ready to call you, Jonelle. This is Mrs. Reyes. Mrs. Reyes, this is Ms. Sweet."

Jonelle smiled and took the offered hand. The grip, soft and weak, belied the overall professional look of the woman standing before her. The tall woman with blond, wavy, chin-length hair was dressed in clothes that looked as if they would cost Jonelle a week's salary.

The pearl gray slacks and pale pink sweater screamed cashmere. The cultured pearls with a large oval diamond around the neck and the diamond stud earrings indicated the woman didn't need to head for the sales racks. A few items detracted from Mrs. Reyes' overall appearance. For all the obvious display of wealth, the hands held no rings. Unpolished fingernails were bitten down to the quick and a makeup line separated the edge of Mrs. Reyes' jaw from her neck, resulting in a disconcerting two-tone appearance. Dirt, or something close to it, stained the pocket of her pants. A heavy hand with the perfume bottle encased the woman in a cloud of cloying scent.

"My office is down here," Jonelle said, her arm indicating the way. Mrs. Reyes stepped in front of her. As they moved away from the receptionist's desk, Jonelle glanced over at Rainey who cocked her head and lifted an eyebrow. She fanned the air with a sheet of paper before turning back to her computer.

"Would you like something to drink, Mrs. Reyes?" Jonelle asked, as they walked down the hall. "We have coffee, soda and water."

"Nothing, thank you. And please call me Sophia."

The door to Jonelle's office was already open. She motioned for Sophia to sit across from her desk. "And I'm Jonelle," she said sitting down. "First, let me say, I'm sorry for your loss."

Sophia nodded. Through thick, black mascara, the blue eyes were dry and clear. Jonelle's nose itched. She stole a glance at her spider plant sitting on the edge of the desk, close to Mrs. Reyes, and hoped the woman's fragrance wouldn't cause it to wilt.

Sophia's eyes flitted around the office. Jonelle waited for her to finish taking in the surroundings.

"I have to admit, Sophia, that I was surprised to hear you wanted to see me," Jonelle said, after the woman's eyes settled once again on her. "Any information you need about your sister's death really should come from the police. Even though the investigation has just started, they know more than I do."

Sophia reached down and opened her bag. She took out a section of newspaper and placed it on the desk. "It says in here that some bum found Susanna. The police told me that you know who that bum is and you're trying to help him." She stabbed a ragged finger on the paper. "I want to know what that bum knows about my sister."

Jonelle touched her gold necklace. She took the paper and turned it around to face her. After a quick glance at the article, she looked up and spoke in a measured voice.

"First off, Mrs. Reyes, I don't see anywhere in this article where the word 'bum' is used. It does say homeless. It's because of him that the police were able to identify your sister as quickly as they did. Also, Luther had nothing to do with Susanna living on the street in the first place. That was *her* choice." Jonelle leaned back in her chair. "So, if the reason for your being here was to voice an opinion about people less fortunate than you, well, congratulations, you've done that." Jonelle rose. "I'll see you out."

Traffic noise from the street below filtered through the window. Somewhere down the hall someone laughed. Jonelle stood next to her desk and waited.

Sophia put the paper back in her tote bag. She clasped her hands in her lap and looked up at Jonelle. "Please," she said. "I'd like to start over. I need your help in finding out about my sister."

After a moment's hesitation, Jonelle sat. "What kind of help are you talking about?" So far, Jonelle wasn't sure she liked this woman but decided to at least hear what she wanted.

Sophia glanced at a silver-framed picture on Jonelle's desk. "Husband?"

"Deceased," Jonelle responded. She didn't feel like telling this woman anything about herself and glanced pointedly at her watch.

Sophia inhaled deeply. "I'd like to hire you to find out how Susanna ended up, uh, living on the street and everything that bum, uh, homeless person, knows about her the entire time she was down here."

Jonelle didn't think she heard right. "Hire me? You sure you want to do that?"

Sophia reached down for her bag and placed it on her lap. She searched inside and brought out a small, brown envelope which she slid across the desk. "There are a few pictures of Susanna inside. The last one was taken about two years ago. I also included the most recent piece of correspondence I got from her, which was a birthday card she sent this summer. I kept the envelope. There's no return address, but it's postmarked Baltimore, Maryland."

Jonelle opened the clasp and removed the items. The top picture showed two young girls together, possibly in their teen years, smiling broadly for the camera, their arms around each other's waist. Jonelle looked from the picture to Sophia and back to the picture. "You're twins?" she asked. Jonelle had never seen Susanna's body.

"Susanna was the oldest by eight minutes."

"Well, well," Jonelle said. She thought it interesting that Burt didn't mention Susanna was a twin when he left the voicemail. Wait until she saw him the next time. Jonelle studied the other pictures, trying to see if she could detect a difference between the sisters. "Mind if I keep these two?" Jonelle selected a recent one of the sisters together and another of Susanna standing under some cherry blossoms near the Lincoln Memorial. Cherry blossoms. That meant Susanna had visited the area before.

"Was Susanna from this area?"

"No," Sophia replied. "Born and raised on the Upper Peninsula in Michigan." She looked at the photos in Jonelle's hand. "I'd like the pictures back when you're finished with the investigation."

"Tell me, were there any differences in your appearance that would tip people off as to who was who?"

Sophia looked up at the ceiling. "Hmm. I'm trying to remember how it was when we were growing up. It's easier now because I wear my hair short and the last time I saw Suze her hair was down to her shoulders. She also dresses a bit, uh, flamboyantly. If you know what I mean."

"Not really," Jonelle said. Never one for making a fashion statement, Jonelle needed more of an explanation. If Susanna dressed like Jonelle's friend Adrienne, the woman would stick out like diamonds in a plastics factory.

"She liked wearing loose-fitting, blousy-type clothes. You know, kind of '*Annie Hall*'. I know that's old school, but you get my meaning," Sophia said.

Jonelle wrinkled her nose. "That's not what I'd call '*flamboyant*,' but I understand you guys had different tastes in fashion."

"I suppose if you saw us side by side, I'd be a bit shorter and Suze would be a tad thinner." Sophia's face flushed. "That's what would be visible anyway."

Jonelle honed in on that last remark. "What about what someone couldn't see right off? Any scars, moles—anything that would distinguish the two of you?"

The phone ringing on the desk startled them both. Jonelle glanced over at the caller ID display. It was Burt. He'd have to wait.

"It can go to voicemail," Jonelle said. "About those hidden from view identifiers. You were saying?"

Sophia sighed and busied herself with putting the remaining pictures and envelope back in her purse.

While she waited for a response, Jonelle studied the woman some more. Her smooth forehead, shining under the office lights, indicated a stress free life. However, a slight eyebrow twitch made Jonelle wonder.

"This is embarrassing," Sophia said, "but I guess they already found out when they did her autopsy."

"Found out what?"

Sophia sighed. "For our eighteenth birthday we decided we were going to stop being good mid-western teenagers and live more dangerously." She averted her eyes. "So, we got tattoos."

Jonelle laughed. "Is that all? Shoot, grandmas are getting tats nowadays. What did you guys get?"

Sophia hugged her bag close to her chest. "I almost chickened out, but I finally agreed to a tiny, red rose. I have it on the back of my right shoulder. Susanna was always more daring than me. She decided to go all out and got a smiling red fox tattooed on her right hip."

Jonelle pursed her lips tight to hold in the laughter. She didn't want to further embarrass the woman sitting before her and now glowing a bright red.

"Okay, I'll take your case. Just so we understand each other, if at any time the police tell me to back off, I'll have no choice but to do so since it's an open murder investigation."

Sophia sat back in her chair. "Thanks. Will you, uh, be talking to that homeless guy."

"Probably." No need for her to know she'd already contacted Luther.

After quoting the agency's rates and required down payment, Jonelle turned to her computer and pulled up a client form. "Is Susanna Quinley her full name?"

"Now it is. She was married before but it was so short and filled with grief for her that she went to court and got her name legally changed back to Quinley. Her rat-bastard of a husband's name is Barrington Kelly. Barrington, can you believe it? Who names their kid, Barrington? We always called him plain old Barry. The prick."

Jonelle swiveled toward the woman, eyebrows raised. The voice and demeanor had changed. Up until this point Sophia had maintained such tight control. Curious. Jonelle turned back to the computer screen and continued typing.

Sophia cleared her throat. "Sorry. It's just that he was so mean to her."

"Mean in what way?"

She hesitated briefly before continuing. "Suze didn't go into a lot of detail. What I do know for sure is that the police were called to their home on several occasions."

Jonelle sat back in her chair and thought about that for a moment. It could explain Susanna's leaving, but not how she ended up without means of taking care of herself. Jonelle typed a note on the form to check police reports for possible domestic violence.

"Do you know where Barrington, uh, Barry, lives now?"

"I don't know exactly where he lives, but last I heard he was in private practice, working as a psychologist somewhere in DC." She snorted. "Lord help his clients."

"Great. I'll check with the American Psychological Association. See if they know where he practices. That'll help me locate him."

"Do they give that information out? Phone numbers and such?"

"Depends," Jonelle said. "What's his specialty? I'll tell them I'm looking for a referral."

Sophia giggled.

"Problem?"

"Well, last I heard he dealt with men's issues. You know, stuff like … uh … erectile dysfunction."

"Oh." After two beats both women burst out laughing.

"Thought they had pills for that," Jonelle gasped, still trying to control her giggles.

"Guess he gets his clients when the pills stop working," Sophia said.

Jonelle pushed her box of tissues toward Sophia who took one and dabbed her eyes.

"Whew," Jonelle said, feeling a lot better about Sophia. "Back to the business at hand." The giggles started again.

"I'll need your sister's last known address and where she worked," Jonelle managed, after they both stopped laughing. "If she had any friends here that she might have mentioned. Or any concerns about any individuals. I'm assuming you told the police all you know?"

"I don't know anything about her life down here. As I said, we were born and raised in Michigan, in a small town on the Upper Peninsula off of State Highway 28. It's a pretty little town. We get our fair share of tourists every year."

Jonelle remembered Luther's comment that Susanna complained about the heat and humidity in this area.

"After Suze graduated Michigan State she went back home and got a job working in local government," Sophia said. "About that same time, I left home and after graduation went to work in Traverse City. That's where I met my husband … um, ex-husband that is." She looked at the naked ring finger.

"What kind of government job?"

"She started out working as a clerk in the city commissioner's office. While there she rose through the ranks rather quickly.

It seemed that every time I got a letter from her, she mentioned another promotion." Jonelle detected a hint of pride in Sophia's voice.

Smart, educated and a long way from home. "What was the last job she had?"

Two beeps on Jonelle's desk phone stopped Sophia from answering.

"Sorry," Jonelle said, looking over at the phone. "That's from the receptionist. She must have something important for me." She held up an index finger. "One sec." Jonelle picked up the phone and tried not to sound annoyed. "I'm kinda busy now Rainey." Jonelle listened to the receptionist tell her that detective Burton needed to speak to her about the victim's sister. "Tell him Mrs. Reyes is sitting here now and I'll call him later. Thanks." After she replaced the handset, Jonelle spread her hands in apology. "I should have told her no interruptions. Now where were we? Oh yes, your sister's last job in Michigan."

Sophia shook her head. "You know, I haven't even told my mom about Suze. Mom's recovering from advanced stage breast cancer, and I wanted to be sure the body really was my sister's. We were all she had left after my dad died five years ago." Sophia's eyes moistened. "I can't believe Susanna's gone."

Jonelle pointed to the box of tissues. Sophia smiled and shook her head.

Aware Sophia hadn't answered her question, Jonelle repeated it. "Do you know the last job Susanna held in Michigan? Was she still an office worker of some kind?"

"Office worker? Not exactly. Susanna was always good in math and very business savvy. The last job she had up there was City Treasurer."

Jonelle stared open-mouthed. How in the world did a high ranking local government employee end up homeless and murdered on a Baltimore street a thousand miles from home?

CHAPTER 9

The next evening, Jonelle persuaded Adrienne to keep her company on her second surveillance job. Doris Henshaw suspected her husband of having an affair and wanted irrefutable proof of infidelity before deciding what steps to take in the marriage.

"So, let me get this straight," Adrienne said as she sat on the sofa while Jonelle placed a digital camera in a backpack. "First, we're gonna go spy on some woman's husband and then you wanna go get something to eat? What if he heads out to a strip club or something? I'm not going into no nudie place."

Next to the camera, Jonelle inserted a small recorder and her Beretta into the backpack. "Tonight, I want to see where he goes," she said, zipping up the bag. "The wife claims he leaves home around ten at night, saying he's meeting friends for a quick drink."

"So how come she doesn't go with him?"

"He tells her after working all week he needs a night out with the boys. According to Mrs. Henshaw, his nights out with the fellas have become more and more frequent, and last longer and longer."

"Ahh. So she wants you to find out about these 'fellas,' right? " Adrienne asked.

"Right," Jonelle said. "That's why she hired the agency. According to Mrs. Henshaw, he doesn't come home until very early in the morning. She's tried waiting up for him but always falls asleep. Don't worry," she said, noticing the stricken look on Adrienne's face. "I'm not watching the place for more than a couple hours. I'm hoping once he leaves the house, he goes straight to the girlfriend."

Adrienne shook her head. "Why do people go through all that? If he's not happy, just leave the woman already. Am I gonna get a cut for helping you out? I mean, you're really taking advantage of this best friend business. What if I already had a date lined up for tonight?"

"All I heard from you this past week was how Michael was getting on your very last nerve, so I figured you had room on your social calendar. Throw me that sweater. It might get cold this evening."

Adrienne frowned at the beige cardigan, then lobbed it at Jonelle. "You gonna wear that? You look like you're going for a job interview at the phone company."

Jonelle rolled her eyes to the ceiling. "These slacks are comfortable. We may be sitting in the Jeep for about an hour or so."

Adrienne sat back against the sofa and crossed her legs. "Great. But I'm betting the dude ends up with his buddies at a naked lady place. That, or trolling the streets."

Jonelle pointed to Adrienne's black leather pants and zebra striped top. "In that case you'll blend right in." She hooted with laughter.

"Oh ha ha. Funny girl. I'm serious. What do we do if he goes to see Betty and the booty shakers, huh?"

"Just be cool. I'll figure something out if—and that's a big if— instead of going to a girlfriend's house he ends up somewhere funky instead."

"Fine."

"Grab your stuff. We've got about twenty minutes to get in place before he goes out."

Both women decided against taking Jonelle's Jeep. "I can't get comfortable in that thing," Adrienne had said. Jonelle agreed the gray Saab would be less conspicuous. After removing her camera she placed everything else on the back seat. Jonelle then gave instructions on how to get to the client's address. Less than thirty minutes later, Adrienne pulled into a spot three cars down from the residence, on the opposite side of the street.

At ten o'clock on the dot, an outside light came on and Jonelle observed a tall, thin white man leave the small bungalow. "That's him," she said. He wore jeans positioned low over his protruding belly and a light colored turtle neck sweater. An unzipped leather bomber jacket completed his outfit. He paused on the porch and lit a cigarette.

"Looks like an average guy," Adrienne said.

"Hmm. Most of them are. When he pulls out, keep at least one car in front of you. I don't think he's expecting to be followed, but you never know."

The man ambled to the end of his sidewalk and strode up to a dark Toyota truck. He got in, waited for two cars to pass and pulled out.

"Okay," Jonelle said. "Let's go."

"Roger dodger," Adrienne said with a giggle. "I got a feeling this is gonna be fun."

After several miles passing through tree-lined residential streets, Henshaw pulled up to a concrete and glass high rise building and parked in a spot close to the entrance.

Adrienne whistled. "That's not what I expected from Mister Middle Class. You sure he's screwin' around?" Adrienne eased her car in a space marked "Visitor."

"Don't park here," Jonelle said. "You're sitting under a light." She pointed to a darker area next to some trees. "Over there."

Adrienne backed into a space several feet away from the left side of the entrance, in between a white Lexus and dark BMW sedan. From their vantage point they had a clear view of the building's foyer. "Looks like a classy place," Adrienne said, cutting off the engine.

They watched Henshaw approach a uniformed man standing outside. After a few words, the doorman tipped his hat and opened the glass doors.

Jonelle frowned. "Gotta agree with you. This is not what I expected. Wait here." She placed the camera in the glove compartment and scooted out of her seat in time to see Henshaw walk up to a desk. He signed something, leaned over and spoke to the man dressed in the same hunter green uniform with gold epaulets on each shoulder.

"Hey," Adrienne said, leaning her head out of the window. "What do I do?"

Jonelle ignored the question and hurried to the entrance. She smiled at the doorman and reached out to open the glass doors. "May I help you ma'am?" he asked in a deep voice.

Jonelle pretended not to hear and went for the door. He moved over, blocking her way. She watched Henshaw enter an elevator. After the doors closed, she faced her questioner.

"Hi," she said. The doorman's dark eyes bored into her. His face didn't match her smile. "I had a meeting with Mr. Henshaw earlier, and he forgot something. I need to give it back to him."

The doorman held out his hand. "I'll make sure he gets it."

"Um, no offense Mr. uh,"—the badge read Rodrigo—"Rodrigo, but I'd rather give it to him in person."

Rodrigo shook his head.

"Listen, I'd hate to tell him that he's missing his valuables just because you won't let me inside."

Jonelle noticed a slight twinge of indecision in the man's eyes. She eased forward, but his voice stopped her.

"You can't go inside without permission," he said, holding up his right hand. "I'll call upstairs and have him come meet you."

"Why can't I wait in the lobby? It's cold out here."

"I'll need to check with the resident first."

A high pitched scream pierced the night. Startled, Jonelle lurched forward and into Rodrigo, pushing him off balance into the door. Another shriek followed.

Rodrigo regained his balance and ran down the sidewalk toward the sound of a woman's cries. Jonelle grabbed the handle before the door closed and made a beeline for the lobby.

The man at the desk rose from his seat, but before he could say anything, Jonelle clutched at her neck. "Rodrigo needs help out there," she said, breathing heavy as though she'd run two miles instead of walked twenty feet. "Sounds like one of your residents is being attacked."

He sat and reached for the phone on the desk.

"No time," Jonelle said, "he needs help *now*. I'll call 9-1-1."

She couldn't call him by name because the area above his breast pocket was blank. Jonelle guessed his age at somewhere between fifty-five and sixty years. She almost felt sorry for him as he tugged on the collar of his uniform as if it suddenly became too tight. He peered around Jonelle. She turned and followed his gaze. No sign of Rodrigo.

He squared his shoulders and came from around the desk and rushed to the entrance doors. Two things struck her. One, the staff knew Henshaw, identifying him as a frequent visitor, and two, so much for the building's security. Jonelle waited until he opened the glass doors before she turned the register around and picked out Henshaw's name on the sheet, also noting that he was visiting room 727.

Jonelle hurried to the elevators and pressed the "up" button. She tapped her foot on the marble floor, praying the elevator would arrive before Rodrigo and his co-worker returned. A soft *ding* and on her right an empty elevator opened. Jonelle entered and punched 7.

Once the doors closed, Jonelle wondered what she'd say to whomever answered the door. As the lift rose past 3 and then 4 the crumbs of an idea formed in her mind. She didn't need an elaborate ruse; Henshaw knew nothing about her. She'd walk up, knock on the door and feign embarrassment and shock at arriving at the wrong room. Or something like that.

After exiting and quickly determining where she needed to go, Jonelle headed in that direction. As she turned the corner a man and woman approached from the opposite direction. She recognized Henshaw and next to him a tall redhead clutched his arm. Almost the same height as Henshaw, the redhead's emerald green spaghetti-strapped dress looked as if one chocolate peanut candy nugget could burst it's seams. A coat of the same color hung loose from Henshaw's other arm.

Henshaw nodded as they passed.

Jonelle managed to return his gesture and muttered a weak, "Good evening." The two kept going, heading in the direction of the elevators.

The situation called for fast thinking. "Oh darn," she said out loud, turning to follow the couple. "I can't believe I left my, uh, package in the car. Now I have to go back down and get it."

Henshaw and the woman looked at each other, and then at Jonelle. Henshaw shrugged.

Jonelle stood on the opposite side in the elevator and watched the couple's reflection in the shiny brass panel next to them. Henshaw's date leaned into him as the three rode down in silence.

When they arrived on the Lobby floor, Jonelle stepped to the back. Henshaw motioned for her to precede him, but she'd glimpsed Rodrigo and his co-worker talking next to the desk.

She shook her head. Neither man paid any attention to Henshaw and his date as they paused while Henshaw helped his date with her coat. Jonelle pressed her thumb on the *door open* button and waited for Henshaw and the redhead to reach the building's double doors before exiting the elevator.

"Hey. Wait a minute Miss," Rodrigo said when he noticed Jonelle.

Jonelle rushed to the doors. "Thanks, guys. You saved me from having to hold onto his personal items."

Almost running to catch up with the couple, Jonelle felt Rodrigo's eyes on her back. "You two have a great evening," she shouted at Henshaw. Jonelle waved. Henshaw half turned and waved back. His date stared straight ahead.

Jonelle rushed to the Saab. The car was empty. Puzzled, she reached for the handle, and pulled. As she did so, Adrienne rose up from the back seat.

Jonelle swallowed a scream. "Oh my God. You scared the crap out of me. What the hell're you doing in the back seat?"

A self-satisfied look covered Adrienne's face. "You can thank me later. What did you find out?"

Jonelle waited for Adrienne to come around to the driver's side.

"Thank you for what? And keep your eyes open for Henshaw. I followed him and his sweetie out of the building, so unless there's another way in and out of this place, they should be coming along any minute now. And I have a feeling they won't be taking his truck." She grabbed the camera from the glove compartment.

Almost as if on cue, a silver Lincoln Town car approached, the redhead in the passenger seat. "That's them," Jonelle whispered to Adrienne. "We have to follow. See where he goes." Jonelle snapped several pictures as the Lincoln crept by.

"By the way, what was all that noise? I heard somebody scream, but I don't see any cop cars."

Adrienne giggled. "That's why you need to thank me. I had to distract that guy, so the only thing I could think to do was, well, let 'er rip. So I did."

"You're the one who screamed?"

Adrienne nodded. She kept her eyes on the Lincoln in front of her and the satisfied look on her face.

"Didn't Rodrigo catch you?"

Adrienne stole a quick glance over at Jonelle. "Who the hell's Rodrigo?"

"Never mind. Hey, watch it. He's turning left at the light."

"I see him," Adrienne said, also making a left turn. "Anyway when that dude in the organ grinder's monkey suit came running up, I told him someone tried to grab me but I fought the guy off with my five-inch stilettos. He wanted to call the cops but I told him I was all right and nothing was stolen."

Jonelle stared open-mouthed at Adrienne. For tonight anyway, she admired her friend's act first, think about it later attitude. "Wonder where they're going?" Jonelle asked, her eyes back on the road. She looked out the passenger side window. Regular street lights gave way to the high density sodium kind. Liquor stores materialized on every other corner. "This area doesn't look familiar. Don't lose him."

The gray Saab followed until the car pulled in front of a low rise building with a large parking area that began in front and curved around back. The neon symbol above the curved entrance to the building depicted two martini glasses, outlined in blue neon, crossed at the stem. "Liquid" red and green lights flowed from one glass to the other. Spotlights shining on a hand-painted sign below the image read "Topsey Turvey Club." Jonelle took several pictures.

After two beats, both women looked at each other and howled with laughter.

"Shh," Jonelle gasped. "We don't wanna call attention to ourselves. See if you can park close. He's seen me but not you, so we should be okay."

It wasn't hard keeping the big sedan in sight. The parking lot, though busy, wasn't filled to capacity yet. That probably happened sometime around midnight. Jonelle slid down in her seat as Adrienne passed the parked Lincoln. Three aisles later, she maneuvered the Saab into an empty slot.

"I knew we'd end up in some nudie bar. I just knew it," Adrienne said, slapping the steering wheel.

"Hey. It's no big deal." Jonelle raised her camera. "There they go. Great. I'm getting some good shots." After Henshaw and his date entered the club, Jonelle turned serious. "Damn. I'm not dressed for this place. Tell you what. You go—"

"Oh, no," Adrienne said. "I'm not going inside by myself. That guy had jeans on. You'll be all right." Adrienne pointed out the window. "Look at that, willya. There're two more couples going in. What kinda guy takes a date to this kind of club?"

Jonelle shrugged. "Maybe this place isn't so bad," she said, looking around. The bland pale brick front could pass for a family restaurant. "Looks okay from the outside. I need to see for myself how intimate those two are. Can't take the camera though." She stored it back in the glove compartment. "I'm ready. Let's go." She undid her seatbelt and got out. Adrienne remained in the car.

Jonelle looked down. "Well?" she asked through the window. Her hand motioned for Adrienne to follow. "Come on," she hissed.

Adrienne's lips pursed in a straight line. "Can't I just wait in the car?" she asked, her voice muffled by the window.

Jonelle shook her head. "I need you as backup in case something happens."

She glared at Jonelle and flung her seatbelt aside. She got out and slammed the door behind her. "Fine," Adrienne said, her voice tight. "Let's get this over with. How long you gonna be anyway?"

"Not long. I just need to see their interaction. See how cozy they get." Jonelle turned and followed the mixed group of patrons up to the club. Adrienne's heels clicked a few feet behind.

"Looks like they're taking money and checking ID."

"Great. I'm actually gonna have to pay for this?"

Jonelle looked over her shoulder. "Will you please stop complaining? I've got money for both of us. The client's paying my expenses for this job."

Behind her, Adrienne sighed theatrically. Jonelle stood at the entrance and rummaged in her purse for her driver's license.

The tall, beefy man dressed in black T-shirt and black jeans, held up his hand. "No need to show me your ID and there's no charge for women. Any of your male friends want to come, the cover is twenty dollars." Jonelle didn't know whether or not to be insulted that he didn't want to see her identification. "Why no charge for women?"

"This is a reputable club. We like to encourage female clientele."

"Do you need to see my ID?" Adrienne asked. She held up her license.

"Thanks," the man said, glancing at it and returning her smile.

The aroma of cooked beef and fried onions took both women by surprise. Adrienne sniffed the air. "Hey, that smells good."

After her eyes adjusted to the dim lighting, Jonelle searched the expansive room for signs of Henshaw. She spotted him over on the far right, one arm looped around the girlfriend.

"Now you got your answer," Adrienne said. "Let's go."

Jonelle stared in disbelief. "You kidding me? I'm not leaving yet. I'm hungry so let's sit down, order a drink and something to eat."

"What about your claustrophobia?"

"If I start to feel weird I'll head for the door. Concentrating on something, like eating, helps so I should be okay."

A young woman overflowing in a black lace top bustier and very tight leather shorts strode up to the two women. "Did you ladies come for the show or would you like something to eat."

"Eat," Jonelle and Adrienne said in unison.

"Fine. You can sit in the back where the main dining area is, or I can serve you out here in the entertainment section."

"I vote for the dining area," Adrienne said. "I have no desire to watch Betty and the booty shakers up close and personal." Adrienne indicated the dancer entwined around the pole on the stage closest to the two women.

The waitress frowned at Adrienne. "Her name's not Betty. That's Amber."

Adrienne poked Jonelle in the ribs. "I'm guessin' the synapses aren't firing on all cylinders tonight," she muttered.

"Huh? You want Schnapps?"

"Just ignore her," Jonelle said as Adrienne rolled her eyes.

Jonelle checked the club's layout. Three circular stages formed a triangle instead of a straight line. The requisite pole occupied the center of each. Above each stage a different colored spotlight illuminated the dancers. Blue on the left, red in the center and yellow at the far end. Dancers performed in time to music piped in from overhead speakers.

A few customers eyed the women as they were escorted to a table with cutlery and drinking glasses already laid out. From

Jonelle's vantage point, if she pushed her chair back a little, she could still see Henshaw entwined around his date.

The waitress took their order for drinks—a vodka and tonic for Jonelle and an apple martini for Adrienne. After the waitress left, Jonelle crinkled her nose in distaste at her friend's choice of drink. "Really? An apple-tini? Since when do you drink those things?"

"Since I got dragged into spending my Saturday night in a perv palace, that's when."

"This place isn't what I thought it would be," Jonelle said. "Look around. Nobody in here is naked."

"Whatever," Adrienne replied, nose buried in the menu. "I'm gonna order the biggest steak they got, with fries. And a salad with blue cheese dressing. What about you?"

After the waitress delivered the drinks and took their food order, Jonelle kept her eyes on Henshaw. He moved so close to the redhead's face it looked as if they were sharing the same breath. Jonelle removed her cellphone. "I need a few more shots and this is less conspicuous than the camera," she said in response to Adrienne's raised eyebrows. Henshaw leaned in and kissed his date. "Gotta move closer. Look," she said, holding her cellphone out to Adrienne, "since he hasn't seen you, why don't you go over there and take a few pictures without them noticing what you're doing."

Adrienne opened her mouth and then shut it again as the waitress returned with two plates of food. Jonelle placed the phone on her lap. After making sure her customers didn't require anything else the waitress pointed to the phone. "Those aren't allowed in here," she said.

"I'm not taking pictures," Jonelle said. "I have to keep my phone ready in case I get a call from one of my kids."

Adrienne coughed on the word *kids*.

"You're supposed to keep it muted and in your purse. Those are the rules."

"Fine," Jonelle said. She dropped the phone inside her bag. The waitress turned to go, looked at the two women over her shoulder and started to say something else. Instead, she shrugged and wandered off.

"Good thing getting involved is not in her job description," Jonelle said around bites of steak.

"Kids, huh? Fast thinking. By the way, this is really good food. Shame the so-called entertainment is lousy."

Jonelle ate and kept her eyes focused on Henshaw. "Actually, I was thinking the entertainment over there is pretty good. Look! No! Don't look. See that?"

"Thought you told me not to look," Adrienne grumbled.

"Henshaw is doing all he can to consume that woman's face. Wonder what her name is?" Jonelle's hand wrapped around the phone. She checked around for the waitress. Not seeing her, Jonelle set the phone on video, tapped the screen and aimed it at Henshaw's table. "Damn. Too far. I gotta get closer." Jonelle tucked the camera under her sweater and slid around to the back of the club. As she focused in on Henshaw's table next to the stage with the yellow light, Jonelle opened the cardigan and recorded him feeding food to his date. Satisfied, she rushed back to her seat.

A few minutes later, the redhead looked at her watch. Next, she cupped Henshaw's face in her hands. After another long kiss, she got up, gave him a finger wave and headed behind the stage area.

"Well, I'll be damned," Jonelle said as the scene played out before her. "Henshaw's girlfriend is part of the entertainment." She finished her drink. "This job's done."

"Really?" Adrienne asked. "You finished with him already?"

With the phone on her lap, Jonelle replayed part of the video and nodded. "Picture's a little dark but you can see who's who and what's what. Mrs. Henshaw wanted proof of her hubby cheating on her and I've got more than enough evidence. One surveillance case down, one more to go." Jonelle swirled the ice around in her glass and contemplated whether to order another one.

Adrienne solved the issue when she asked the waitress for the check. "I hope you don't need my help on this other case," she said to Jonelle, "'cause I'm not sure I like some of these new experiences you keep getting involved in."

"The other stakeout is easy. It's the big case I want to concentrate on."

"You got a real case? What is it?"

"Finding out how Susanna Quinley ended up as a homeless person. And ... who killed her and why."

CHAPTER 10

On Monday morning Jonelle sat in front of her computer and looked up the town in Michigan where Susanna worked. She pulled up the website, scrolled through the images and tried to get a feel for the town of Oldenberry. If the photos were an indication of the entire area, the place was very attractive: wood and stone lakeside homes, many with their own docks. Dense wooded areas wrapped around several small waterfalls dotting the landscape. A few more clicks and she landed on the local government site.

"Let's see what we have here," Jonelle said. She selected the link to the city commissioner's office and discovered the contact address and telephone number. She swiveled her chair around, picked up the receiver and dialed the 800 number. After a few rings a chirpy "Hello, commissioner's office," sounded in her ear. Jonelle got right to the point.

"Good morning. My name is Jonelle Sweet and I'm a private investigator with Shorter Investigative Services here in Baltimore. I've been hired by Sophia Quinley Reyes to investigate how her sister, Susanna Quinley, came to live in Maryland." Jonelle didn't want to mention Susanna's death to this miscellaneous voice over the phone. "Mrs. Reyes informed me that Ms. Quinley was the city treasurer. Is that correct?"

The silence on the other end stretched for so long that Jonelle wondered if she'd been cut off. "Um, hello? Are you still there?"

"Yes. I … uh … need to let you speak to someone else. Hold please."

Jonelle frowned at the phone. The voice on the other end had gone from happy to guarded at the mention of Susanna's name. Jonelle wrinkled her nose in distaste as the hold music featured Barry Manilow straining on and on about having made it, or something to that effect.

Just when she thought the song was over, it started again. Midway through the second iteration, Barry was cut off by a man's voice on the other end of the line.

"This is Chief Commissioner Norman Finkleberg. I've just been informed you're investigating Susanna Quinley. What is this about?"

Jonelle decided telling the man information that was public knowledge wouldn't hurt anything. "Ms. Quinley, Susanna, was killed less than a week ago. The police are investigating how and why she died." Jonelle hesitated. No need to mention Susanna lived on the street. "My job is to uncover how she ended up living here in Maryland. In order to do that, I need to know about her life up there."

Labored breathing came through the line. The man sounded as though he was having a heart attack. "Hello? Mr. Finkleberg, are you all right?"

"No," he said weakly. "This is too shocking. And on top of everything else. Oh, my God."

"Tell you what. I don't think we should discuss Susanna over the phone. I'd like to come up and talk to you. And anyone else who may have known her." Jonelle reached in the top drawer for her day planner and glanced at the current week. "I'm free later this week. I'd like to find out as much as possible as soon as possible, if you're available." Plus, she wanted to talk to him before his health gave out. Poor guy sounded sick.

Once his breathing settled, they set up a meeting for Thursday morning. That would give Jonelle enough time to fly up there Wednesday, rent a car and look around a bit first.

The only concern she had was the distance between the Detroit airport and the Upper Peninsula. Finkleberg assured her it wasn't as bad as shown on the map.

"Most people fly into Detroit's Wayne County Airport, and connect into Sault Ste. Marie. From there you can rent a car. It's only about sixty miles to the town." Finkleberg took Jonelle's name, telephone number and email address and said he'd make a reservation for her at the best bed and breakfast in the area. She started to request accommodations for two days, then decided to add Friday, just in case. "I'll email you the specifics," he said.

After explaining her plans to Rainey, the receptionist agreed to make plane and rental car reservations for three days and leave the return trip open in the event Jonelle decided to stay an extra day. "I can close the Henshaw case right now," Jonelle said, standing next to Rainey's desk. "I'll type up my report and add copies of the photos and video I took of him and his date. I'll need you to send everything by registered mail to Mrs. Henshaw, along with the invoice."

Rainey nodded. "No problem. Do you want me to get the forms ready giving you permission to take your weapon on the plane?"

"Almost forgot that. Definitely. The last thing I need is a hassle from the TSA."

Rainey scribbled a few notes. "You know the gun must be unloaded and locked in a case, right?"

Jonelle nodded.

"Anything else you need before you go, Jonelle?"

Jonelle looked up at the ceiling. "I'm not sure what to do with the Polly Cole case. I'm committed to her every night this week, except weekends."

"What did you plan on doing with that case when you agreed to go to Michigan?"

Jonelle felt her face get warm. "I honestly hadn't thought that through. I was too excited about the prospect of going up there and talking to people who knew Susanna." She shrugged. "Any advice?"

Rainey sat back in her chair. She tapped a yellow pencil against her chin.

Jonelle squinted at the receptionist. Was there a pencil stuck in her hair?

"Hmm. How long have you been on this case?" Rainey asked.

"About a week. The kid has gone nowhere in all that time. 'Course with my luck, the first night I'm not there, she'll bolt." Jonelle fiddled with her necklace. "Hey. Do you think maybe Ben could help me out this week? It'll get him away from the dreaded diet for a while. Think I'll ask him." Jonelle turned to go.

"Hold it a sec," Rainey said. "While I agree that of the two guys Ben is the best choice, you still need to approach this the right way. Let me think on this a minute."

Jonelle passed the time by pacing back and forth. After the third pass, and judging by the look on Rainey's face, she stopped. As she stood above Rainey she noticed that wedged in the receptionist's ash blond bouffant was not just one, but two pencils. The yellow implements penetrated the spray-stiffened hair on opposite sides of her head.

"Uh, Rainey," Jonelle said.

"Hush. I'm still percolating on this."

Jonelle knew better than to go against Rainey's wishes, especially while percolating was in progress. She wished Marvin would buzz or the phone would ring. Something.

After what seemed an eternity, Rainey pointed a finger in the air. "Got it."

"Finally," Jonelle said under her breath.

"How about this. He's been almost unbearable because of that darn diet. He complains that all his wife packs him for lunch is a salad or hard boiled eggs. Stuff he wouldn't touch on a normal basis. Plus the woman is kinda sneaky. She keeps his credit cards so he can't buy his lunch and I suspect he doesn't have much cash on him either." Rainey smiled. "So, how about you offer to pack him three days of good, substantial Ben-style meals and keep them in the fridge here for him to take when he covers for you. What d'you think?"

Jonelle frowned. "I think getting between a husband and wife is a bad idea. Besides, do you really think I can buy his time for a few sandwiches?"

Rainey held Jonelle's gaze.

"Oh right," Jonelle said. "Forgot who we're talking about."

"It'll only be for a few days. Just 'til you get back from the north country."

Jonelle still wasn't sure the food idea was a good one, but she couldn't think of anything else. "Guess it'll have to do. And you make it sound like I'm going to Alaska."

Rainey stuck another pencil in her hair. "Might as well," she said. "Isn't this place near Canada?"

Jonelle nodded.

"I rest my case," Rainey turned and looked at the clock on the wall beside her desk. "Ben should be back before noon. I'll say you need to see him. Okay?"

Jonelle agreed. She started to mention the pencils but figured Rainey would either remember or the sheer number would cause them to begin falling out of her head. She started down to her office, turned and came back.

"I almost forgot. I know I fly into Detroit, and then connect to that Sue something place. Once I arrive there, how far is it to Susanna's hometown?"

Rainey turned to her computer. After rapid fire key tapping, she confirmed what Finkleberg had already told Jonelle.

"How big is this airport and why's it called Sue Saint Marie?" Jonelle frowned. "Never heard of it."

Rainey spelled it for her which confused Jonelle even more. Seeing her perplexed look, Rainey added, "I think it's Native American or French. Maybe both. I'll make sure you get a car with a good GPS."

The morning passed with few interruptions. She typed up the Henshaw results and a status report on the Cole case. Ben agreed to take over the one remaining assignment. "Maybe I'll get lucky and the kid'll make a run for it the first night," he said.

"Just call the mom if she does," Jonelle reminded him. "If she wants you to notify the police, that's okay. Nothing else."

Ben gave her a grocery list and instructions on what to make for two nights of surveillance work. "Better make enough food for three nights, in the event you're delayed." He even teased her when she told him where she was going.

"So, you're takin' your snow boots and snow pants, parka … all that stuff, right?"

"What is it with you guys? You act as if I'm going to the North Pole."

"You pretty damn near are. Better pack your passport in case you wander across the border. No telling what those Canucks will do to you, you being an illegal alien and all." He snorted and left before she could fire back a retort.

With travel arrangements made and her cases taken care of, Jonelle sat back and concentrated on what she'd learned from her brief conversation with the city's commissioner. While he expressed shock at the news of Susanna's death, his reaction seemed a bit extreme. She couldn't wait to find out what she'd uncover once she started asking questions about why Susanna left such an important job.

CHAPTER 11

Except for some minor turbulence, the flight into Detroit's Wayne County airport posed no problems. Jonelle made it to her connecting flight's gate with forty-five minutes to spare. She used the time to power up her laptop and familiarize herself with the area where Susanna grew up and rose to prominence as city treasurer.

A cloudless sky greeted Jonelle as she left the Sault Ste. Marie terminal and headed out to the rental car lot. She buttoned up her wool parka against the sharp chill in the air. The bright sun caused a sneezing fit. She dug in her bag for tissues and sunglasses, plugged in the address of the bed and breakfast Finkleberg had emailed her into the SUV's GPS and headed out.

In Baltimore, the trees were just beginning to change color. Here, in the Upper Peninsula, the leaves were vibrant, the air more crisp and clean smelling. Jonelle tried to find a radio station that played soft jazz but soon gave up and turned it off. She settled back in her seat and with one hand on the wheel relaxed into the drive.

"Girl, you are definitely not in Baltimore anymore," she said as she admired the view in front of her. A quick glance at the vehicle's clock assured Jonelle she had plenty of time before her agreed check-in time at the B and B, so she pulled over onto a scenic overlook turnoff. After a few moments admiring the view, she reached into her bag and pulled out her digital camera. Once outside, she snapped photos of a waterfall cascading between trees hugging both sides of the shoreline. The deep reds and yellows of the leaves reminded Jonelle of colored balls of cotton. A short distance away, a wooden bridge snaked low over the river and connected to the opposite bank. A small carved sign warned of black bears in the area.

Jonelle's mind wandered to the last conversation she had with Sophia. She'd informed Sophia where she was going and when she'd return. "You're not going to bother my mother, are you? I said she wasn't well," Sophia had said.

"You did tell her about Susanna, right?" Jonelle had thought for one awful moment that Sophia still hadn't informed her mother of Susanna's death.

"Of course, I have," she'd said, an edge of impatience in her voice. "It's just that ... I don't want her upset."

Jonelle was a little peeved that Sophia had assumed she wouldn't know how to handle herself. "I'm not planning to interrogate your mother, but I do have questions and she may have some of the answers," Jonelle had said, dismissing Sophia's words as the reaction of a still grieving sister. "If I see that your mom is getting upset, I'll back off. I have no desire to cause her undue stress."

Sophia wanted Jonelle to promise to let her know all about the meeting as soon as possible. Jonelle agreed and reminded Sophia that she'd produce a report on what transpired on the Michigan trip and how Susanna ended up in Baltimore.

After several more miles of good highway and better scenery, a "Welcome to Moose Country," sign greeted Jonelle as she entered the town of Oldenberry where Susanna had lived and worked. Most of the hotels and lodges she passed had signs out front depicting anglers landing fish in pristine lakes and rivers, and snowmobiles barreling through the snow. Other signs displayed on both sides of the road advertised wildlife refuges and bear ranches. Jonelle wasn't sure what a bear ranch was. She smiled as she thought that if Adrienne were with her, her friend would make some kind of crack about saddling up a grizzly.

A quick glance at the GPS reminded Jonelle she had approximately five miles to cover to reach the bed and breakfast. Deep rumbling in her stomach prompted her she hadn't eaten since breakfast. A log cabin style restaurant appeared on the right and she pulled in and parked.

Jonelle entered the eatery, noted the "Seat Yourself" sign and immediately drew stares not only from three men occupying space at the counter but also two women seated at a corner table. From the look of things, she was the only person of color. Jonelle selected a booth near the front.

"Just visitin'?" the waitress asked, not meeting Jonelle's eyes and setting a paper placemat and napkin covered utensils on the table. She didn't wear a name tag over her regular street clothes.

For a brief moment, Jonelle thought of telling the woman she was thinking of moving there, just to get a reaction. She decided against it. Best not to antagonize people who might provide needed information.

"Yes, I am," Jonelle said. She pulled a menu from the wire holder on the table.

"I'll give you a few minutes," the waitress said. As she walked away Jonelle realized the woman hadn't given her name. The restaurant's polished wood décor gave off a warm feeling in stark contrast to the chilly reception she'd received. Jonelle thought about selecting a salad and maybe a bowl of soup, then decided to hell with it. She was hungry.

The waitress approached the table again with an expression somewhere between gastric upset and migraine headache. After ordering a "Benjy's Special Burger" done medium well with the works, fries and coffee, Jonelle decided she might as well begin her investigation with the forty-something woman standing in front of her.

"Before you go, I'd like to ask you a quick question."

The waitress hesitated. The look on her face said questions weren't in her job description, but being polite to customers was. "Okay," she said, drawing out the word.

"I'm here to see Norman Finkleberg," Jonelle said. "Do you know him?"

The waitress visibly relaxed. "Sure," she said with a warmer smile. "Norm's a regular customer. He always orders the steak and cheese sand with onion rings and large coke."

"That's nice," Jonelle said, not really caring what the man's eating habits were. "I'm here to talk to him about Susanna Quinley. Was she also a regular?" No need explaining the woman was dead, at least not yet.

The waitress blanched. Her eyes darted all around the restaurant, finally landing somewhere behind the counter. Jonelle turned in time to see a heavyset balding man shake his head. Mumbling, "Gotta get your order in," the woman hurried off. The bald man followed the waitress through swinging doors behind the counter.

Jonelle spent the next fifteen minutes checking emails on her phone and playing digital scrabble. She looked up as the scent of fried meat and potatoes announced the arrival of her meal. The waitress placed the food on the table. "Smells good," she said. From the pockets of a washed out brown cardigan came small plastic bottles of ketchup, mustard and relish. She tore the check with the words, "pay the cashier," and dashed off before Jonelle had a chance to say anything else.

The first bite of the burger reinforced how hungry she was. Although delicious, there was something a little different about the flavor. For one awful moment Jonelle conjured up images of all the signs she'd seen around about black bear. Hunger won out against the possibility that what was between the buns wasn't beef. That and the fact the food she was eating was the best she'd tasted in a long while almost took away her curiosity about the waitress' reaction at the mention of Susanna's name.

Jonelle finished her coffee and held up the cup. The waitress hurried over with the pot. As she filled the cup, Jonelle asked, "I didn't offend you before, did I? You seemed upset when I mentioned Susanna's name."

"Nope. No problem. No worries. Norm will answer all your questions. I don't know nuthin'." She scurried away again.

Jonelle sighed and shook her head. She sat back and slowly drank the hot, soothing coffee. As she did, she glanced around, amused that the remaining two men in the café kept whispering and stealing glances at her over their shoulders. Each time she caught them looking, she flashed them a smile.

Finished with the meal, Jonelle left a generous tip and walked over to the cash register next to the entrance to pay her bill. Instead of the waitress, the bald man took her money and gave her change without comment.

"Please tell the waitress I didn't mean to upset her," she said.

"She ain't upset," he replied, looking at a point beyond Jonelle's left shoulder.

"That's good 'cause all I wanted was to find out if she knew Susanna Quinley." She studied the man's face, looking for a reaction.

His eyes slowly came back to Jonelle. "Everybody knew Susanna. This is a small town and she was pretty high up in the government. She always had a smile and a good word for everyone she met. That is, until …" He clamped his mouth shut.

Jonelle waited for him to finish.

He shook his head. "You need somethin' else?"

"You started to say something about Susanna," Jonelle persisted. "Can't you at least tell me what happened? Do you have any idea why she left?"

His knuckles turned white as he gripped the sides of the small counter. A slight redness crept up his neck.

"You best talk to Norm Finkleberg. I shouldn't even have told you what I did. We all made a pact never to talk about that woman again. Not until she's dead and buried." He held Jonelle's gaze. His fingers relaxed and the corners of his mouth curled up. In that moment, Jonelle knew that he knew Susanna's fate.

CHAPTER 12

The trip from the restaurant to the Lakeside Bed and Breakfast took less than ten minutes. Finkleberg said the proprietors, Joshua and Michelle Hunt, had reserved one of their best rooms for her.

A gravel driveway curved away from the Victorian home. In front of the peach colored, wood-sided structure, a wraparound porch contained three white-washed rocking chairs and a swing. As Jonelle sat in the rental she counted three stories and four gables in the front of the house. A large stone chimney crept up the northwest corner of the outside of the home. She left her vehicle and grabbed her tote bag from the back seat. The open gate to the white picket fence welcomed Jonelle down a flagstone walk with mulched flower beds on either side. She paused and imagined how pretty the effect would be in spring and summer, then continued onto the porch.

She used the anchor-shaped brass knocker to tap twice on the door. A few moments later, a young woman with shoulder length, softly curled auburn hair and light brown eyes opened the door. "Hi. I'm Jonelle Sweet and I believe Norman Finkleberg made reservations for me to stay a few nights."

"Of course. Welcome and please come in. I'm Michelle Hunt."

"Thank you," Jonelle said as Michelle ushered her into the foyer. "What a lovely home you have. I think wood walls and floors give a place such a nice, warm feel."

Michelle nodded. "I'll keep that in mind when all this needs polishing." As the two shared a laugh, Jonelle decided this young woman was a vast improvement over the locals she'd met so far.

Michelle led the way up highly glossed stairs. "Red oak" was the answer to Jonelle's question about the kind of wood. On the landing Michelle removed an old fashioned skeleton key from her skirt pocket, opened the first door on the left and stepped aside. Jonelle entered a large room dominated by a king-sized four-poster bed, marble-topped vanity and a sitting room situated in an alcove. Two hunter green wing chairs flanked a small round table.

"Hope you're comfortable here," Michelle said. "I usually serve tea and coffee in the parlor around four, and you're invited to sit by the fire. If you'd like something stronger, I have red and white wine. Tomorrow's breakfast includes French toast and waffles, juice and coffee or tea. You're welcome any time between seven and nine. The only other guests we have are a couple who are visiting us for the fifth time and they're late risers. I only mention this for you to decide if you want company for breakfast."

Jonelle placed her overnight bag on an antique wooden trunk at the foot of the bed. "I like getting an early start, so breakfast for me is closer to seven," she said. "However, I may take you up on that offer of afternoon coffee."

Michelle nodded. "I'll leave you to get settled then." With that, she smiled and left the room.

Jonelle pulled off her shoes and flopped down on the bed. In all probability in a town this size, Finkleberg had spread the word about Susanna and the reason for Jonelle's visit. She hoped Michelle wouldn't shut down when she started asking questions.

After a brief nap, followed by a splash of water on her face, Jonelle changed into a blue, crewneck sweater. A quick comb through her shoulder-length hair, and she was presentable enough to go downstairs.

Halfway down, Jonelle heard voices. She plastered a smile on her face and descended the rest of the way. On the left was the sitting room where the smell of coffee greeted her. Michelle stood next to a couple seated together on a large, leather couch.

"Glad you could join us, Jonelle. This is Mr. and Mrs. Wickham. Bernie and Beatrice this is Ms. Jonelle Sweet." Michelle lifted an eyebrow.

To her credit, Jonelle continued smiling as she faced two adults dressed alike. Husband and wife wore matching yellow long sleeve shirts, brown corduroy pants and black clogs. Bernie wore his black hair short and parted down the middle, while Beatrice sported her brown shoulder length hair teased on top and flipped up at the bottom. Both looked to be somewhere in their early thirties. Jonelle glanced at Michelle whose eyes had widened slightly. The corners of Michelle's mouth twitched. She excused herself and left the room.

"Coffee smells good," Jonelle said, trying to retain her composure.

"It is," the Wickhams said in unison.

After pouring herself a cup and selecting a piece of pound cake, Jonelle sat in an armchair and pretended to be interested in Bernie and Beatrice's bird watching exploits. A few minutes after explaining the mating habits of the Gray Jay and Yellow Warbler, Bernie and Beatrice excused themselves saying they had more adventures planned the next day.

Jonelle closed her eyes and settled deep into the leather chair. While the couple seemed nice, their constant repeating of each other's words grated heavily on her nerves. As she was about to doze off, Jonelle heard someone moving about. She opened her eyes, somewhat disoriented until she remembered where she was.

"Hope I didn't disturb you," Michelle said. She carried a tray with the silver coffee service and the remaining cake.

"Not at all. Didn't realize I was this tired. I should be upstairs." She stretched her arms above her head. "Tell me something," Jonelle said as Michelle started to leave. "Do the Wickhams always dress alike?"

Michelle smiled. "From the very first time they came here. In spite of their little, uh, habit, they are two of the nicest people you could meet."

"They seemed pleasant enough once you got beyond that whole lookalike thing." Which reminded her of why she came to this part of Michigan in the first place. "Can you sit for a minute? I don't know how much Mr. Finkleberg told you about why I'm here." Jonelle took a deep breath. "Susanna Quinley was found dead in Baltimore and her sister, Sophia, would like me to investigate how she came to live in Maryland. Sophia gave me permission to ask questions about her sister from everyone who knew her."

From the look on Michelle's face, the news about the death came as no surprise.

Jonelle continued. "The police are investigating the murder, but if you don't mind, I'd like to find out what you know about Susanna, to get some idea of what kind of person she was."

"I don't know anything about what happened with Susanna or why she left," Michelle said, gripping the sides of the tray.

There was that attitude again. First the waitress and now Michelle. "What about Susanna in general. Did you know her personally?"

Michelle sighed and positioned the tray on the coffee table. She sat in the middle of the sofa.

Jonelle waited.

"We grew up together," Michelle said in a voice so soft Jonelle had to lean forward to hear. "I've known the twins since we were all in the fifth grade."

"What was she like growing up?"

Michelle studied her hands clasped tightly in her lap before answering. "Everything we did was typical kid stuff … at first." Michelle paused. The grandfather clock ticked steadily as Jonelle waited for Michelle to continue.

"I mean, the only thing that really stuck out was that they didn't dress the same. You know how mothers are, especially back then. Twins not only looked alike, they dressed alike. But not those two."

"Maybe the parents wanted them to express their individuality. I can see that."

Michelle leaned back against the sofa. "Oh, they expressed themselves all right," Michelle said. "In fact, their 'expressions' got them in a boat load of trouble over the years." She stared up at the ceiling. "I remember this one time, they grabbed little Jimmy Turner on his way home from school. They dragged him into the woods, stripped off his clothes and left him to run home naked."

"Well, jeeze," Jonelle said, fingering her necklace. "How old were they?"

"About eleven or thereabouts. Jimmy musta been six, seven at the time."

"Did they hurt him?" Jonelle asked.

"I don't know for sure, but rumor was they forced him to play ring around the rosy with nothing on for quite a while." Michelle shook her head. "Their daddy found out and made them apologize. But that was just the beginning. Other people accused them of doing, uh, weird stuff over the years." Michelle grabbed a rust-colored throw pillow and hugged it to her chest.

Jonelle needed to hear more. "Like what?"

"Well. One time one of their neighbors accused the girls of mutilating some chickens. She claimed she saw the twins hanging around her chicken coop acting strangely. After she chased them off, she found three of her best laying hens with their necks broken. The girls denied everything, but their daddy paid for the dead birds." Michelle tucked her legs under her body.

"Oh, they could be all sweetness and light when they wanted to, but if they suspected they were wronged in some way, well, they tried to get even."

"And they did all this together?" Jonelle asked.

"At first. See that's another weird thing. In elementary school, they were thick as thieves, did everything together. Once they got to high school things changed. Instead of harassing everybody else, sometimes they directed their anger at each other." Michelle shuddered. "I stopped hanging with them altogether by then. They were starting to creep me out. Big time."

Jonelle didn't know what to think. She was getting an entirely different picture of the woman from the one Luther said he knew. "In what way?"

"I remember the first school dance we went to. It was sophomore year and most of us went with friends since we didn't have dates. Anyway, by that time Sophia and Susanna hung out with different people. Sophia ran around with a faster crowd, while Susanna was in the popular group. You know, cheerleaders, pep club, that clique."

Never a member of either group, nevertheless, Jonelle smiled in agreement.

"Everybody was dancing, having a good time. All of a sudden, there's all this yelling and things crashing and banging on the floor. We rush over and there they are, punching and pulling each other's hair. Most of the kids were taunting them, egging the fight on. That kind of thing. The rest of us were stunned."

Jonelle felt pretty shocked as well. "What happened next?"

"The chaperones broke it up. From that point on though, I kept hearing how much the sisters really didn't like each other." Michelle stood, pillow still hugged against her chest.

"Do you know what they were fighting about?" Jonelle asked.

Michelle avoided Jonelle's eyes as she slowly shook her head.

"You sure? I mean, I know how kids talk. What did you hear?"

The look on her host's face told Jonelle the woman was struggling with how much more to reveal. Michelle's nails picked at the fabric of the pillow. "This is just rumor."

"I understand," Jonelle said, hoping her tone would encourage the woman to keep talking.

"See, Susanna, being a cheerleader, was dating a really cute guy on the JV basketball team." Michelle giggled nervously. "God, I sound like I'm still in high school." She paused and her eyes took on a dreamy look. "Several of the kids said Sophia went around telling everyone that she and Joshua had sex. Josh claimed he *thought* he was uh, being intimate with Susanna. Susanna confronted Sophia and well … that's how it started."

Jonelle frowned. Something wasn't right. "I thought you said they didn't dress alike. Seems like people could tell who was who."

Michelle smiled slyly. "Except they were really good at mimicking each other's mannerisms."

The tiredness Jonelle felt earlier had almost evaporated. She needed to hurry up to the room and her laptop to make notes. She didn't want to forget anything Michelle had said, especially since she had every intention of confronting Sophia about the stories when she returned to Maryland.

"Well, guess I better go," Jonelle said, covering her mouth to stifle a yawn. "The guy Josh. That's your husband's name, right? Coincidence?"

Michelle blushed. "Same guy. He's changed a lot since then."

Jonelle wondered about that. "Anything else you remember about that night?"

"Not really. Except the one thing that has always bothered me about that fight at the dance was what Sophia said at the time." Michelle picked up the tray. She smiled sadly at Jonelle. "The last thing I heard Sophia scream at Susanna that night was that she was tired of being a double and that no matter how long it took, people were gonna look at her and see *only* her."

CHAPTER 13

Even after learning the disturbing information about the Quinley twins, Jonelle fell asleep almost as soon as her head hit the pillow. She woke refreshed the next day, surprised she'd slept so well. Strange beds usually meant sleepless nights.

After a quick shower, she walked downstairs and into the antique-laden dining room. While the initial effect of all that dark wood evoked warmth and coziness, Jonelle felt that if she stayed at the B and B more than a few days, she'd need more space to breathe. Michelle walked through the door from the kitchen and greeted Jonelle. If last night's conversation bothered her, she gave no indication of it.

"Did you sleep well?" she asked with a smile.

"Absolutely," Jonelle responded. "The mattress was the right firmness and I was sound asleep as soon as I turned off the lights." The sweet smell of maple syrup filled the air. "Boy does that smell good."

"Hope you enjoy it." Michelle placed the covered dish and caddy with syrup close to Jonelle. A glass of orange juice and carafe of coffee were already on the table. Jonelle removed the plate's silver dome. Underneath were a few triangles of French toast, two squares of Belgian waffles and three sausage links. With all that food staring at her, Jonelle wondered if her host had noted her size and cooked accordingly.

"I like to make sure all my guests get a hearty meal each morning," Michelle said, as if reading Jonelle's mind.

Michelle lingered at the table while Jonelle poured coffee and drizzled syrup on the toast and waffles. After taking a few sips of juice, she invited Michelle to sit down next to her.

"I probably shouldn't, but …"

"Please. I like company when I eat." Jonelle really didn't care for conversation at breakfast, but if that produced more information about Susanna, she'd suck it up.

Michelle's fingers smoothed out non-existent creases in the tablecloth. Jonelle decided to help her hostess get started. "I'm sorry I didn't get a chance to meet your husband," she said.

The worry lines that crept across Michelle's forehand disappeared. "Oh, that's no problem. Poor guy's keeping late hours this time of year with all the early tourists getting a head start on the fall colors and the hunters stocking up on equipment. We own a combination gun shop and hardware store on the edge of town," she said in answer to Jonelle's raised eyebrows.

Jonelle swallowed a few bites of toast, drank more coffee and waited for Michelle to continue. When she didn't, Jonelle gave a little push. "I don't know if I mentioned this yesterday, but whatever you tell me in the course of my investigation is kept in the strictest confidence."

Michelle nodded.

"When I see Norman Finkleberg this morning, I'll ask him to tell me everything he knows about Susanna Quinley and what happened when she worked for him. I won't tell him about our conversation, but I may ask him if he knows anything about Susanna and Sophia's early days here." Jonelle didn't want to belabor the point. If Michelle was going to say anything else, she'd just have to wait the woman out.

Michelle sighed. "I'm not a bad gossip. But you're real easy to talk to and I guess, well, things just spilled out." She shrugged. "It's been a long time since Sophia left the area. As soon as she did, Susanna seemed to really get her life together.

Went to Lake Superior State University, got a good job, married a local guy … well that didn't end so good. They were barely married two years before they got divorced. Darn! There I go again." Her face flushed a deep crimson.

Jonelle waved her hand in the air. "Don't worry about it. Sophia told me a little about Susanna's ex-husband. Apparently he's a psychologist and lives somewhere in my area." No need to tell Michelle about Susanna's most recent lifestyle.

Michelle sat upright in her chair. Her eyes widened in disbelief. "Psychologist? Barry is a psychologist? How on earth did that sleazebag …" She stopped. Her hand flew to her mouth. "Sorry. Slipped out."

"I haven't met him yet," Jonelle said. "When I get back to the office, the first item on my agenda is to try and track him down. Unless of course, you happen to know how to reach him?" Jonelle had a feeling that would be too easy and she wasn't disappointed.

"God, no," Michelle said. "Good riddance is what I say. Very few people missed him when he left. A psychologist, huh? Well who'd a thunk it!"

Jonelle filed away the response to Susanna's ex. She made a mental note to ask Finkleberg about the husband. "Tell me," Jonelle said, "do you think Susanna's leaving had anything to do with why Sophia moved away?"

"No. In spite of her weird personality glitches, Sophia was really very smart. They both were. Sophia got a full scholarship to Michigan State and I heard she married some rich guy and became a troll."

"Huh? A what?" Jonelle sat back in her chair and stared at her host.

Michelle smiled. "That's what we Yoopers—those of us who live on the UP—call people who live below the Mackinac Bridge. Think I heard somewhere that she moved to Traverse City."

Yoopers and trolls. Jeeze. Jonelle wanted to hear more about those "personality glitches" but stopped when she heard footsteps on the stairs, followed by the Wickham's appearance in the dining room. After absorbing their identical blue slacks, red, blue and green checked shirts and brown loafers, Jonelle finished her breakfast and bade everyone goodbye. "Sorry to rush off, but I have a meeting soon and I need to gather my stuff. Thanks for a wonderful breakfast, Michelle." The two grinned at each other the way friends do when they share a secret.

A quick trip off the main drag and two streets and twenty minutes later, Jonelle found herself in front of the county government office. Norman Finkleberg's directions were spot on. It seemed as if everything in this town was either ten or twenty minutes away. Jonelle waited for a few moments to gather her thoughts as to what information she needed from him.

As she stared out the window of the rental at the building's plain gray façade, Jonelle imagined a minimum security prison, minus the razor wire. Coincidence? Maybe.

Bright sunshine filtered through the gold and crimson leaves on the large oak trees standing on either side of the concrete walkway. She parked the car in the lot at the side of the building and walked up to the entrance. In between the two sets of doors, a suite directory highlighted names and room numbers. Even though he'd given her his location, Jonelle examined the list to make sure.

Next to the entrance, a sign ordered, "Check In Here." Only one person stood ahead of Jonelle at the information desk, an elderly woman paying for a dog license. "It expired. That's why I had to come all this way," she complained, answering a question Jonelle hadn't asked.

The young man behind the desk couldn't have looked more bored than if he had been wearing a large sign with the word printed in big, bold letters.

"Good morning. I have an appointment to see Norman Finkleberg."

"Name?" he asked barely looking at her.

"I just told you," Jonelle replied, trying hard not to smile.

He stared open-mouthed at her.

"Oh. You mean *my* name? That right?" She waited a bit to make sure the man's mouth closed before she added, "My name is Jonelle Sweet and I have a ten o'clock meeting. Please tell Mr. Finkleberg I'm here"—she looked at the brown nameplate on the counter—"Herman."

Herman pushed his wire-framed glasses up his nose, grabbed his phone and announced Jonelle's name to whoever was on the other end. Hand still on the receiver, he cocked his head over at several rows of black plastic chairs. "He'll be right out."

Fighting the impulse to congratulate Herman on saying a complete sentence, Jonelle wandered over to a chair opposite the desk. Ten minutes later a frazzled-looking, balding man rushed out from a door behind the clerk. "Where …," he began. Herman pointed his pen at Jonelle and she stood, arm outstretched.

"Mr. Finkleberg? I'm Jonelle Sweet."

His eyes opened in surprise as he looked her up and down. She could tell he was taking in her dark skin and height. He straightened his already straight tie and shook her hand. Gray eyes met her gaze, and then just as quickly looked away. "Yes. Of course. Please follow me."

Uh-oh, Jonelle thought. Guess I should've sent a picture.

Jonelle expected to see a large open room with many desks and instead she found herself in a long hallway. She passed a door on the right with "*Treasurer*" stenciled on the opaque glass.

That reminded her to ask if she could question Susanna's replacement. A quick left turn and facing her was another glass and wooden door with, "*County Commissioner*" stenciled in black. They entered and walked through one more reception area where he opened another door that led to his inner office.

"Please have a seat," Finkleberg said, going around the large wooden desk and indicating a maroon leather chair across from him.

A scent in the air caught her attention as she eased into the offered chair. She sniffed the sweet, smoky aroma and looked over at the commissioner. "Smells like the tobacco my gran smoked in her pipe."

He pushed his thick, black horned-rimmed glasses back on his nose. "Sorry if it bothers you," he said, reaching in a desk drawer. He pulled out a can of air freshener. "Let me just spray a little bit of this around."

"No, please don't," Jonelle said, hand raised to indicate he shouldn't press the button. "I rather like it. Brings back fond memories of snow cones and running barefoot in the grass." She smiled at him.

Finkleberg returned her smile. His shoulders relaxed and he leaned against the high backed chair that nearly swallowed his slight, almost gaunt frame. "I'm not supposed to indulge in here, but sometimes things get so frantic, I don't have time to rush outside."

Jonelle waved his comment aside. "No need to explain. I can imagine things have been quite hectic for you, considering all that's occurred the last several months. Which brings me to why I'm here."

Finkleberg pushed thin wisps of hair across his head. "Right. Before you ask your questions, I'd like to know how Susanna died. So far, the details of her death haven't traveled up here yet."

Jonelle couldn't tell him everything so she decided to give him information he could find in a newspaper. "She was found next to a Dumpster in an alley between a sandwich carry-out and a liquor store. Her throat was cut and she didn't have any identification when she was found. We, that is, the police, initially discovered her name through an, uh, associate of hers. Media coverage produced her twin sister Sophia, who provided more details. As of right now, that's really all I know. I'm friendly with the lead detective and he's promised to keep me informed of any developments."

A frown creased Finkleberg's face. "Does that mean you're working with the police?"

"Not really. Sophia contacted me and wants me to find out how her sister ended up so far from home. I'm here to learn all I can about Susanna's life up here."

He shook his head. "Sophia. Never thought I'd hear that name again. What is it they say? A bad penny always turns up." He shrugged. "Something like that, anyway."

Sophia again. Appearances were definitely deceiving. The questions for Sophia were piling up. Odd how people were more willing to talk about her rather than discuss Susanna.

Jonelle needed to stay on point. "So, tell me about Susanna. How was she to work with?"

His eyes stared off in the distance. "She was a good worker for quite a while and seemed to blossom as a person, especially after Sophia left town. Never late. Smart as a whip. I swear she absorbed information faster than an Asian kid soaking up words at a spelling bee. Sorry, don't mean to offend."

Jonelle didn't feel the need to speak up for all minority groups, so all she did was shrug.

Finkleberg loosened his tie. "Susanna moved up the ladder quick and things were going great." He paused, a slight smile on his face as if remembering good times.

As she watched him, the grin melted. "Things changed a few years ago, when Susanna married Barry. Sophia came to the wedding as matron of honor with her new husband. Everyone held their breaths, wondering what would happen with the twins, but they got along great. Two years after the wedding, Susanna got a divorce. Sometime after that, she started missing work here and there." He paused.

Finkleberg's eyes clouded over. "There's not much I don't know about in this town. I say this to point out that what I'm about to tell you isn't rumor. Police were called to Susanna and Barry's home several times. Domestic disputes," he added in response to Jonelle's unasked question. "Next thing you know, Barry left to go to Johns Hopkins for his doctorate and Susanna applied for and received an uncontested divorce."

"How did the divorce affect her?"

"At first, she seemed happier. Things got better at work. What's that old saying? 'God's in his heaven and all's right with the world'? Well that didn't last long." He sighed. "One day, about five months ago she and Rosemary didn't show for work."

"Who's Rosemary? Another sister?" Jonelle didn't want to deal with yet another Quinley.

He shook his head. "Rosemary was one of two secretaries in the treasurer's office. After Susanna divorced Barry, the two of them started hanging out together." Finkleberg took off his glasses and rubbed the bridge of his nose. "One day, neither showed up for work. We called each one's home and got no answer. The next day when we still didn't hear a word from either of them, I sent my assistant to Susanna's house to check on her. When he didn't get an answer to his knock, he called the police. Once inside they discovered she'd gone. A quick check of the premises revealed empty clothes closets." He hesitated so long Jonelle thought his mind had wandered.

"Were you able to find Rosemary?"

He replaced his glasses and leaned forward, elbows on top of his desk, fingers tented under his chin. "No sign of Rosemary either and it looked as if she'd also left in a hurry."

"Do you have any idea why the two would leave like that?"

Finkleberg reached for a manila folder that sat on the right side of his desk. He opened it, scanned the contents and closed it again. "We had an audit scheduled for the week they both went missing. As county treasurer, Susanna knew about it of course. After the auditors finished going through the records, they discovered over $350,000 missing from the town's coffers." Finkleberg tapped his fingers on the folder. "It seemed as if our treasurer and her secretary had stolen the money."

"Wow," Jonelle said. Not only was it a mystery how Susanna ended up on the street, now it seemed as if the woman had embezzled a lot of money. "How'd that happen?"

"Based on the audit, the scheme was simple in its plan. And it worked because we trusted her. Never would I imagine she'd be the one to steal from the town. Sophia maybe. But not Susanna." He looked wistful.

Finkleberg explained how the scheme worked. "Susanna wrote personal checks from the government account which collected from transactions such as property taxes and fees from parking tickets to dog licenses. Apparently she established separate accounts at two local banks, converted the money into cashier's checks and deposited them into the accounts."

According to the commissioner's investigation, Susanna made false entries in the county's accounting records to make it look like legitimate expenses.

"Once we found out what was going on, we went back and discovered things that should have tipped us off but didn't. Like all the overtime Rosemary worked, when none was needed. We found out later from the other secretary that customers would complain they weren't being credited the correct amount on their taxes."

"Why didn't she tell anyone?"

"She said Rosemary told her people were always complaining, and being the newest secretary in the office, she didn't press the point. Guess she should have." He peered at Jonelle. "We've been told no money was found on Susanna's body. I'm going down to coordinate with the local police. It's vital the town get all its money back."

While Jonelle appreciated his concern over the town's funds, she found it curious that he wasn't interested in who might have killed Susanna, or why.

"Does anyone know what happened to Rosemary?"

Finkleberg nodded. "That's about the only good result in this whole mess, though I guess 'good' would depend on your point of view." He smiled at the perplexed look on Jonelle's face. "Rosemary Wilkins was caught at the Canadian border and now sits in prison."

"She have any of the money?"

"When Wilkins was apprehended, she had $20,000 in her possession. In exchange for a guilty plea and a reduced sentence, she confessed that Susanna was *supposed* to ship an additional $30,000 in cash sent to a delivery box number. Can you imagine that amount of money delivered by UPS? What a dimwit. She blames everything on Susanna and is pissed she got screwed."

By all accounts that left over $330,000 that Susanna had managed to escape with undetected. The question now was, where was the missing money? Susanna couldn't stroll into a bank with that much money if she had no permanent address. Luther told Jonelle he knew Susanna had a lot of money and she needed his help hiding it. Luther also said he never actually saw any money. When she returned to Maryland she had to find Luther and make him tell her everything.

Jonelle stood and paced around the office. "Helps me think," she said as his eyes followed her around the room. "Did Rosemary give the police any indication where Susanna went or what happened to the rest of the money?"

He shook his head. "Rosemary said that after they split up, Susanna told her she was getting as far away as she could." He frowned. "Wait a minute. Rosemary did say something a little peculiar. I discounted it at the time, but now, I'm not so sure."

Jonelle stopped pacing. She fingered her necklace and waited for Finkleberg to finish.

"She said Susanna told her she knew someone down south who could not only help hide her, but also help her hide the money."

"Rosemary said that?"

He nodded.

"Who was this someone down south? Did Rosemary have a name for this person?"

"No and we believed her. Rosemary is not the sharpest thorn on the bush." Finkleberg's voice rose. "Why Susanna bothered with her is a mystery to me." He softened his tone. "Once Rosemary was caught, she told us everything she knew. Her mother said Rosemary told her to expect a package but didn't say what was in it."

"Was she telling the truth?"

Finkleberg nodded. "Rosemary's mother was very upset when she found out what happened. She agreed to inform us if she received a package and she never did."

"The whole thing sounds farfetched. But it is kinda clever. All that money hiding in plain view somewhere on a shelf just waiting for the owner to go get it." Jonelle raised her eyebrows. "You guys did check, right?"

"We had no choice. Checked every friggin' delivery store on the UP. Nothing."

The two of them sat quietly, each absorbed in their own thoughts.

"What about your relationship to Susanna?"

Finkleberg squirmed in his chair. "What do you mean by '*relationship*'?"

"I mean, how did the two of you get along?" She paused.

"We got along fine."

Jonelle studied the man before her. She watched his body stiffen and waited for him to continue.

"We had a good working relationship."

When he didn't provide more information, she moved on. Even though he seemed convinced Rosemary had told the police everything, Jonelle wasn't so sure.

"Would it be possible for me to ask Rosemary a few questions? Is she incarcerated nearby?"

Finkleberg regarded Jonelle through narrowed eyes. "We only have one prison in the state that houses women. She's a Level I prisoner at the Women's Huron Valley Correctional Facility located in Ypsilanti."

"Where's that?"

"It's about thirty-six miles west of Detroit, just outside of Ann Arbor. But you'd be wasting your time. Rosemary was really contrite when she was caught and the police chief told us she couldn't wait to tell all she knew."

Yet, the woman headed for the border, Jonelle thought. After doing a quick calculation of how much extra time she would need to visit Rosemary in person, she tried a different tack. "If I understand the way the prison system works in most areas, those in minimum security must have a few extra privileges, am I right?"

After a slight hesitation, he nodded.

"So, do you think I could call her? I'd identify myself and tell her I'm helping Sophia find out more about Susanna. Rosemary may not know that Susanna was murdered."

"She probably doesn't." He leaned back in his chair and stared up at the ceiling. "Tell you what," he said, looking back over at Jonelle. "I know her lawyer. I'll give him a call, have him contact you at the Lakeside B and B. If he agrees, the two of you can work out the logistics."

"Fair enough," Jonelle said. "Can I talk to the person who replaced Susanna? I'd like to find out what, if anything, she can add to what I already know."

Finkleberg was shaking his head even before Jonelle stopped speaking. "No. *He* doesn't know any more than what I've already told you. He didn't live in this county at the time, so he doesn't even know Susanna."

"Okay," Jonelle said. Something else nagged at her. "What about the ex-husband? Is it possible he might shed some light on the missing money?" And, Jonelle thought, the man now lived "down south," another reason for Susanna to head there.

Finkleburg's high-pitched laugh resounded through his office. She waited for him to finish.

"Sorry about that," he said. He wiped his eyes with his pocket handkerchief. "Guess you don't know the full history of Barry and Susanna. To say it was a volatile marriage is putting it lightly. In hindsight, it's difficult to imagine two people who should not have gotten married when they did, least of all to each other."

Jonelle nodded. "I've heard rumors that he was abusive. And that the police were called to the home on several occasions. Still, people sometimes resolve their differences after some time has elapsed."

He swiveled back and forth in his chair, a bemused look on his face. "Rumors, huh. I'll bet. Well, let me set the record straight on a few things."

From the sly look on his face, Jonelle could tell he was enjoying himself.

"First off," he said, "Barry never physically hurt her. Most of his 'abuse' involved the venom that came out of his mouth. Susanna was the one who used her fists and threw things. Poor guy ended up black and blue on several occasions."

Jonelle's eyes widened. "You mean *she* hurt *him?*"

"Sometimes," Finkleberg said, eyes lighting up with mischief. "Or you could say she was just defending herself, which is an excuse I hear from some people around here. Others say she started more than half of their battles."

"I'll be damn," Jonelle said. "Speaking of the ex, do you have any idea where he lives?"

"Sure," Finkleberg said. "We still send each other Christmas cards. I have his address at home."

CHAPTER 14

On the way back to the B and B Jonelle decided to eat lunch at a different restaurant. She'd ask a few more questions about Susanna and Sophia to see what new information she could uncover about the two women.

A few minutes later she came upon two restaurants, one on either side of the main road. Owing to the town's prominence as a tourist destination, Oldenberry had more than its share of eating places. Since she didn't feel like making a left turn, Jonelle pulled into the gravel lot of the "Contented Moose" restaurant on the right. Like the other eateries she'd seen, this one also advertised bear burgers. Jonelle burped as she thought about the earlier meal. Decision made, this time she'd order a large salad.

Jonelle entered an outdoorsman's dream. Animal heads and fish bodies adorned the wooden walls. "Pity I don't know any hunters or fishermen," she mumbled looking around the half-filled restaurant. A small woman in jeans and red flannel shirt approached the podium set up near the door.

"Sit anywhere, Miss. Know what you want or would you like to see a menu?" she asked.

"Well, I've never been here before, so I'd like a menu please." Jonelle ambled over to a table for four against the wall.

The waitress trailed behind. "Okay," she said with a shrug once Jonelle sat in the chair next to the wall. "I only ask 'cause we ain't got much variety around here now that the tourists haven't really come in yet. Next week we open our menu up, so to speak."

Jonelle ordered a chef salad, thousand island dressing on the side and while she waited for her food to arrive, checked out the few diners in the place. Most of them reminded her of the Wickham's but, to her great relief, without dressing alike. Her eyes settled on a dark-haired woman sitting four tables away. The woman stared at Jonelle with frank interest. Jonelle stared back, determined to see which one would stop looking first. It was a silly game she and Adrienne used to play when they caught people staring. Usually, the others stopped looking first. Not this woman. She matched Jonelle's stare.

The waitress, whose nametag said "Jenny", returned with Jonelle's salad and coffee, which meant Jonelle broke eye contact first. Jonelle thought she saw a faint smile on the dark-haired woman's lips.

"I'll leave you the carafe, in case you want more coffee," the waitress said.

"Who's that lady over there?" Jonelle asked, nodding to the woman who had returned to eating her meal.

"That's Ayasha," Jenny said, without looking. "She's a regular here. She's really harmless, but if her staring makes you nervous, I can put your food on the other side of the table."

"She do that a lot?"

The waitress nodded. "She can spot a tourist a mile away. It's some kinda game she plays. People around here just ignore her."

Jonelle studied the woman a bit longer. "Native American?"

"Yep. She's full-blooded Chippewa. Her family runs the river boat casino down the road. You musta passed it on your way here." The waitress turned to leave.

"Hold it a sec. Ask her if she'd like to come over here and join me."

Jenny frowned. "You sure about that? Nobody's ever asked before." She lowered her voice to a whisper. "Some people say her elevator doesn't go all the way to the top. If you know what I mean."

"Yeah, I get it. Actually, I find her interesting."

"Suit yourself," Jenny said with a shrug.

Jonelle's eyes tracked the waitress's progress as she walked up to Ayasha. Although she couldn't hear what was said, the waitress turned and pointed to Jonelle. Ayasha gathered her things with Jenny's help and ambled over to Jonelle's table.

From a distance Jonelle couldn't tell the woman's age. This close, Ayasha appeared about her own age. Thick black hair hung mid-way down her back and glowed to a high sheen. A generous smile displayed large white teeth.

"Glad you could join me," Jonelle said. "The waitress said your name, but I wasn't sure I heard right. Is it eye-e-sha?"

"Nope. It's ah-yah-sha. Means 'little one' in my native language. Not so little now though, huh?" Again she flashed that dazzling smile. "I really should be eating what you're eating," she said pointing to Jonelle's salad. "But these burgers are really great. Would you like to share some of my fries?"

Jonelle shook her head. "I'm doing penance for sampling the local fare when I first arrived yesterday."

The two women munched in silence. Jonelle felt a little like the person who chases after something, and when caught, doesn't have the faintest idea what to do with it. She cleared her throat. "Um, I suppose you've already figured out I'm new here."

Ayasha nodded. "I heard you've been asking a lot of questions about the Quinley twins. Or, as some in my circle call them, 'tweedle-dum' and 'tweedle-dee.' Those are the cleanest names I can give you right now."

So far, Ayasha seemed okay. Only one way to find out for sure.

"You might also know that I'm here to discover as much as I can about Susanna's background," Jonelle said. She added quickly, "And whatever you can tell me about Sophia. I understand the girls were close when they were children, but drifted apart in their teens."

Ayasha crammed several fries in her mouth. Jonelle munched salad and topped off her coffee while waiting for her guest to finish chewing. "Well," Ayasha said, using her hand to cover a soft burp. "'Scuse me. Never knew anything about them really until middle school. Had a few classes with both of 'em but they stayed pretty much to themselves and only hung out with their white friends. Neither one of them socialized with us 'Injuns'".

"What about in high school? Did you know them better?"

"Sophia a little bit more than Susanna. They pretty much hung around with their separate cliques. I do know they continued to get into trouble, though it was typical stuff by then." Before Jonelle could ask, Ayasha added, "Stuff like getting busted for shoplifting, drinking alcohol in cars with their friends. Some drugs. Like that." She gave Jonelle a knowing look.

"Can you give me more specifics?" This was getting interesting.

Ayasha gave a short laugh. "Once, they got busted trying to sell nickel bags of marijuana on the south side of town. They operated on different streets, but hell, look around at how small this place is. Imagine it. Two blond lookalikes selling drugs. Might as well hold up a sign for crissakes." She snickered.

The image that flashed in Jonelle's mind made her smile. "I thought Susanna was the 'good' one. She sold drugs, too?"

Ayasha rolled her eyes. "Oh please. Neither one was what you'd call 'good.'"

"What else can you tell me?"

Ayasha looked off in the distance. "The first couple years, some brainiac in the school system thought it would be cute to have the girls take all the same classes. They found out pretty quick that was a very bad idea."

"Why?"

Ayasha looked smug. "They would sit together and talk all during class. They'd laugh and giggle with each other; totally not pay attention. Little things started happening to the teachers. Papers would go missing; things on the desks moved around. One teacher found all her school supplies super glued together. Finally the school decided to separate them. Their daddy went to the school board, but this time other parents complained and he couldn't do anything about it. Quinley argued nobody could prove the vandalism was the twin's fault. But everybody knew it was them."

A clear picture of the two formed in Jonelle's mind. "I heard about what they did to a little boy. Took his clothes and harassed him. Did they do stuff like that when they got older?"

Ayasha tucked thick hair behind her ear and leaned in closer. "There were a few incidents that spread from my part of town."

Jonelle glanced around and noticed the two were now the center of attention. "Are you finished with your meal?" she asked.

"Sure. You in a hurry?"

Instead of answering right away, Jonelle caught the waitress' eye and made the sign for the check. "No, but I think you and I can talk better someplace more private." Jonelle paid for her meal and offered to pay for Ayasha's. "I already paid. But thanks." As the two left the restaurant, Jonelle felt eyes boring into her back. She hesitated, contemplating whether or not she wanted to resume their conversation in her room at the B and B. Ayasha settled the issue.

"There's a really cute park nearby where we can sit and look over at the waterfall. I need to take my car 'cause I may have to leave in a hurry to get to work on time. Where's your car?"

"Over there," Jonelle said, indicating the Ford Escape.

"Mine's the dusty blue Explorer at the end. I'll wait 'til you pull up behind me."

Jonelle settled the SUV behind the Explorer and used the time alone to try and unravel all the information she'd been told so far. It seems everyone in town had their opinions about the twins, but she hadn't come close to figuring out how Susanna ended up with Luther. Even accounting for the fact that Susanna's ex went to school at Hopkins and was still living somewhere in the area, it still didn't explain how a woman with more than a quarter of a million dollars ended up on the street. And where was the money?

The blue Ford put on its left turn signal and drove down a narrow dirt drive. A rustic sign announced the community park with another replica of a moose carved into the wood, taking up half of the signage. Jonelle followed Ayasha onto a paved lot and parked next to her. Three other vehicles, all pickup trucks, filled the rest of the lot.

Both women pulled over at the same time. Ayasha pointed to a picnic table in a small clearing. "We can sit over there," she said.

Jonelle got in step with Ayasha. Neither woman said anything until they sat down across from each other.

"I hear you're investigating Susanna's death," Ayasha said. "That right?"

Jonelle knew word travelled fast in small towns, but even this seemed like some kind of record. "To tell you the truth, I'm not investigating her *death*. That's up to the police. What I'm doing at the request of her sister is investigating her life. I'm trying to figure out how she got from here to Maryland."

"Yeah, okay. But she was murdered right? And you're working with the police, right?" Ayasha's eyes sparkled.

Jonelle nodded. A tightness started in the pit of her stomach. She remembered the waitress's words about the woman sitting across from her. "As a private investigator, sometimes I do work with the police. In this case I need to find out as much as I can about Susanna. Whatever I find out I'll share with the detectives in Maryland."

Ayasha placed elbows on the table, her fists under her chin. She leaned in close, eyes still bright with interest. "So, what happened? How'd she die?"

Jonelle decided to keep her answers short. "Someone cut her throat."

"Whoa." Ayasha sat back. "You know, if someone had told me one of 'em would get themselves killed, I would've picked Sophia as the victim. Or, hell, I'd even pick her as the, uh, perp. Isn't that what murderers are called? She was the wild one; the one who kept getting into trouble when Susanna went around acting like she was getting her life together."

Time to turn the interview around, Jonelle thought. "Could you tell the difference between the two?"

Ayasha shifted position. "Well, Sophia preferred her hair shorter than Susanna. People said it was Sophia who initiated all the crazy schemes. That's one of the reasons why their daddy made sure Sophia went away to college. Guess he hoped that when they separated each would straighten out." Ayasha shrugged. "Guess it worked, 'cause we heard Sophia married some rich guy."

"Speaking of marriage, what do you know about Susanna's husband, Barrington?"

Ayasha looked perplexed at first. "Oh, you mean Barry?" She shrugged. "Apparently, he was supposed to be,"—her fingers formed air quotes—"gifted and talented."

For someone who sounded like a conduit for even the hint of gossip, Jonelle figured Ayasha knew more about the man than she let on. "So, tell me what you know or have heard about the relationship between those two."

"Nuthin' to tell. Didn't know the dude personally." Ayasha's gaze turned back to the waterfall.

"I heard," Jonelle said, grabbing the woman's attention again, "that there were several domestic calls to the police. You know anything about that?"

One side of Ayasha's mouth curled up. "Yeah. I did hear where they had a lot of knock down drag out fights and the cops were called to break it up. Next thing I heard, he left town." Jonelle studied the woman in front of her. It sounded as though Ayasha was sad about him leaving. Though she wondered what their relationship was, if any, Jonelle had to focus back on Susanna.

"I've already heard about the fight between the two girls at the prom. Were you there?"

"That fight? That was nothing. Yeah, I was there and a lot of us thought the whole thing was staged. They were both active in the school's theater group, did you know that?" Jonelle didn't. She motioned for Ayasha to continue.

"That whole business most of the white kids started about Sophia being jealous and all was crap. The girls liked to jerk everyone's chain … make people think of that whole good twin, bad twin thing. Truth is, they were more alike than people thought." Ayasha paused and glanced around the park. Jonelle sat quietly. After a few moments, Ayasha turned back around.

"I remember a few times seein' 'em around town, heads together, whispering and stuff, but as soon as they saw someone from school, they'd split apart like a bolt of lightning struck between them. I also noticed that same weird stuff whenever the school selected that year's play. In case you're wondering, I was a part of that whole scene, but never on the talent side. Of course." There was that slight smile again. "As it turned out, I was more interested in the technical side anyway, especially the lighting."

She leaned in again with that gleam in her eye. "You'd think that if they were all that competitive against each other, that it would show up whenever auditions were held for the lead, but it didn't. If one twin tried out for a particular role, the other would content herself to try out for a lesser part. Or even agree to helping with makeup and costumes, that sort of thing."

"No arguments? No yelling or screaming?" Instead of getting a clearer picture of the Quinley twins, things were getting more confused.

Ayasha shook her head and stared at Jonelle with raised eyebrows.

Jonelle waited for her to continue and when she didn't, asked another question. "Do you think maybe their erratic behavior had something to do with not only selling, but also taking drugs?"

Ayasha stood so quickly, the table shook. "Some folks around here think me and the boys have a problem with drugs. Well, we don't use any more."

"Who're 'the boys'?"

"Cousins. We're not all that close, 'cause they're into some really funky stuff." She scanned the parking area. "I gotta get back to work."

"Before you go, I'd like to know your last name."

"Why?"

"For my own satisfaction since you've given me so much useful information."

She blinked several times before almost yelling, "Yazzie."

Jonelle watched her stomp off. No wonder people thought she was nuts. Jonelle shook her head. While the information Ayasha gave her was interesting, that's all it was. The clearest sign Jonelle had so far of why Susanna left was because of the money she stole. Ayasha left before Jonelle could explore what, if anything, the woman knew about the embezzlement.

All the way back to her room, Jonelle mused over everything Ayasha said. When she parked in front of the B and B she noticed hers was the only vehicle there. In spite of that, she still called out when she let herself into the home. "Hello? Michelle?" Disappointed Michelle didn't answer, Jonelle was relieved the Wickham's didn't answer either. Just to be sure, Jonelle checked the dining room and found no one inside. The couple's bizarre habit of dressing like twins was weird, and she'd had her fill of twins, at least for today.

She climbed the stairs to her room, intent on making notes of her interview with Ayasha while waiting for afternoon tea. Standing on the landing, Jonelle noticed her door slightly ajar.

Her breath quickened as she tiptoed to the door. She put her hand against it and pushed. Two drawers in the bureau were open; Jonelle knew she'd shut them. A quick search inside revealed several items rearranged but nothing missing. When she left that morning, she'd placed her briefcase on the chair next to the small table. The briefcase now sat on top of the table.

Her laptop and notebook were where she'd left them. But, the top of the computer was up; she knew she'd closed it. Someone had entered her room and gone through her things.

CHAPTER 15

Puzzled at who, and why, anyone would want to go through her belongings, Jonelle sat on the bed and thought about the people she'd talked to since she arrived. The man and woman at the first restaurant were the only two who seemed unwilling to answer her questions and who appeared a bit hostile. In this town, secrets were impossible to keep and she felt sure everyone knew where she was staying. Jonelle grabbed her camera and clicked a few pictures. For what purpose, she wasn't sure, but it made her feel better. She photographed the open bureau drawers that held her clothes, as well as the open laptop and notepad.

Noise from downstairs caught her attention. She tiptoed to the door and listened. Not hearing a conversation, Jonelle walked out onto the landing and called out. "Michelle, is that you?"

Michelle appeared at the bottom of the stairs. "Hope I didn't disturb you, I just came from shopping."

"Not at all," Jonelle said. "When you have time, I'd like to show you something in my room."

"Sure. Give me a few minutes to put the groceries away." Michelle walked away and Jonelle returned to her room and waited. Jonelle remembered when she returned from the park she entered the front door with just a turn of the knob. Anyone could have entered. But why go through her things?

By process of elimination, Ayasha was in the clear, as well as the waitress from the Contented Moose. The city commissioner had plenty of time to leave his office and search her room, but why go through her things? He seemed forthcoming with all the information about Susanna. That left the unpleasant restaurant owner and waitress at the first place she stopped when she arrived.

A gentle knock at the door. "Come on in," Jonelle said.

Michelle entered carrying two mugs of something steaming. "Thought you might like a cup of tea," she said.

"Sounds great. Let's sit by the window." Jonelle took the offered mug from Michelle over to the small table. Michelle sat across from her.

"So, how'd it go today?" Michelle asked with a smile.

Jonelle recited abbreviated accounts of her meetings with Finkleberg and Ayasha. At the mention of the woman's name, Michelle frowned. "Where did you meet her? She's not someone I would have introduced to you."

"I had lunch after I left the commissioner's office. She was sitting alone at a table so I asked her to join me. Have to admit she was a bit odd."

Michelle looked down in her cup. "That's an understatement. She and other members of her family have had more drug related run-ins with the law than I can count." Michelle raised her eyes and gazed at Jonelle. "I wouldn't put too much weight into anything she told you. She might've been stoned."

"Hmm. Maybe. Tell me something. I've heard bits and pieces about the father, but nothing about the mother. What can you tell me about her? I understand she's not in the best of health."

After a few sips of tea, Michelle put down the cup, sat back in the chair and stared out the window. Jonelle waited.

"Not sure what I can say about Mrs. Quinley that would help you find out about Susanna," Michelle said.

Jonelle waited for her to continue but when Michelle didn't say anything else, Jonelle wondered what happened to the woman who had no problems spilling information before.

"That's okay. I probably should talk to her myself anyway. One more thing, Michelle," Jonelle said. "When I came back to my room this afternoon, I discovered someone had gone through my things. I know it wasn't you." At least Jonelle hoped not. "I could tell someone rifled through my clothes"—she pointed to the still open dresser—"and tried to get into my computer but it's password protected, so they didn't get anything. This notebook here,"—Jonelle waved it at Michelle—"was on top of the laptop when I left, but I found it on the desk when I returned."

She waited a few beats before adding, "Do you have any idea who would want to invade my privacy like this?"

The color drained from Michelle's face. "No one could've done this. Are you sure?" Michelle's eyes swept over the space.

"Actually, it would have been very easy for someone to search my room. When I got back, your front door was unlocked and the door to my room was open. So, if this place isn't locked what's to stop someone from walking in?" Jonelle lowered her voice and smiled softly at her host. "Someone did this and I've been sitting here trying to figure out who it could be."

Michelle rose and wandered around the room, one hand on her hip and the other placed against the side of her face. "This has never happened before. Sure, a lot of people know you're here … and why, but I've never had to lock the doors before." She frowned. "Usually, I'm always here, or if I have to go to the store, my husband looks after the place." A huge sigh escaped her. "Josh said he had to run out for a few minutes. Since we didn't want to inconvenience you or the Wickhams, we decided to leave the front door unlocked. We've done it many times before with no problems." She stopped pacing and sighed. "Guess I'll have to change that policy. I'm so sorry."

"Do you think the Wickhams might know something?" Jonelle asked.

Michelle shook her head. "They left this morning shortly after you did and were still gone when I left to go shopping. It's usually"—Michelle looked at her watch—"around now when they return."

"Any new arrivals today?"

Once again Michelle shook her head. "No one else is due until tomorrow and they're also return guests. I don't get this."

Michelle crossed her arms. In a quiet voice she asked, "Would you like me to call the sheriff?"

Jonelle stood. "No. Not necessary. Nothing was taken, so I guess no harm done. It's a little past three, so I think I'll go pay a visit to Mrs. Quinley. This is really the only chance I'll have to talk to her since I'm leaving tomorrow."

The lines around Michelle's mouth deepened. "I'll make sure no one enters your room while you're gone."

CHAPTER 16

After Michelle left, Jonelle gathered her notebook and stuck her laptop in a dresser drawer. She left the B and B without seeing anyone and once inside the rental, plugged Mrs. Quinley's address into the GPS system. That done she called to alert the twin's mother of her imminent arrival. Jonelle wondered how much information Sophia disclosed to her mother about Susanna's death. Several minutes later Jonelle arrived in front of an enormous log cabin situated next to a crystalline lake that flowed on as far as she could see.

Jonelle stepped out of the vehicle and stood on the side-walk leading up to the front door. The home towered over its closest neighbors a few acres away and illustrated more than anything what little she knew about the family's status in the town. No sooner had Jonelle stepped onto the porch's bottom step when the front door opened. A tall, thin woman with short, white hair, stood ramrod straight and peered down at Jonelle. The olive green cashmere turtle neck outlined a protruding collar bone. Dark brown wool slacks hung on her slight frame and ended on the instep of brown leather clogs. Jonelle guessed the woman's gaunt appearance was more a result of the disease swirling through her rather than some type of chosen diet. "Mrs. Quinley?"

"You're the detective lady from Maryland."

"Yes. I'm here about—"

"I know why you're here," Mrs. Quinley interrupted. "Sophia called me, though it was hard to understand her. She said she had a bad cold. Plus, you can't keep anything from the people in this town." She looked past Jonelle. "You might as well come in before the grapevine explodes." At that, she turned and walked inside. A brief whiff of something medicinal enveloped the air in her wake. Jonelle noticed the pink scalp showing through the woman's thin hair and was surprised there were no servants milling about.

"We can sit in here," Mrs. Quinley said, pointing to the right at what looked like a sitting room off of the foyer. Sarah Quinley eased down into a dark green leather wing chair with brass studs around the sides and armrest. A thin arm pointed to a matching leather sofa directly opposite. "Have a seat."

"Thanks." In spite of the woman's frail appearance, she radiated strength and confidence. Cool, blue eyes never left Jonelle's face. The first thought that came to mind was that the woman sitting before her was used to intimidating people.

Jonelle cleared her throat. "First, let me say I'm sorry for your loss. I can't imagine how painful it must be to lose a child."

Sarah's eyes flitted around the room. "Have you experienced a death in your family?"

"My husband died suddenly, last year."

"A child's death is worse. Much worse," Sarah said. She faced the window and gazed out at the trees. The pause stretched on for several seconds. Jonelle had already decided to break the silence when Sarah crossed her legs and looked directly into Jonelle's eyes.

"What do you want to know?"

On the way over Jonelle had debated what types of questions to ask and whether or not she had to tread softly because of the woman's health. She didn't need to worry. Sarah gave the impression she could handle whatever was thrown her way.

Jonelle took her pad out of her bag. "I've received conflicting information on how close the twins were while growing up. Some said they were inseparable until they entered high school and drifted apart. What do you remember about that time?"

Sarah's face twisted into a tight smile. "The girls didn't make friends easily. I suspect it was more a case of the other parents not wanting their children to play with them. My late husband owned a lot of property around here and he ran his businesses with an iron hand. So, with few others wanting to be friends, they relied on each other. I tried to ease the burden a bit, by dressing them different, you know, so as not to emphasize their sameness, but it didn't work. At first, Sophia seemed stronger and dominated Susanna. The trouble they got into was usually initiated by her with Susanna following along like a happy puppy."

"Did it stay that way?"

"Around the time they turned thirteen, Susanna came into her own and rebelled when anyone tried to intimidate her."

"I heard a story about them undressing and harassing a boy when they were young. True?"

A brief nod.

"And the incident with the dead chickens?"

A frown this time. "No proof my girls did that."

Jonelle didn't press the point. "One other story told to me involved a high school dance when the two fought each other over a boy one of them dated. Also true?"

"They never denied it."

"Are there any other instances you can give me about the girls' relationship to each other?"

Sarah clenched her hands in her lap. "They did typical teenage stuff. They got closer when they went to college."

"I thought they went to different schools."

"Sometimes space is what's needed to realize how much people mean to each other."

"What about drugs? Someone told me the twins were seen selling drugs. I know a lot of kids indulge, but not many actually end up selling." Jonelle watched Sarah's reaction. Instead of getting angry, she looked as if she welcomed the question.

"My girls were always curious about things. Always playing make-believe. I think that's why they gravitated to theater arts in school. So, yes, they experimented and they also admitted to me and their father that they occasionally sold to their friends. But not on the street. They wouldn't do anything as common as that."

Jonelle recalled Ayasha's words about the twins selling drugs in town but decided not to press the point. Very few parents knew the full extent of their children's involvement with drugs.

"I also heard that Susanna had a difficult marriage. That the police were called to the home on several occasions and both husband and wife shared the blame for the alleged abuse."

Sarah's cool façade cracked a little. She frowned and shifted her eyes away from Jonelle. "Whatever you heard is a lie. Susanna told me it was Barry who mistreated her. Calling her names, belittling her in public. Once, she said he hit her."

"Did she say how that happened?"

Sarah uncrossed her legs. "I don't want to talk about it. Besides, what does that have to do with her death?"

"Nothing. However, I'm going to track Dr. Kelly down when I get back and ask him these same questions. I'd like to know what you know, before I get his input."

"*Dr.* Kelly. That's rich," she snorted.

Jonelle waited for Sarah to elaborate, but when that didn't happen, she moved on to the real substance of the interview. "Norman Finkleberg said Susanna and an accomplice embezzled $350,000 of the county's money. Susanna fled but her co-conspirator was caught and is sitting in jail. Do you know why Susanna took the money?" Jonelle looked around the massive room.

Anger clouded Sarah's eyes. The lines around her mouth deepened as she rose from the chair and stood above Jonelle. "That's a lie. I'm sure it was that other woman's fault. Susanna didn't need the money. We have plenty. My husband left us well off and when I die everything will go to my girls." Realizing what she said, Sarah's eyes watered. "Well, I guess now it will all go to Sophia.

"This so-called interview is over." She turned and stomped out of the room.

Jonelle exhaled a burst of air and followed. Way to go.

Sarah stood next to the open door. "That poor excuse of a secretary probably masterminded the whole thing," she said.

Jonelle faced Sarah. "They only found $20,000 when she was caught, so, where's the rest? Rosemary said Susanna took all the money and was supposed to send her an additional $30,000."

"That's another lie," Sarah said, arms crossed tightly in front of her chest.

"How can you be so sure?" Jonelle didn't want to argue, but she had to make a point. "I understand this must be difficult. But, Susanna was the treasurer and had direct access to that amount of money. Also, why did she leave? And why go all the way to Maryland? Especially since her ex-husband lived in the area and according to you, he abused her."

Sarah's cool façade cracked as she wiped a tear from her eye. "I wish to God I knew."

CHAPTER 17

Worn out from her encounter with Sarah Quinley, an exhausted Jonelle perked up when an envelope with her name handwritten on the outside, sat on the table in the foyer of the bed and breakfast. She tore it open and read the note from Winston Hackett, attorney. The message stated that Rosemary Wilkins was available to talk to her for a half hour tomorrow. The only stipulation was that he be present. Jonelle rushed up to her room and changed Friday's Baltimore plane reservations to a later time. Next, she called Rainey and advised she wouldn't be in the office until Monday morning. Rainey informed her that Burt had called twice, no emergency, and to call when she returned.

A quick check of her room assured Jonelle no one had gone through her belongings. That done, she contacted the lawyer and they set up an appointment for two thirty at the correctional facility. Hackett gave Jonelle directions on what to do when she arrived.

After packing most of her things in her overnight bag so as to save time in the morning, Jonelle sat on the bed and jotted down interview questions to ask Rosemary. She wondered why Susanna needed an accomplice instead of doing everything herself. Rosemary might shed some light on that as well. A soft knock interrupted her thoughts.

"Come in," she said.

Michelle entered alongside a tall, outdoorsy type man with a full ginger beard and hazel eyes. His thick hair reached almost to his shoulders.

"This is my husband, Josh," Michelle said. "I wanted him to meet you before you checked out tomorrow."

Josh smiled and held out his hand and Jonelle shook it. The handshake was warm and dry and not too firm. Before she got the chance to invite them to take a seat, Josh went over, pulled out a chair from the desk in the alcove and sat down. Michelle blushed a little before sitting across from him. Jonelle found his actions off-putting, then reminded herself that the man lived here.

"So," he said, smile still plastered on his face. "I've been hearing a lot about you from the folks in town. As the owner of the only hardware slash gun shop in town, I double as one of the local places where people get together, to, let's admit it, gossip."

Not sure of what reaction Josh expected, Jonelle merely nodded.

"I understand you know how Susanna died. Care to share that information?"

Something about the man's tone set Jonelle's teeth on edge and for a brief moment she wondered if he was the one who'd gone through her things. She glanced at Michelle who had started biting her nails. "The only thing I know is that she was found with her throat cut. The man who found her was a homeless person."

While Josh's lips smiled, his eyes didn't. "Oh come on. I'm sure you know more than that. What did she look like?"

"She looked dead," Jonelle said, without missing a beat.

The smile on his face faded as the lines hardened around his eyes.

No doubt about it. Josh gave off an odd vibe. Susanna's painted face wasn't in the news and she wasn't about to let this obnoxious man learn anything other than the barest of details. Still, she wondered if he knew more about the murder than what he let on. If so, how'd he find out?

"I didn't see the body," Jonelle continued, "but I'm sure it wasn't pretty. Can't imagine a cut throat would be, with all the blood, exposed bone and so on." Jonelle heard Michelle gasp.

"Just curious," he replied. "She always wore far too much makeup. We used to think she carried that whole actor thing too far. If you know what I mean." He winked at Jonelle.

Jonelle stole another glance at Michelle, who had taken the hand from her mouth and lodged it around her own neck.

"Not really. Don't wear much myself," Jonelle said. "As I told Michelle I'm here at Sophia's request to see if I can find out how Susanna ended up in Maryland. So far, I haven't been able to find anyone who can explain that to me. The only possible connection is that her ex-husband lives in the area, although I understand the two were estranged."

Josh glanced at his wife, who turned away. "Have you talked to Barry?" he asked.

Time to end Josh's interrogation. "Not yet. Tell me, Josh. Why all the interest? You're the first person who wanted to find out more about what I know, rather than why I'm here." She smiled. "Is this just curiosity on your part, or ... something else?" Jonelle kept the smile on her face, though even she could hear the strain in her own voice.

Josh rose from the chair. "Finkleberg told you why she left. Stole money that belonged to this town. Her and that little bi ... " He looked at his wife. "Never mind."

"You're right. Finkleberg told me about the embezzlement, but he said he has no idea as to why she ran all the way to Maryland. Especially since her accomplice headed for the Canadian border. You have any thoughts on why she chose to go south?"

Josh strolled over to the chest and touched the top drawer. The one that was ransacked. Next he ambled over to the door and shrugged. "Beats me. Maybe she wanted to see the cherry blossoms again." He snorted. Michelle walked up to him and put her hand on his arm.

"We've taken up too much of Jonelle's time," she said. "We'll leave now and let you get your rest." Michelle shot her husband a warning look.

"Just a sec. How do you know she went to see the cherry blossoms?" Jonelle asked.

"We all did as part of a high school trip. Didn't Michelle tell you we were all in the same class?"

"Not in so many words. Though I did hear about a fight at a dance."

Pleased the smirk disappeared from his face, Jonelle continued. "Tell me. In your, uh, dealings with the twins, how did you tell them apart?"

Josh paused, hand on the door knob.

"We need to let Jonelle get her rest," Michelle said, staring at her husband.

The annoying grin returned. "Oh," he said. "I'm guessing you know about the rose and the fox."

CHAPTER 18

She ate her last breakfast at the B and B alone. Michelle had served her and left with a terse, "Have a safe trip." Jonelle flew into the Detroit airport and picked up the rental car reserved for her by the agent in the Sault Ste. Marie airport. With almost an hour on the road she gathered her thoughts as to what information she needed from Susanna's accomplice, Rosemary Wilkins.

A blue sign with white letters proclaimed, "Women's Huron Valley Correctional Facility" as Jonelle pulled off the highway and headed down a two lane access road. If it wasn't for the guard tower protruding to the left of the main entrance, coupled with the multiple rows of razor wire adorning the top of the high chain link fence along the far sides, the nondescript building would fit in well at any industrial park complex in any city.

Jonelle followed signs directing her to the visitors parking on the right. She locked her rental car and strode to the building where she announced her name and passed through two security checkpoints. The guard at the last check informed her that Winston Hackett had not yet arrived to escort her to the visiting room. Jonelle checked her watch. She was a few minutes early and her window of opportunity was short if she was to make the six p.m. flight back into Baltimore's BWI Airport.

No sooner had she sat on one of the gray plastic chairs than a slender man approached with arm outstretched. "Ms. Sweet? Winston Hackett. Sorry I'm a little late. I've been with two other clients here which is why I agreed to meet you today. I make it a point to see everyone on a regular basis and today is the day for my assigned appointments. So, tell me again why you'd like to speak to Rosemary."

The man's no-nonsense manner reassured Jonelle he wouldn't waste time. "I visited the town where Susanna Quinley and Rosemary embezzled money from the town's treasury." Jonelle didn't bother with *alleged.* Nothing was alleged once someone was tried and convicted. "As I stated on the phone, a person or persons murdered Susanna. The police are investigating the crime and I'm here because her sister wants to know how Susanna ended up in Maryland. I'm hoping Rosemary can shed some light on that."

"Hmm." Hackett opened his briefcase and pulled out a folder. Jonelle waited while he read a few sheets and wrote some notes on a lined pad. "Okay," he said, a quick smile covering his face. "Follow me to the visiting room."

Two-tone walls, light gray on the top half, dark gray on the bottom, flanked Jonelle's trek down the hall. They passed several doors and stopped at the one marked "8" stenciled in black. An armed guard unlocked a heavy door with a rectangular window in the center. The guard didn't speak as she stepped aside to let them enter. Inside, a metal table with four chairs sat in the middle of the room. As Jonelle and Hackett entered, a young woman with very long, dark blond hair looked up. If the woman before her hadn't been wearing prison-issue blue shirt and pants, Jonelle would have pegged her as a second grade teacher.

"How are you Rosemary? This is Ms. Jonelle Sweet, the private investigator I told you about," Hackett said.

Rosemary's pale blue, defeated-looking eyes watched Jonelle's every movement. Jonelle noticed Rosemary's nails were bitten down, with dried blood around the cuticles.

"I suppose you know that Susanna is dead."

Rosemary flinched.

Jonelle would have eased into the reason for her visit, but didn't want to waste time. "I'm here at Sophia Reyes' request. She's Susanna's sister."

"I know."

Jonelle took out her notepad. "Do you mind?" She looked first at Hackett, who shook his head. Rosemary shrugged.

"I'll get right to it. Did Susanna ever mention any connection or affiliation to anyone living in Maryland? Or maybe Virginia or Washington DC?"

Rosemary raised her hand to her mouth and quickly brought it down again. "She knew her ex lived somewhere down there. When we split up, I thought she was going to Canada. That's what we agreed on. But she lied. She played me for a fool."

Jonelle stole a glance at Hackett whose eyes never left his client.

"I understand you worked for her and the two of you often shopped and had lunch together."

"She'd gone through a crappy marriage and I'm a single mom." Rosemary's voice cracked. "We bonded right away. She was so smart. So nice to me. Told me how I should dress if I wanted to be more than a secretary. And she helped me out with Jason, he's my two-year-old."

Damn. "Is Jason your only child?"

"Yes. His daddy couldn't keep a job and hardly gave me anything for child support. If it wasn't for me gettin' him that job with the county, I would've had even less. It's gonna be hard enough for Jason when he grows up, bein' part native and all. Sometimes when I was a little short on cash, Susanna would loan me some." She glanced at her lawyer. Out of her peripheral vision Jonelle saw him nod slightly.

"All this mess was her idea. She said no one would ever catch on and when they found out we'd be long gone. I wouldn't have any more money worries. She said she knew how to hide the cash so no one would ever find it … or us. Claimed we'd always be protected."

"She used the word, *protected*?"

"Yeah."

"Do you know what she meant by that?" Jonelle felt Hackett shift next to her. She waited for his objection, but none came.

"She never said, and I didn't ask." Rosemary sat back in her chair and crossed her arms. "I should've known better. My mom always told me you don't get something for nothing in this world." Rosemary leaned forward, hair falling over her face. She shook her head over and over.

"I'm no Einstein, okay?" she said, head down and voice muffled. "But I shoulda known we'd be found out pretty quick. As soon as we didn't show up for work, I knew they'd send someone to find out where we were. Hell, before that we were there every day and always on time. Susanna insisted on it. The only time I missed work was when either me or my son was sick and I always called in."

Jonelle scribbled in her pad. "What happened to your son when you left?"

Rosemary looked up. "I took him over to my mom's two nights before we decided to … take off with what we had. Once I felt it was safe enough, I was gonna have her bring him to me."

Jonelle frowned. "But Rosemary—"

"I know, I know. I'd be getting her involved, too. I wasn't thinking about nothin' but the money and doin' better for my kid."

Something stirred inside Jonelle. "Tell me, what day did you leave for Canada?"

"Real early Tuesday morning."

Jonelle sensed Hackett move again in his chair, but the lawyer remained quiet.

"Why didn't you leave Friday night? That would have given you the entire weekend. No one would've noticed you were gone until Monday."

"Susanna said she had some arrangements to make Monday."

"What kind of arrangements?"

"I don't know. I didn't ask. I was so anxious about what we were doing that I spent the whole week throwing up. I should've backed out. A little voice kept telling me not to do this, that it was wrong. But Susanna insisted everything would work out fine."

Hackett cleared his voice. "Sorry, but time's up Ms. Sweet."

"Right. One more thing. What did Susanna say about her ex-husband? Were they in communication? Did she know where he lived?"

"The only thing she really said was that they worked better as exes than as a married couple. She never mentioned if she knew where he lived. And I didn't care. We were supposed to go to Canada, but she tricked me."

"What about the mother? Sarah Quinley? I understand you met her."

Rosemary crinkled her nose in distaste. "That snobby old … I know she's sick and I shouldn't talk about her that way, but she treated me like I was supposed to kneel down and kiss her feet or something."

"Did you get the impression that she knew anything about what you and Susanna had planned?"

Rosemary opened her mouth, then clamped it shut and shook her head. "Naw. Susanna only wanted me to meet her."

That didn't fit. "Why?"

Pale eyes glanced over to the far wall. "I don't know."

Jonelle thought she did, but didn't press the point. Hackett stood and Jonelle followed suit. "Thanks for talking to me, Rosemary. I appreciate your time."

"Time's all I got, Miss."

Jonelle and the lawyer stood outside the visiting room door. She held out her hand and he shook it. "Thanks for allowing me to talk to her. I feel real sorry for her and her son."

"I know. She's really a nice kid who got used by someone a helluva lot smarter than she. I don't mean to talk ill of the dead, but maybe we've got a little karma thing going here."

"Maybe."

Jonelle waved goodbye and followed her escort down the hall. So far, no one was able to determine exactly why Susanna fled to Maryland, but her connection to the area was clear. One of the first things Jonelle would do when she got home was contact Barrington Kelly.

As Jonelle headed down the highway toward the airport and the flight that would take her back to Baltimore, she wondered again about the real relationship between the sisters. After she talked to Kelly, she'd meet with Sophia and clear up a few things.

Several hours later, an exhausted Jonelle let herself into her condo, glad for the quiet that greeted her. She took a quick shower and fell into bed. Before sleep overtook her, she wondered why it was no one asked *why* someone wanted Susanna dead.

CHAPTER 19

After a weekend at home spent digesting the information she'd learned in Michigan, Jonelle sat in her office on Monday morning and fired up her computer. Even though she'd gotten Barrington Kelly's home address in Alexandria, Virginia, from Finkleberg, she wanted her first contact with Susanna's ex to occur in his office. She didn't have to search long before she found his practice on K Street in Northwest DC. That told her one important thing: the high profile and expensive area of the city indicated the good doctor had achieved some measure of success. She noted the telephone number and address and had picked up her office phone to place the call to set up a face-to-face when her cellphone chirped.

The incoming text was from Burt. His "FYI" recorded what forensics found in the substance that coated Susanna's face. Jonelle had assumed it was just regular store-bought makeup, but Burt's text indicated something different. The ingredients he listed were: shortening, cornstarch, white flour and glycerin. Except for the glycerin, somebody could've been making a cake. Even with all the questions swirling through her head, Jonelle didn't want to contact Burt now, so she texted, "jst rtrnd, bsy, cntct ltr". First item on the agenda was Kelly. She dialed the number and waited.

A bubbly voice on the other end announced, "Doctors Schein, Morrow and Kelly may I help you?"

Jonelle remembered Sophia's description of Kelly's specialty and grinned to herself. She hadn't thought through how to impress upon the receptionist her need to see Kelly without giving away the reason. The voice inquired, "Anyone there?" prompting Jonelle that since she figured Finkleberg would've given Kelly a "heads-up" anyway, she'd just announce who she was.

"Yes. Hello. I'd like to speak to Dr. Kelly please." After giving her name, but not the reason for her call, stating it was personal, Jonelle waited on hold. A few moments later, the voice came back on the line and stated Kelly wasn't available at the moment. Jonelle left her name, office and cellphone numbers. Before she disconnected, Jonelle added an "in reference to" with just one word: Susanna. She noted the time and decided to give him until five o'clock tomorrow to return her call. Knowing it involved Susanna, Jonelle bet it wouldn't take him that long.

She'd no sooner noted her calendar to call Kelly on Tuesday when Rainey buzzed from the front to let her know Mrs. Reyes had stopped by to see if she had time to meet with her. "Of course," Jonelle replied. "She knows the way, Rainey, so go ahead and send her back." Sophia was next on her to do list. She wanted to give her client the details about the trip to Michigan. The unannounced visit saved her a phone call.

Jonelle stood as Sophia entered and gestured to the guest chair. "I'm glad you stopped by. I was going to call and fill you in on my trip to the Upper Peninsula." Something was different about Sophia and Jonelle couldn't put her finger on what it was.

"Hope you don't mind my coming in without an appointment, but I was anxious to find out how it went," Sophia said.

Then she remembered what Sarah had told her. "How are you feeling? Your mother said when you called, you had a bad cold."

"Oh, that." Sophia cleared her throat. "I think it was only a twenty-four hour bug."

Jonelle described her visit to Finkleberg's office. "When did you know about the embezzlement charges against Susanna?"

Sophia crossed and uncrossed her legs before responding. "I found out when the Oldenberry police contacted me to try and find out where she was." Sophia failed to meet Jonelle's eyes.

"Why didn't you tell me?"

"Because I didn't think the police contacting me had anything to do with how she ended up dead in Maryland."

Jonelle studied the woman sitting across from her and realized what the difference was in Sophia's appearance. To Jonelle's eye, it looked as though Sophia had more makeup on than before. While that wasn't an issue, it reminded her of what Burt said about the paint on Susanna's face.

"Maybe. But since you hired me to find out about your sister, whatever you know or find out that pertains to her, you need to inform me. Okay?"

Lines appeared through Sophia's heavy makeup. "I'm not holding anything back."

"I'm not saying you are," Jonelle said. Tension hung in the air like low hanging clouds preceding an approaching storm and Jonelle didn't like the feeling. She took a deep breath and recited the shorthand version of her trip to Michigan. Her review of the interview with Sarah made Sophia wince, but she held her tongue. It wasn't until Jonelle mentioned Rosemary that she got more of a reaction. Sophia's eyes widened and she leaned forward, her face just inches from Jonelle's.

"What did she tell you about … my sister?"

Jonelle leaned back to put more space between them. She told Sophia everything Rosemary said about the money and Susanna's plan to send Rosemary the rest of her share. Jonelle studied the woman before her. Her client seemed more upset about Rosemary than the fact Jonelle still didn't know what pulled Susanna to the streets of Maryland.

"Have you ever met Rosemary?" Jonelle asked.

Sophia paused. "I was living in Traverse City when Susanna got her promotion. She never mentioned her co-workers. Why should she?"

Jonelle tried another tack. "Did you know of your sister's plans in the embezzlement?"

Sophia blanched. "Of course not. How could you—"

"Don't get upset," Jonelle interrupted. "I had to ask. So, you're saying you didn't know anything about Susanna's life in Oldenberry after you left, is that correct?"

Sophia tightened her grip on her bag. This time, her eyes stared into Jonelle's own, lips pressed in a tight line. Jonelle waited for the outburst.

"I thought I hired you to find out why my sister ended up down here and her relationship to that … whatever. Seems like I'm wasting my money," she said, voice tight.

"I know why your sister left, and you're right, I don't know yet how she ended up here. The logical answer is Kelly so I've left a message and I plan to interview him on what, if anything, he knows. Whatever he tells me will dictate my next move." Jonelle shrugged. "But, if you'd rather I not pursue this any further, fine. I'll tell Rainey to render you a final bill." Jonelle turned to her computer and pulled up Sophia's form. She turned back to her client, eyebrows raised.

"I don't know why you have to be so difficult," Sophia said. She opened her handbag, took out a tissue and dabbed her nose. The affected gesture irked Jonelle and she took a deep, impatient breath.

"The only way I get information which may lead to finding answers to what happened is to ask questions. Of everybody that may even have the slightest bearing on the case. I asked you about Rosemary because she hinted that you and Susanna got closer after her divorce. She said she didn't know how much—if anything—you knew about what Susanna had planned, so I had to ask." Jonelle paused, waiting for Sophia's reaction.

Sophia wadded the tissue and looked around for someplace to deposit it. Jonelle reached down and held the trashcan out to her. "Thanks," she said. She threw the tissue in the can.

After she replaced the wastebasket, Jonelle leaned back in her chair and waited for Sophia to say more. She didn't have to wait long.

"Look. Susanna and I got much closer after I left to go to college. For some reason I can't really explain, our relationship was a little rocky in high school."

"Did it have anything to do with drugs? Someone told me you two used to sell drugs in different parts of the town."

Sophia's eyes widened in shock.

"Who told you that?"

Jonelle shrugged. "The *who* isn't important. Is it true?"

Sophia nodded. "That whole episode was just teenage rebellion stuff. Once we discovered how dangerous dealing was, we stopped. It wasn't worth our lives. Most of the people who bought were Indians—I mean Native Americans. They have a problem with drugs you know."

So do whites, blacks, Asians and every other group on the planet, Jonelle surmised. She let the drug issue go.

"I was also told—and I can't tell you who told me—that when it came to spousal abuse, that Susanna sometimes slapped her husband around. Do you know if that's true?"

A crooked smile played on Sophia's lips. "You *did* learn a lot in those few days, I see. Neither me nor my sister take crap from anyone."

The hardness in Sophia's voice wasn't lost on Jonelle. "So, she was capable of violence. Is that right?"

"If necessary." Sophia held Jonelle's gaze.

One of the things Jonelle learned from her uncle was that to get at the answers you needed, sometimes you had to ask the unexpected questions. "So tell me. How well do you get along with your husband?"

Sophia seemed taken aback. "What does that have to do with anything?"

"Just curious. Especially considering what you just said about not taking any 'crap'."

"My husband and I have a great relationship."

Sophia placed her right hand over her left. Jonelle had already noted the absence of a ring.

Jonelle waited for more information and when none was forthcoming, decided to stay on this theme. "Do you have any children?"

A head shake.

"What's your husband's profession?"

Sophia shifted in her chair and turned her gaze to the office window. Jonelle waited.

"If you must know, Martin is a lawyer." Again, Sophia seemed reluctant to divulge any more information than she had to. Jonelle glanced at the clock. She didn't have to be anywhere anytime soon.

"Private practice or does he work for a firm?"

"He's employed by the local utility. Look, I don't see what this has to do with Susanna."

Jonelle glanced once more at Sophia's left hand.

"Why no ring?"

Sophia continued covering her left hand with her right.

"I don't like to travel with my expensive jewelry. Especially when I'm in a place like this."

Yet, the first time we met you had on an expensive looking necklace, Jonelle thought.

"You know, I assumed you're staying here by yourself, but just to be sure, is your husband with you?"

Another head shake.

A quick check of the computer screen revealed the hotel where Sophia was staying. Right on the pricey Inner Harbor.

"How long are you staying in Baltimore? I could always keep you informed about the status of your case if you needed to return to Michigan."

"As long as it takes. The police won't release my sister's body while they still consider her evidence. I'm not sure I like the way you do things down here. I get the feeling that they're not telling me everything they know."

If you only knew the half of it, Jonelle thought. Before she could pivot off this line of questioning and back to the task at hand, Sophia beat her to it.

"Tell me about the … uh … homeless person. He found Susanna and I understand he's not even in custody."

"He had nothing to do with your sister's death," Jonelle said. "He tried to help her when he found her wandering on the street, so—"

"I don't care about that," Sophia interrupted. "He must have found the money by now." Her eyes narrowed. "I also heard you're supposed to be a friend of his. Do you think he'd tell you what happened to the money?"

Jonelle shifted her weight in the chair.

"Luther told me that Susanna claimed she had a lot of money and needed his help hiding it," Jonelle said, feeling as if she'd just betrayed a good friend even though she and the homeless man were not on that level. "He doesn't know where it is."

Sophia sat up. "So he claims he hasn't found it yet? And you believe him?" The look on Sophia's face showed she wasn't impressed with Jonelle's investigative skills.

Jonelle held both hands up, palms out. "Now just hold on. She was killed before she told him."

A coldness appeared in Sophia's eyes. "I bet he found it and is waiting until things settle before he grabs the money for himself."

Jonelle shook her head. "I doubt that. Why all the concern about the money? When it's found, it'll go back to Michigan. Listen, Luther really cared for your sister. He was devastated when she was killed."

Sophia's eyes softened a little.

"My guess is that the money's still hidden somewhere. Maybe she opened a bank account and its sitting in there for all we know." Jonelle remembered the code written on the piece of paper. "The police are looking at every angle."

In a flat voice Sophia said, "It's not in a bank."

Now it was Jonelle's turn to be skeptical. "How do you know that?"

"You can't open a bank account without a fixed address."

"True. But if she contacted her ex, she could use his address," Jonelle said, thinking out loud. "Although, to deposit that amount of money you'd have to have ID. The police are checking all the banks and so far, nothing."

Although sparring with clients was not Jonelle's favorite thing to do, it did open up several avenues that she hadn't thought of before. Why did Sophia seem more interested in retrieving the money than Finkleberg? Surely the woman knew the money, if found, had to be returned to the county. And why should she care?

"One of the things Rosemary said that I found curious was that Susanna was supposed to send her the rest of the money she promised her. What I can't figure out is why? Why not just give the woman everything upfront? They could go their separate ways and not bother with each other again. Rosemary said Susanna had planned to screw her all along. Does that sound like your sister?" It occurred to Jonelle that Susanna would probably do the same thing to Luther.

Sophia looked at her hands. "Maybe she wasn't one hundred percent sure she could trust her. By keeping some of the money in reserve, so to speak, that meant the little secretary would keep her end of the bargain. I know Susanna shouldn't have done what she did, but that's irrelevant at this point."

"That 'little secretary' has a child."

"Some half-breed I heard."

"That make a difference to you?"

Sophia shrugged.

Let it go, Jonelle. "Your mother told me you were all well off. Your father had a lot of money and made sure the three of you would be well taken care of. Plus, your mother said that when she passed away, you two would share her estate. So, why take the money in the first place?"

Sophia rubbed her temples. "I can't answer that," she said, her voice barely above a whisper. She stared into the distance. "Maybe it was the thrill of doing something dangerous."

The cloying fragrance of Sophia's flowery-scented perfume started the beginnings of a headache, just behind Jonelle's right ear. By her own reckoning she had about ten more minutes before the mild ache turned into a full-blown migraine.

"Tell me about the last conversation you had with Susanna. When was it? How did she sound? What did you two talk about?"

A deep sigh escaped Sophia's lips. "It was six months or so ago. I knew she was still bummed that her marriage didn't work out, even though she wasn't happy when she and Barry were together. She admitted she was depressed. She felt stifled in that small, one-horse town. She claimed there wasn't much to stimulate her … intellectual or otherwise." Sophia chuckled. "That's my sister for you. Always wanting something more. Something better."

"She could've moved. She had the means to do so. She didn't have to steal money from the town where she grew up." Jonelle didn't care for Sophia's cavalier attitude about the whole situation.

Sophia's eyes formed into slits. "Maybe," she said.

"Besides feeling trapped in Oldenberry, any other indication she was about to do something drastic?"

Sophia looked down at the bag sitting in her lap. "No. Not that I recall."

Jonelle didn't believe her. "What about your mother?"

Sophia looked up sharply. "What about her? She has nothing to do with this."

"I realize that. But your mother isn't well. Wouldn't Susanna care what this would do to her health? Your mother's still living in that town and has to face the people there knowing what her daughter did to all of them."

For the first time since she sat down across from Jonelle, Sophia looked sad. "That's the worst part of all this."

CHAPTER 20

After a somewhat stressful conversation with Sophia Reyes, all Jonelle wanted to do when she got home was make a quick dinner, take a long bath and curl up with a good book. Instead, she loaded her backpack with junk food and water, took a hot shower, watched a few hours of mindless TV, and went to her surveillance job. The one encouraging part of the day was the call from Barrington Kelly who agreed to meet with her tomorrow in his office. To help pass the time, Jonelle planned on going over the questions she wanted to ask him about Susanna. And Sophia.

While she was in Michigan Ben reported absolutely nothing happened at Polly Cole's house. "Thought I might have a little excitement Thursday night when I saw a light in the front go on around two thirty in the morning. About twenty minutes later, the light went off. No one went in or came out. Figured she couldn't sleep and went into the kitchen to grab a bite to eat. Or whatever. Bottom line is nothing happened. Nada. Nein. Zero. Zippo," he'd said before Jonelle cut him off.

In a way she was glad Ben subbed for her for a couple nights. That would provide a different vehicle in the area. Even though Mrs. Cole said she'd given a few discreet neighbors a 'heads-up' that Jonelle and her Jeep would be watching the house, Jonelle wanted to be sure that someone out of the loop wouldn't get suspicious and call the police.

The cool night ushered in the sound of chirping crickets. Jonelle passed by the craftsman bungalow the first time, looking for a spot that would give her a good vantage point. As she approached the house for the second time, she noticed brake lights on a car parked at the curb ahead of her, its front wheels angled out. "Thank goodness," she said, slowing to a stop.

Headlights shone in her rearview mirror. She engaged her Jeep's blinker to signal her intent to pull into the vacated space. The vehicle behind her didn't move. Jonelle put her arm out the window and waved the car on. It didn't work; the car stayed behind her. "Idiot," she muttered.

Only after Jonelle had backed into the space did the car pass. Annoyed at the driver's actions, she glanced out her side window, intent on throwing the occupant a dirty look. The vehicle crept past. As it moved on, she noted two people in the gray sedan. A whiff of marijuana floated through her open window. Jonelle smiled to herself. Even if a person had never smoked the stuff, everyone knew that distinctive smell.

Jonelle perked up at the possibility the boyfriend had arrived and tonight the daughter would bolt. It'd be great if she could catch the guy in the act of sneaking into the house, thereby resolving the second surveillance case and allowing her to focus on Susanna. *Two* people in the vehicle bothered her. Would the guy bring a friend? She waited for the car to come back and park, but nothing happened.

Jonelle checked her watch. Only eleven thirty. She groaned. It was gonna be a long night. She settled down and pulled out her notebook. She'd already gotten some sense, although contradictory, of Barrington Kelly. With pencil in hand, she scribbled a few questions. Most of them focused on Kelly's last contact with Susanna.

Finkleberg must've contacted Kelly about the missing money when Susanna fled. If Susanna had contacted Kelly, surely Kelly would've let Finkleberg know. What if Kelly knew about the embezzlement? Would he help his ex or turn her in? Jonelle made a note to call Burt to see if the Michigan cops had arrived about Susanna and if he'd learned about her ex.

Jonelle pulled her backpack from the floor onto the seat and scrounged inside for a bottle of water and bag of chips. As she opened the bag, approaching headlights illuminated the inside of the Jeep. Jonelle stopped herself from sliding down in the seat; she wanted a good look. As the car closed in on her location, she noticed the same gray sedan with the same two guys she'd seen earlier. She sniffed. Yep, the sweet, smoky smell of weed hung in the air.

This time, the person in the passenger seat turned and stared at her. Dark hair drooped over his forehead and ran down his neck, hiding his collar. The car continued down the street.

The guy didn't look like any young girl's boyfriend. He resembled someone whose mugshot would appear on the news. She wanted to follow to see where they went or at least get a look at the license plate. If she left and the kid bolted, then what? How would she explain she'd failed at such a simple task? She shoved the key in the ignition. The hell with it; those guys sent her intuition button into overdrive. If Polly Cole's daughter made a run for it, well, she'd make some excuse. If those guys were planning something illegal, she couldn't sit by and let that happen.

The Jeep turned over and Jonelle sped down the street, intent on picking up where they were headed. Up ahead, brake lights flashed as the car made a right turn. She pressed the accelerator. At that time of night and on a Monday, there wasn't much traffic. The one constant thing this neighborhood used for traffic control was stop signs. Sure enough, a stop sign ahead forced the sedan to a halt. Jonelle used one hand to scribble the license plate on her notepad before she noticed the rental car sticker. Damn. The car sat there. Jonelle waited. What were they doing? Jonelle glanced at the glove compartment where her Beretta lay.

The squeal of tires alerted her and she watched the sedan make an abrupt left turn and speed down the street. No point in following now. She had the license plate and would forward the information to the police department if necessary. Still. Jonelle felt the men had things on their mind other than robbing the neighborhood where she happened to be watching. Plus, she hated coincidences.

She made her way back to Polly Cole's house. Nothing looked out of place as she pulled into the same spot. Settled in once more, Jonelle believed the men had nothing to do with Polly's daughter, and burglars wouldn't slow down and draw attention to themselves. The only other possibility was that they were following her.

CHAPTER 21

After having spent most of her fledgling PI career with her butt ensconced in plastic chairs in various waiting rooms, Jonelle was happy to relax in a plush, upholstered chair in the reception area of Schein, Morrow and Kelly. The petite Asian American woman behind the curved, wooden reception desk smiled at her again. "Sorry for the delay," she said, showing even, white teeth beneath bright red lipstick. "The doctor is still with his last client."

Jonelle returned the smile. "No problem. I'm not in any particular hurry."

A few minutes later, a male voice interrupted her as she read about the latest exploits of yet another celebrity couple she never heard of.

Jonelle looked up as a man of medium height and slender build approached. "Ms. Sweet?" he asked. Since the only other person there besides herself and the secretary was an elderly man, Jonelle thought his question somewhat redundant. As she stood to greet him, the first thing she noticed was his sad, what they used to call bedroom, eyes. Those eyes took her by surprise, as did the rest of his rather ordinary appearance. Somehow he didn't match up with the man she supposed someone like Susanna Quinley would date, much less marry. She was glad she'd swiped a business card that displayed his picture since she wasn't sure she could remember what Kelly looked like after she left.

They shook hands and Kelly indicated a long hall to the right of the secretary. "Follow me to my office?"

"Sure," Jonelle said. "Lead the way."

Plush, gray-green carpeting muffled their footsteps. In between closed doors on both sides of the hallway were posters of abstract paintings. Jonelle wondered if they were supposed to be substitutes for those, "what do you see" blotches she'd heard psychologists used, then remembered he wasn't that kind of head doctor.

Kelly opened a door with his name in raised, pewter lettering and suggested she sit in a black, leather chair in front of his desk. He went around and sat in a similar but high-backed chair. Jonelle noted the prints on the walls in his office resembled those in the hall. She took in the wine-colored leather sofa against the left wall. Floor to ceiling bookcases covered the space behind Kelly's desk. Framed photographs faced him, preventing her from seeing the subjects. A three-sectioned, two-drawer mahogany file cabinet filled the area under the one window. A tall, yellow vase with streaks of red splashed through it perched on top of the cabinet. To her disappointment the flowers inside looked fake.

"So," he said, drawing her attention back to him. "You're here to talk about Susanna."

Jonelle liked it when people got right to the point. "Yes. The first thing I'd like to know is how you found out about her death. Did you hear about it on the news? Read it in the newspapers?"

He shook his head. "Not from the papers. I only read the *Wall Street Journal.* I seldom watch local news because frankly, all they're about ninety percent of the time is reporting crime. No," he said, picking up a pen and holding it horizontally between the fingers of both hands, "I first heard about her death from Norman Finkleberg."

"Did he also tell you what she's accused of?"

"He said she stole money from the county." He made the statement as if he'd just been asked to describe his favorite sweater.

"You're not surprised?"

He shrugged.

Jonelle waited for him to elaborate. When he didn't, she decided to back up and start with what she'd heard when she was in Michigan. "I understand you two had a rocky marriage. Is that a fair assessment?"

Kelly turned and looked toward the window. "We never should have married. I lusted after her all through high school, like most of the other guys. She was so pretty. So popular. Of course I never thought she'd go out with someone like me. But, one day, I got the courage to ask her to a movie and she said yes. My feet didn't hit the ground all week." He paused, a slight smile of remembrance on his face. "We dated off and on all through high school and right before college we decided to go ahead and get married. Our parents were against it, but you can't talk to kids." He hesitated again. After a few seconds, he turned and faced Jonelle.

"Truth is, they were right. We were awful together. Argued from day one. I seemed to annoy the hell out of her just by breathing."

"Tell me about school. I heard the twins sold drugs. Were you into that scene?" The doctor didn't look the type, but one never really knew.

"I don't do drugs. Never have, never will."

"You knew she did though, right? Did it bother you?"

Kelly blinked several times. "I knew and no, it didn't bother me. She wasn't addicted or anything. They stopped dealing when things started getting a little, uh, hairy in the places that attracted that sort of people."

"'They?'"

"Sophia got involved in that nonsense for a while also."

Jonelle didn't think that selling drugs in high school would provoke someone into killing one of the women years later, yet she knew people killed for far less.

"Were they ever threatened? Did the other dealers object to them selling on their turf?"

"I have no idea. They weren't serious. To them it was another way of pushing everyone's buttons."

Although no one had mentioned it in Michigan, Jonelle wondered if that lifestyle carried into the twins' adult life.

"Do you know if Susanna, or Sophia for that matter, continued their involvement with drugs?"

Kelly's eyes widened. "Of course not. That all ended years ago."

Jonelle appreciated his candor and wondered if that was a personality trait of his position. She decided to press on. "I heard different rumors about how you and Susanna sometimes argued to the point the police were called. Some say you not only verbally, but also physically abused her, while others said she fought you. Physically, I mean." Jonelle watched his expression.

Those hazel eyes gave up nothing, though the sides of his mouth curled down a bit.

"I don't hit women. Never have, never will. Whenever Susanna felt she wasn't winning whatever argument *du jour* she'd throw things … whatever was at hand. Occasionally her fists connected with my nose." A sad smile crossed his face. "Two years or so later, we'd both had enough." He gave a harsh laugh. "Funny. The only thing we agreed on was divorce."

"Why did you come all the way to Maryland for school? There are many prestigious colleges between the Upper Peninsula and here."

"True. But I got a full scholarship to Hopkins. My parents weren't as rich as Susanna's. They couldn't help with my education. If I wanted a better life for myself, I had to do it on my own. Besides, I wanted out of that place. Too many eyes. Too many wagging tongues." He cocked his head to one side. "I bet you noticed that when you were there. Am I right?"

Jonelle agreed. "Very close-knit community. I guess that's one reason why Finkleberg was so shocked at what Susanna did. Did she ever give you any indication that she'd steal from the town?"

He shook his head and turned to gaze toward the window again. "The police kept asking me who would do such a thing to Susanna. I knew they considered me a suspect until I produced a solid alibi."

"Mind telling me what it was?"

He smiled ruefully. "I was hosting a birthday party for a friend of mine on my boat. It's moored in southwest DC. At least twenty people vouched for my whereabouts."

Kelly put the pen on his desk and picked up one of the framed photographs. "My girlfriend hates that I still have this, but Susanna was a part of my life." He turned the picture so Jonelle could see. It was of the two of them, taken on their wedding day.

"Very nice," she said. "I know what you mean. You can't flick your emotions on and off like a light switch. It takes time."

Kelly replaced the photo in the exact spot on his desk. "So. When Finkleberg told me about the missing money, I refused to believe she'd done it. Not until he said they arrested that other woman and she confessed."

"When was the last time you talked to Susanna?" Jonelle watched him carefully. Finally, she noticed a slight change in his eyes.

"I haven't seen her since I left Michigan. That was years ago."

"I understand, Dr. Kelly. But what I'm asking is, have you talked to her? Communicated with her in any way, either on the phone or maybe by email?"

He sighed. "I told the police I got a phone call from Susanna about five, six months ago. She said she was coming to the area to, uh, look for another job and wondered if she could stay with me for a while. I told her no. That I was involved with someone and we were living together."

"Is that true?"

He frowned. "Of course."

"Did she say why she was looking for another job?"

He shook his head.

"How did she react when you rejected her suggestion?"

"Typical Susanna fashion. She got mad. Called me a spineless wonder, said I should grow a pair, etcetera, etcetera." He glanced at his watch. "I'm sorry, but I have another client scheduled in a few minutes."

"Okay. Just a few more quick questions. Did she know anyone else in the area?"

"Not that I'm aware of."

"The biggest thing that doesn't add up is why, after you rejected her request to stay with you, she chose to come here anyway and live on the street? Why would an attractive white woman, with money no less, want to live with a scuzzy-looking black guy on Baltimore's mean streets?" Sorry, Luther.

"I have … ," his voice cracked. "I have no idea."

He stood. Jonelle followed suit.

"What about Sophia?"

Kelly started to come around his desk and stopped. "What about her?"

"Did you two get along?"

He shrugged. "Not really. She'd left the U.P., after high school."

"True. But she came back for your wedding."

"And left right after. So, if you don't mind … " He walked over to the door and held it open.

"You talked from time to time. Right?"

A flash of anger in his eyes. "What makes you think that?"

"Because she told me what your specialty was. How would she know unless you told her?"

"Susanna must've said something."

Jonelle didn't buy it. "But you said the only contact you had with Susanna was about six months ago. She'd already left Michigan under a cloud of suspicion. So, how would she know anything about you, unless the three of you kept in contact with each other."

Kelly looked as if he was having second thoughts about telling Jonelle anything. She waited for his response. She didn't have to wait long.

"Okay. This is how it happened. Right after Susanna called—"

"How long after?" Jonelle interrupted.

"Not sure. Couple days maybe. Anyway, I got a message to contact Norm Finkleberg. He and I remained friends after I left. He told me what happened and asked if I knew where she was. I told him she'd called me, wanting to stay with me a while but I turned her down. I said I had no idea where she was staying. Norm said he'd contacted everyone else in the family and they claimed they didn't know where she was either."

"When did Sophia contact you? Before or after you talked to Susanna?"

Kelly returned to his chair, leaned back and gazed at the ceiling. "After. All this was after. If I'd known what she'd done, I'd have said she could stay with me, and then when I got the call from Norm I would've told him where she was."

Jonelle didn't believe him. Even though Susanna stole the money he still had strong feelings for her. Why else would he hold on to their wedding picture?

"What happened next?"

He rose again. "Nothing. Until a few days ago when Norm called to say he'd heard from you and you said Susanna was killed. I already knew, of course. Sophia told me."

"How?"

"Excuse me?"

"Did she call you at home or here on your work phone?"

"Here. Of course." He stared pointedly at his watch.

"Thanks for your time." She held out her hand and they both shook. Instead of exiting through the door she entered, Kelly walked around her to another door Jonelle hadn't noticed before.

He opened it and pointed down a short, narrow corridor. "Follow the hallway to the first corridor on the left. That leads to the elevators. Most of my patients prefer leaving this way."

Jonelle smiled at the word *patients*. "That's okay. I've got nothing to hide."

They shared a laugh. Out in the hall, Jonelle remembered she forgot to ask Dr. Kelly when he last had a face-to-face with Sophia.

CHAPTER 22

Although Jonelle felt her meeting with Kelly provided her with a few bits of information about Susanna, it still didn't answer the question of why his ex-wife ended up on the streets of Baltimore. Even though he appeared helpful, Jonelle couldn't shake the feeling that the good doctor was holding something back.

And where was the 330,000 dollars? When Jonelle arrived at her office the next day following her meeting with Kelly, a message from Adrienne waited. Adrienne had promised Jonelle she'd talk to one of the doctors at the university's teaching hospital to see if they could explain what kind of person would kill someone in such a horrific manner and then smear paint on their face? Not only that, why go to all the trouble of making some? Why not just buy paint or makeup at a store?

The message advised that a Doctor Frances Pope could spare a half hour with her. Since her last job was working security on the campus, Jonelle knew exactly where to find the building that housed the office. She avoided a detour over to her former place of work; she didn't want to explain her career after she left. She'd heard her former colleague Tyrone had found himself a girlfriend and according to Adrienne, the two were getting serious. Good for him. When she worked there, she knew Tyrone had a soft spot for her.

Her eyes scanned the clogged street. Classes had resumed over a month ago which made finding a good place to park a hit or miss proposition. Had she gone over to security they'd have given her a parking pass.

With a sigh, she aimed for the large covered lot. She took a ticket and grumbled about the prices posted on the side of the structure. She found a spot near the top, locked her Jeep and hustled down to the entrance, skirting traffic on her way to the doctor's office. She had five minutes to spare before her appointment.

Once inside the building, she decided to take the stairs to the next level. The metal door opened onto a long hallway. She took a deep breath and hightailed it down the hall. At this rate, she wouldn't have to worry about formal exercises to lose weight. Her job as a bona fide detective was all she needed.

She knocked on the doctor's door. A soft "come in" later and Jonelle found herself just a few feet from the doctor's desk.

A small, light-skinned African American woman with close cropped hair and freckles running across her nose smiled at her. "Ms. Sweet?"

Jonelle nodded. The pleasant-looking woman sat behind a desk piled high with papers. On the walls several framed documents occupied space with several "grip and grin" photos. Shelves of various sizes overflowed with books.

"Students have another hour until I consult with them although"—Dr. Pope looked at her watch—"they usually start lining up about now." The doctor left her chair, motioned for Jonelle to sit across from the desk and locked the door. She didn't speak until she returned to her seat.

"Ms. Roth indicated you had a few questions about a victim that you're consulting with the police about. I advised her that all I'd be able to do is provide you with some basic generalities. I'd need to know a lot more before I could make a more thorough observation."

"I realize that, so thank you for taking the time. I guess all I really want is your impressions on what was found on the woman's face."

Jonelle explained the white makeup, and what it was made of. "I'm not tracking down the perpetuator or anything. I only want to know what kind of person would do something like this."

Dr. Pope explained again that she didn't do pop psychology and criminal psychology was not her specialty. Still. "Did you see the face yourself?"

Jonelle shook her head.

"Were any other marks on the face?"

"A black substance covered the eyes and mouth. How big of a difference does that make?"

The doctor turned around and pulled a large book from her bookcase. With a frown she flipped several pages until she found what she was looking for.

"Ah, here it is. There's a condition called coulrophobia. Basically, it's a fear of clowns … well not so much clowns per se. It's more the idea that you have a normal-sized person with a painted face, unusual clothes and oversized feet. The natural instinct is to wonder what's under all that."

Jonelle had never heard of it and asked the doctor about the spelling.

"Sometimes the makeup can function as a type of mask. It can hide a person's true identity as well as give them the opportunity to adopt a new one. Perhaps it was the killers way of saying they knew this person was not who she appeared to be."

That last point hit home. Susanna was trying to hide something. But how did the killer know that? Up until now Jonelle was going with the assumption that a stranger might have killed Susanna.

"So, you think maybe the face painting has to do with hiding something, like clowns do?"

Doctor Pope smiled. "Not in the basic way. One of the things that people find most disturbing about clowns is that they have two sides. They are not always happy; they can be downright creepy and scary. A lot of people identify with that."

"Hmm." Jonelle's eyes wandered around the cluttered office. "The deceased is a twin of the person who hired me to find out how her sister ended up on the Baltimore streets."

Concern clouded the doctor's eyes. "Does the sister wear a lot of white makeup?"

"Not white, exactly. Just a lot of it. I visited the area where the victim was from and there are several Native American tribes in the area. What about the possibility that it was some kind of native ritual?"

"Anything's possible, but I would have expected the color to be something other than white. Say, red for example, if whoever did this wanted to make a particular point. In most cultures white reflects innocence and purity. Though black around the eyes and mouth suggests power, death, evil and mystery … something negative."

Jonelle pondered that a moment. "There's another thing. She was also a member of her high school theater group. Do you think that could be a connection?"

Doctor Pope shook her head. "Without knowing more about the victim, I can't really say. Sometimes face painting is considered sexual, but I don't see evidence of that from what you described. What I find most interesting is the fact that you said the substance on her face was homemade. You can buy theatrical makeup anywhere."

"So why do you think he went to all the trouble to make it?"

"Maybe he was smart enough to realize tracing special makeup would be easier than buying the ingredients at a drugstore. So, it tells me your murderer is somewhat intelligent."

And that the murder was premeditated, Jonelle thought.

"Have you talked to the surviving twin? Does she have any ideas?"

A loud knock on the door interrupted them. "Just a moment," the doctor called out.

"She claims she doesn't know why."

"Claims?"

Another knock, more insistent this time. "Hold on a moment," Doctor Pope shouted. She rolled her eyes. "Don't you believe her?"

"Honestly? I'm not sure."

"Hmm. This is pure speculation, but anyone who takes the time to manipulate a body isn't too concerned about getting caught and that makes him—or her—very dangerous. You say the victim was a twin?"

Jonelle's stomach clenched. What if the killer had personal issues with Susanna?

"Do you think the surviving twin is in danger?"

"I can't say for sure but it doesn't sound like this was a random act. The person who did this might want to do the same to the lookalike." Doctor Pope looked at her watch. "I'm sorry, but I'm afraid I've got to see the students."

Jonelle stood and held out her hand.

"Sorry I couldn't be more help," the doctor said.

"You were very helpful. You've given me a lot to consider."

The doctor nodded. "The door opens without a key, so if you don't mind letting whoever that is, enter?"

Jonelle smiled. "No problem."

On the other side of the door stood a skinny boy whose demeanor and red-blotched face indicated he hadn't been long out of high school. He stared open-mouthed at her.

"Well, don't just stand there," Doctor Pope called to the visitor. "Come on in. You've got twenty minutes before my next appointment."

CHAPTER 23

As Jonelle sat in the coffee shop across from campus, she reviewed her conversation with Doctor Pope. She realized the doctor was at a disadvantage from not conducting her own study, but there were a few things that resonated.

Jonelle hadn't considered the sexual component until the doctor brought it up and dismissed it. The only person she knew of with the opportunity for a physical relationship was Kelly. And maybe Luther. The doctor pointed out the mask aspect and Jonelle thought back to her time in Michigan's Upper Peninsula and her conversation with Ayasha, the only Native American she met. Maybe white was used, not because of the symbolism, but because it was easier to make. As she took another sip of coffee, her cellphone rang. On the other end was an angry Rainey.

"Where are you?" Rainey demanded.

Jonelle wasn't used to hearing that tone coming from the receptionist and it took her back. "Uh. I just finished an interview. Do you need me back at the office?"

"You better believe it. There's somebody yelling into the intercom outside that he needs to speak to you. I'm not buzzing him into this building until I know who he is. I don't like the way he sounds." Rainey went on to say that another of the building's occupants refused to let him in because he looked like a homeless person.

"Sounds like Luther," Jonelle said, gulping down the rest of her coffee. "Tell him to stay where he is. I'm on my way."

Jonelle sped down the road, nervously glancing in the rearview mirror and hoping she wouldn't encounter a policeman intent on proving a point about speeding … or blowing through yellow lights. She quickly pulled into her assigned space in the open lot and nearly toppled over onto uneven concrete as she rushed to the building. A disheveled shape limped off in the distance.

"Luther! Hold on."

He turned around slowly at the sound of her voice.

"I was gonna give you up," he said as Jonelle approached.

"Sorry. I had an appointment," she said, gasping for breath. "If I'd known you wanted to see me." She thought a moment. "Do you still have that pay per use cellphone I bought you last year?"

Luther shook his head. "Lost it. Still had this here card you gimme. That's how I knew where you worked." He looked at the building. "Didn't know it was gonna be like tryin' to get into Fort Knox though." A frown creased his already deeply lined forehead. "That lady that answered is kinda mean."

Jonelle laughed. "Rainey's a sweetheart. Just a little protective that's all." She had no problems with Luther coming to the office, but wondered how the other tenants would react to his being there. Almost as soon as the thought occurred she dismissed it. Who cares? Luther was her client.

She walked up to the building and was about to press the security code when he stopped her.

"Uh-uh. Don't wanna go in there. I just hafta tell you somethin'."

Jonelle looked around. "There's a park about a block and a half from here. Would that do?"

"I know where it's at." Luther shambled off with Jonelle by his side. Neither spoke on the short trip over. Jonelle knew from past experience not to rush him. He'd tell her what he had to in good time.

The word *park* was generous. It basically encompassed a bit of green set off in the middle of the north and southbound traffic on one of the areas busiest streets. The park boasted some trees and a few benches. The sparse grass was dotted throughout with bare spots. Jonelle and Luther sat down on a bench in the center of the median. Luther spied a few indigents milling about and grunted.

Three men eyed them suspiciously. "Do you know who they are?"

"I seen 'em around."

"Would you rather go someplace else?"

"Naw. They just eyeballin' us 'cause they know you don't belong."

Jonelle took that as a complement. She'd have to wait until he decided to speak, although the fact that he came to see her, rather than her having to track him down, indicated whatever it was, was important. She forced herself to rein in her impatience.

"Saw that there lawyer you got me," he said.

So that's why he wanted to see me, Jonelle thought. She tried not to show her disappointment. "What did he say?"

Luther shrugged. "Not much, you ask me. Claims the cops no longer think I'm a … whatchacallit … person of interest."

Jonelle knew the fact that Luther was walking around freely spoke volumes as to whether or not the police had any evidence against him.

"It's about Chester," he said. "He come back finally, but he's layin' low. He's scared that them guys what beat him up is gonna come lookin' for him again."

"He tell you why they attacked him?"

Luther leaned forward, brow furrowed in concentration. "Gotta make sure I git this right 'cause he wasn't too happy he tole me this much." Luther was seized by a coughing fit.

Jonelle fidgeted while Luther got himself under control.

He coughed up something wet and spit it on the ground.

"Chester says he went around tellin' people Suze had a big secret involvin' money," Luther said, once the spasms subsided. "There's no way he knows where the money is, 'cause she never told me. And if anyone would know, I would." More coughing ensued.

"Anyway," he croaked, "one of the losers what hangs out in front of Micky D's near the Harbor was braggin' about some guys payin' him to tell them which guy was Chester. Loser claimed they had somethin' to give Chester. They give it to him all right. He says he was headin' back to the warehouse when he was jumped and they started beatin' up on him."

"Did Chester mention whether or not they said anything to him? Either before they started hitting him, or before they ran off?"

Luther sat back and stared up at the sky. "Chester remembers them callin' his name. When they walked up to him, they asked him if he knew a white lady named Susanna. He had a funny feelin' so he said, no and one of them shoved him into the other one. And back and forth like playin' keep away. Punchin' him and laughin' all the while." Luther hesitated and took several long drags of his cigarette. Finished, he flicked the butt into the grass.

"Chester says while they's beatin' him, he hears runnin' and yellin' and the guys ran off. But not without threatenin' him again."

"Is that all?"

"Here's the thing." Luther reached inside the pocket of not so well-worn, almost clean, jeans and retrieved another cigarette. Jonelle wondered if his pants were one of several pair that she'd given him. For a man who had nothing, the fact that he still could afford to smoke was somewhat amazing.

"Like one?" he asked.

She shook her head. "What else can you tell me?" She waited while he filled his lungs with nicotine and blew smoke off in the distance.

"While they was playin' with Chester, he said they kept askin' him about money. He said he didn't know nuthin' that he was just braggin' is all." Luther shook his head over and over. "Damn fool. Never did know when to keep his mouth shut."

Jonelle stood, intending to pace, then sat again. "They mention any other names besides Susanna's?"

"He says no. And the old fool had sense enough not to mention mine." Luther stretched his legs out in front of him.

"What else does he know about the men?"

"Well, there was two of 'em. And he said they looked Mexican, but didn't have no Mexican accents."

"Dark hair and eyes?"

Luther nodded. "He said long, straight hair. Plus they was kinda husky in build. Chester said they near abouts broke his jaw, they hit him so hard."

Jonelle had more questions. "Did he notice a car?"

"Naw. He didn't pay no attention to them until they walked up to him."

Luther glanced at Jonelle. "He also tole me somethin' about Suze." He paused again.

Jonelle held her breath.

The sound of traffic whooshing by coupled with the occasional *thunk* as a wheel found a pothole reverberated in the air.

"Chester claims the day before she was killed he seen Suze go in one 'a the short-sheet hotels near Pimlico." Luther turned to Jonelle. "Suze didn't like Chester and the feelin' was mutual." He turned back around and gazed up at the sky.

"Chester claims he was curious so he waited and sees Suze come out again, dressed different. And she wasn't alone. She had some guy with her."

Jonelle's heart raced. "What guy? Had he seen him before?"

Luther shook his head. "He didn't know who it was. Never seen him around."

Jonelle tried to control her excitement. "I need to speak to Chester. Can you bring him to me or would it be best if I go see him?"

"None 'a the above."

Even knowing Luther's penchant for being difficult, Jonelle wondered at this latest evasion. Wherever this attitude was coming from, she wasn't in the mood to play games.

After a few minutes of watching traffic and trying not to inhale too much exhaust from cars traveling on both sides of the median, Jonelle was ready to pack it in. She rose from the bench.

"Aw, sit down. Bit touchy today ain't you?"

Jonelle sat. "Not a good day this morning. So, when can I speak to Chester?"

He shrugged.

She set the issue of Chester aside for now. The time had come for Jonelle to ask Luther something that had been bugging her. "What did Susanna tell you about the money?"

He peered sideways at her. "I don't know where it's at," he said.

"I'm not saying you do. I just want to know if she told you how she got it."

A frustrated sigh escaped his lips. "My posse warned me she was prob'ly trouble, but I didn't listen. All she said was she had a boat load of money that had to be hid somewheres safe."

"In order to hide it somewhere, it had to already *be* somewhere. Did she give you any indication where the money was right then?"

He shook his head.

Now it was Jonelle's turn to express frustration. She pulled out her cellphone and found the photo of the paper with the code. She turned it toward Luther. "Does this mean anything to you?"

He took the phone from Jonelle's hand and squinted at the image. "What's that?"

"I was hoping you could tell me."

"Looks like gibberish." He handed the phone back.

"What's really strange about this is while she wanted you to help her hide the money, I know she had it in her possession when she arrived in Maryland. Where was it?"

Luther shrugged. "She didn't give it to me if that's what you're thinkin'."

"Anybody else she was close to besides you?"

"Naw. She didn't like nobody else but me."

"Were there occasions when the two of you were apart for extended periods of time? I mean, you didn't keep watch over her right?"

"We wasn't joined at the hip, if that's what you mean," Luther said.

"How much time would you say elapsed when the two of you didn't see each other? Was it hours? Days?"

He squirmed on the bench.

Jonelle was on to something. "Was there a time when you didn't see her for twenty-four hours or more?"

"Couple times. Here an' there. But she always came back," he said with a touch of pride in his voice.

"So then, it's possible that she stayed somewhere else. Or with someone else. Like at that motel Chester told you about."

"Mebbe. I gots to go." He stood.

"Hold on." Jonelle didn't know how to put it, but the issue of Susanna and Luther's total relationship had to be addressed. "Were you and Susanna intimate?"

"Hell no. What's wrong with you anyway? I was helpin' her that's all."

"Sorry, but I had to ask." Another question bugged her. Burt might know the answer, but she wanted to hear it from Luther.

"How did you wind up kneeling over Susanna's body?"

Luther's eyes narrowed. "What you mean?"

She got right to it. "Were you following her? Her murder occurred some distance from the warehouse, out of view from passing traffic."

"I … I mighta been watchin' her." His feet kicked the dirt. "I wanted to keep an eye out. Didn't want her to … get hurt. So, I followed her but got distracted a few times." He sniffed. "Damn good thing I did before the rats got at her."

Jonelle shivered. "There's something else Chester told you. Right?"

"It don't mean nuthin'. He drinks more'n I do and sometimes his eyes don't work right."

Jonelle stood and faced him. "Tell me anyway."

Luther scratched his left armpit and stared off in the distance. "It don't make no sense."

"Luther." Jonelle's voice indicated she wanted to hear everything.

"He claims he started hangin' around that hotel where he saw Susanna go into that day. And before you ask, he don't know the name. Don't think he can read. Anyway, this time he says he saw her go in dressed like one of them fancy business ladies."

Jonelle tried to tamp down the excitement rising up within her. "Did he follow her inside this time?"

Luther glared at Jonelle as if she'd just sprouted a third eye. "You kiddin' me? He don't go inside nowhere he figures he'd be thrown right back out again. But he was nosey, so he sat down and watched for a while."

He stopped and dug around for another cigarette. Jonelle clamped her lips tight to keep from screaming, *get on with it!*

"He says after a long while he sees her come out. And then he says somethin' strange which made me think that all the while he was waitin' he was drinkin'."

"Strange how?"

"He says he saw two Susanna's leave with the same man he saw before."

CHAPTER 24

The address where Sophia Reyes claimed she was staying and the location where Chester maintains he saw Susanna "single" and "double" were miles apart in location and class. Based on the description Luther got from Chester, Jonelle studied a map of the west side and narrowed down two possible hotels where Susanna, or someone who looked like her, might have stayed. Of the two, the second hotel, The Lancelot Inn, sounded a little better. Though both "one-stars" sounded run-down and threadbare, at least the Lancelot offered coffee and tea in the morning.

Armed with the photo of the twins, Jonelle ignored the unattended, bullet-proofed check-in desk, hurried to the elevator and took it to the top floor. A quick look down the hall showed her two overflowing carts and three open hotel room doors. She peeked into the first door just in time to witness the maid strip off the bedroom sheets. Straightening up, she jumped when she found Jonelle looking at her.

"Sorry. I was wondering if I could ask you a quick question."

"I come back later if you want," the maid said, momentarily confused as to whether she should put the sheets back on the bed or take them with her.

"No. This isn't my room. I'm a private investigator looking for someone." Jonelle pulled out her PI license and shield. A quick glance and the ID looked like a police detective's identification. Next, she held out the picture of the twins.

After a brief hesitation, the maid looked at the picture in Jonelle's hand. She shook her head. "No. Not familiar. So sorry."

"You sure? Blond, thin. They're twins so at some point the two of them may have been together. Along with a distinguished-looking gentleman."

The maid shook her head.

"Do you think your other co-workers might remember her?"

She shrugged.

Around the corner, Jonelle discovered another cart and found someone who displayed a hint of recognition.

The young woman stared at the photo with such intensity that it appeared as if she was trying to imprint the image in her mind. Jonelle waited. If she finally found someone who recognized Susanna, she'd stay there all day if she had to. After a few minutes, the dark-haired woman handed the picture back to Jonelle.

"Looks kinda like the lady that was stayin' here," she said. "But she gone now."

Jonelle nodded. "Do you recall seeing her with someone?" Dare she hope?

The cleaner shrugged. "Only the man with her."

When Jonelle met with Kelly she'd swiped one of his business cards. Fortunately, the card had his picture on it. She showed it to the maid. "Does this look like the man you saw with her?"

The young woman studied the card with the same intensity that she had when she looked at Susanna's picture.

"No. Not him."

Though disappointed, Jonelle tried another way. "Was the man black or white?"

"Brown. Like me, but not like me."

This added a new wrinkle. "About how tall would you say? I'm five foot seven so was he taller or shorter than me?"

"About same."

"Okay. Thin? Fat? Average weight?"

The young woman scrunched her face in concentration. "Not fat, but … how you say?" She placed her arms about two feet out from her sides.

"Heavy? Say like an American football player?"

"Yes, like Falco on Ravens." She grinned broadly, proud to brag about her American culture reference.

"That's great. What about hair color?"

The maid visibly relaxed as she warmed into answering Jonelle's questions. The time between question asked and answered was brief. "Black hair. Real straight and almost pretty. Shiny, like a woman."

Jonelle thought back to Luther's description of what the men who attacked Chester looked like. Could one of them have been with Susanna?

Another maid exited from two doors down and called out. "Esmeralda?" Followed by something in Spanish.

The young woman hastily put the dirty towels away, grabbed clean ones and hurried back into the room with Jonelle on her heels. "Just one more thing."

"Don't want to get in trouble."

"I know. One more question. Did you hear them say anything? If so, can you recall any of their words?"

The young lady shook her head and quickly replaced the towels.

Jonelle sighed. That was all she was getting. "You've been very helpful. Thank you." Jonelle turned to go. Out in the hall, the woman called for her to wait a moment. "I just remember something." She looked quickly behind her and lowered her voice. "The lady say to the man something about the truth. 'I swear I'm tellin' the truth.' Like that."

"'I'm telling the truth'?"

"Yes. Like that."

"Esmerelda!"

"Gotta go."

CHAPTER 25

When Jonelle returned to the agency Rainey was on the phone. She whispered "Any messages?" and was answered with a head shake. Seated in her office, Jonelle dialed the number Sophia had given for her hotel. Jonelle got the front desk and was put through to the room. After several rings and no answer, Jonelle left a message asking Sophia to call when she returned.

A quick call to Kelly's office indicated he was with a client. She left a message asking him to call her as soon as possible.

Next, she went over her notes on her trip to Michigan and got a nagging feeling that something was missing. She reviewed her interview with the girl's mother and debated whether to call and ask if either twin had a fear of or fascination with clowns.

Rainey's buzz decided the issue. Jonelle's client Polly Cole had arrived to settle her final bill. Jonelle walked to the front and greeted Mrs. Cole. "Hope everything's all right," she said. She'd planned on setting up again outside of the house. In fact Jonelle looked forward to it, hoping to flush out the two men from the previous night.

"Everything's fine. I'm completely satisfied with your agency. The shift change I'd requested came through so I'll be working from seven in the morning to three thirty in the afternoon. Times when my daughter will be in school," she said.

"I'm glad we could help. If you prefer, we can mail you a final bill."

Mrs. Cole shook her head. "I can go ahead and settle it now."

Before Jonelle could say anything to Rainey, the secretary had already prepared the invoice. While Jonelle could now concentrate all her energies on Susanna's case, she secretly wanted a few more days to get a bead on the men in the gray rental car.

After a quick goodbye from Mrs. Cole, Jonelle walked back to her office. She'd powered up the computer when Rainey announced detective Burton wanted a quick word.

"Send him back."

She'd barely stacked the papers on her desk when his stout frame stood in the doorway.

"This is unexpected," Jonelle said as she indicated for Burt to take a seat.

"Thought you'd like to know I've been in contact with Norman Finkleberg. Don't believe I need to explain to you who he is. He told me the two of you had talked. I didn't know you'd paid him a visit." An uncomfortable silence hung in the air as Burt fiddled with his "Finding Nemo" tie.

Jonelle's back stiffened. Something in Burt's tone of voice irked her. "You don't need to know since you aren't my client. Sophia Reyes is."

"*Anything* that has bearing on Susanna Quinley's murder says otherwise."

"If that's all you wanted to tell me, you could've phoned."

Burt made a time-out motion with his hands. "Fair point."

Jonelle didn't trust herself to speak so she merely nodded.

"Good. Now to why I'm here. Heard you've been asking questions about the vic at a hotel where it's believed she stayed. True?"

"You *heard*? From who?"

"You're not the only one with contacts on the street. Plus, Susanna's body was discovered a little over two blocks from there."

Jonelle flinched. She hadn't known the exact address where Susanna's body was found.

"Well?" The detective's all-business tone was different from their usual back and forth banter. She wondered what had changed.

"I got a clue from a friend, who heard it from his friend. So I checked it out. Problem?"

"What'd you find out?"

"Talked to a maid who confirmed that Susanna had stayed there for a while." Jonelle took a deep breath. "She also said she was with a man. When I showed her a picture of Barrington Kelly, she said it wasn't him."

"What was the maid's name?"

Jonelle shook her head. "Didn't get that far. I assume you guys talked to the staff, right?"

"Only the front desk. They admitted someone checked in who looked like her, but they had no record of the name. We figured she used an alias. The one thing they did reveal was that she had the manager lock a leather satchel in the office."

"The money?"

"We can only guess. Problem is she left one day and took the bag with her and it hasn't been recovered."

"Crap. So you still have no idea where the money is." It was more a statement than a question.

Burt drew his eyebrows together. "Are you going behind my back on this case?"

"Oh, please. What are you talking about? I told you I have a duty to my client to—"

"Your *duty* as you call it was to find out why Susanna ended up with the homeless. Sounds like the answer was because she embezzled money. So from where I'm sitting, your *duty* is over."

Jonelle stood. "You need to leave before I lose my temper and this ends up in a place where neither of us wants it to go."

A frustrated sigh escaped Burt's lips. He remained seated. "Fair enough. But if I hadn't come over here, would you have told me about going to the hotel?"

"Of course." When she got around to it. "You seem to forget that Luther is also my client, so whatever information I get, remains confidential unless he gives me the okay to tell you." That included the two guys she was sure had followed her. She'd keep that information to herself while she checked out whether or not they had anything to do with Susanna's case.

Her blood pressure returned to normal and she sat. "By the way, I haven't been able to reach Sophia. I was wondering if she's been in touch with you?"

Burt leaned back in his chair. "That's another reason I stopped by. She hasn't returned my calls, so I went to her hotel. She's not there and according to the staff she hasn't checked out. I called Dr. Kelly and he claims he hasn't seen her either. Since you have a penchant for finding out things that sometimes elude us mere police detectives, I thought maybe you knew where she was."

Jonelle shook her head. "Before you came in I tried calling her hotel as well. Got nowhere, but I did leave a message. I can't imagine she'd go back to Michigan without letting us know, but her mother is sick, so I guess that's a possibility." Saying it out loud made sense to Jonelle. She held up a finger to indicate he should hold on. Jonelle found Sarah Quinley's phone number and dialed. While it rang, she said to Burt, "There may be an emergency which is why she didn't tell anyone." After several rings and no answer, Jonelle left a voice message inquiring after Mrs. Quinley's health and asking her to please call when she got the chance.

"I hope she's all right. She didn't look at all well when I was there."

Burt stood. "It makes sense she'd leave in a hurry if her mother needed her. I'll wait awhile for her to call." He held out his hand. "I don't have Sarah Quinley's number. Okay if you write it down for me?"

Jonelle hesitated. She knew what a thorough detective he was and felt sure he already had the woman's number. She played along and wrote the number on a sticky pad and handed it over to him.

"Thanks." He put the note in his coat pocket without looking at it and headed for the door.

"Wait a second. I've got something to ask."

He indicated with his head for her to continue.

"When I first interviewed Sophia, she told me a lot about their childhood together in Michigan. One of the things she said was that the girls had gotten tattoos. Why didn't you mention that to me?"

He shrugged. "Didn't think it was important for you to know. Why?"

"I just want to verify that it was obvious during the autopsy."

"Sure it was. Hold on." Burt pulled out his phone.

"You keep autopsy results on that thing?"

"Of course not. Just unusual or interesting information, in case I need a quick reference. Like someone asking me information that, technically, doesn't concern her." He winked at Jonelle. "For instance, like that note we found on the body." His fingers scrolled through several screens. "I don't see that info but I know I have it. I'll get back to you on that."

CHAPTER 26

A few hours later Burt called Jonelle from his office. "No, she didn't," Jonelle said into her phone. "She had a smiling red fox above her right hip."

"I attended the autopsy, Jonelle. I know what I saw. Problem?"

"Guess I misunderstood. Thanks."

"Sure. I'll talk to you later."

Jonelle pulled up the notes from her interview with Sophia and found what she was looking for. She hadn't made a mistake. Sophia was clear about the types of tattoos the girls had. What did it all mean? Did Sophia deliberately lie? If so, why? Jonelle hadn't mentioned all the details of her relationship with the police, so it was possible that Sophia figured Jonelle would never pick up the discrepancy. Unless. Unless Sophia lied. Why would she?

Jonelle dialed Sophia's cellphone and hotel, and once again no answer. Jonelle stressed the importance that Sophia call back soon and indicating she'd also left a message for Sarah Quinley. That should push the elusive Sophia to check in.

Her mind felt crowded with information from both Luther and Burt, so she forced herself to concentrate on routine paper work. At five o'clock, too antsy to sit around and tired of waiting for the phone to ring, Jonelle grabbed her stuff and rushed down the hall.

"See you Monday, hon," Rainey said, straightening up her desk.

"Goodnight. Have a nice weekend." Jonelle didn't feel like going home. Even with the late hour and on a Friday, another chat with Dr. Kelly seemed in order. That is, if he was still in the office.

Jonelle drove to the Washington suburbs, parked in the Red Line Metro station lot and boarded a train headed in the direction of Farragut West. She hated riding the subway during rush hour and especially on Fridays. She spent the thirty-minute ride contemplating what she'd say to Kelly about the tattoos. She'd ask about any unusual marks on Susanna's body and let him tell her what ink was on his ex-wife's person.

Jonelle pushed through the throng of people on K Street and entered Kelly's building. She hoped someone was still there. As she walked down the hall to his practice, Jonelle no longer cared what anyone thought about her being there. She opened the glass double-doors. The same receptionist with the bright, red smile greeted her, although the smile didn't seem as sparkling as before.

"I'm sorry, but the office is closed now." The young woman stood behind the desk, bag hanging from her shoulder. Jonelle admired the way the receptionist hid her displeasure at having to deal with someone when it was obvious she couldn't wait to leave. A quick glance revealed an empty waiting area.

"Are you here to set up another appointment?"

Jonelle nodded. "I forgot to ask Dr. Kelly something. Since I was in the area, I thought I'd stop by to see if I could ask him a quick question. It shouldn't take more than five minutes or so."

Lines between her eyes marred the woman's perfectly made-up face. "Oh, I'm so sorry. Doctor Kelly left earlier and I'm afraid he won't be back until Tuesday. If you'd like, I can check his calendar for the next available opening." Brown eyes looked questioningly at Jonelle.

"I really don't need to tie up more of his time than necessary. I'm doing inquiries for his sister-in-law about the … uh … situation with his ex-wife." Jonelle turned sideways and leaned on the desk. "Would it be possible for you to give me his cellphone number?" Before Jonelle could complete the question, the young woman was already shaking her head.

"No, I'm afraid not. What I can do is ask him to call you if he checks in. But I doubt that will happen. He had to leave rather suddenly and advised us that should there be an emergency with one of his patients, I was to refer them to one of the other doctors."

That wasn't what Jonelle wanted to hear. Even though he already had them, she left her cellphone and office phone numbers with the suggestion that it didn't matter when Kelly called, she needed to verify some information. The bright smile appeared again and Jonelle wondered if there was some kind of class these people attended to get that look.

Instead of heading for the elevators, she slipped down the hall and around the corner, which gave her full view of Kelly's practice. A few moments later, the receptionist walked down the hall and boarded the elevator. Jonelle stood where she was, occasionally looking at her phone whenever office workers glanced her way. After approximately five minutes when no one else left the practice, she went back.

Jonelle couldn't shake the feeling that Kelly's absence and Sophia's disappearance were connected. Even though Kelly insisted he hadn't seen his ex-sister-in-law, Jonelle didn't believe him.

Since most high-end businesses depended on custodial services to clean the offices, the glass doors to the reception area weren't locked. Jonelle tiptoed inside and slipped down the corridor in the direction of Kelly's private office. She listened for any noise coming from the other closed doors and heard nothing. A quick turn of the knob provided access inside.

Jonelle rushed over to the file cabinets and tried the first drawer. Locked. Damn. No wonder he didn't mind not securing his door. To settle any questions in her mind, Jonelle tried each one and got the same result. She felt around inside her handbag for the small lock picking case. A few clicks later the file cabinet opened.

She flipped through folders of patient names. Nothing looked even remotely related to his relationship with Susanna. She closed and relocked the cabinet. Disappointed, her eyes settled on his desk drawers. All five were locked. A few minutes later, she'd picked three locks: one in the middle and one on either side.

Situated in the center of the middle drawer, a black leather-bound book with "Day Planner" embossed in gold took up most of the space. She flipped through it. Most entries for the month held names and times and none mentioned Sophia or Susanna. However, a notation in the margin for today mentioned "Norm arrives." Interesting. In the back of the book were sections for notes and names, addresses and telephone numbers. Jonelle sat and slowly thumbed through each page, searching for … she wasn't sure what. She stopped at the entry for Norman Finkleberg, took out her notebook and wrote his home address and telephone number.

A few more pages and Sophia's name popped up with an address and telephone number, which Jonelle also noted. She'd compare both to the information Sophia had given her that first day. She didn't find anything on the hotel where Sophia was staying. Jonelle closed the book and placed it back in its original location. A few pens, sticky notepads, stapler and paperclips were the only other items.

She moved on to the side drawers. Brochures, pamphlets, a small tape recorder and spiral bound notebooks took up most of the space in each one. A glance in the last drawer on the right divulged only one article: a large manila envelope. Blank on the outside and after turning it over, discovered it was sealed. She held the envelope up to the light but couldn't read the contents.

With the envelope tucked under her arm, Jonelle put her ear to the door and, hearing nothing, stepped into the narrow hall. She noted the names of the other two doctors; the third door didn't have a name. She opened it and a motion sensor light illuminated the area.

A copier stood in the center of the room. Open, gray metal shelves hugged the walls from the floor to approximately six feet high. As she expected, similar manila envelopes overflowed from a box on one of the shelves. She tore open the one from Kelly's office and glanced at four pages. One was a copy of a rental car agreement; a handwritten entry on the bottom indicated another invoice was coming. The name on the signature line was illegible. So, why was the document in Kelly's possession? Two other pages contained hotel information with the words "pay now!" written at the bottom.

Jonelle's hands shook with excitement. One hotel was the Lancelot and the other was a hotel she hadn't heard of, but was also on Baltimore's west side. The fourth document held an itinerary with the departing location in Oldenberry, Michigan and the arrival in Baltimore. Jonelle frowned at the copier, trying to figure out the machine. When she placed the first document on the glass and pushed a button, a red light came on, reminding her to input her code. "Dammit!"

She grabbed the sheet off the copier and swiped a clean envelope from the shelf, peered up and down the hall just to be sure and closed the door behind her. A sense of urgency gripped her as she navigated her way back to his office.

Her first thought was Sophia had rented a car and given the invoices to Kelly. But the signature wasn't familiar. And why want Kelly to pay? Jonelle frowned at the hotel invoice. The name printed at the top was not the one where Sophia was staying. Another note, this one attached by a paperclip also stated "pay now!"

A sigh of frustration escaped Jonelle. Instead of getting closer to figuring out the mystery of Susanna living on the street, the answer was slipping away. She picked up the last piece of paper again and scrutinized it more closely. At the bottom of the itinerary someone typed "Women's Huron Valley Correctional Facility" the name of the women's facility where Rosemary Wilkins was incarcerated. She flipped the paper over. Nothing else was typed and there were no handwritten notes. She grabbed her phone, held it as close as she could and snapped multiple shots of all the pages.

Jonelle replaced the contents in order in the new envelope, sealed and placed it back in the drawer. She used the same tools to secure the locks and tried the drawer handles to make sure. Rather than deposit the torn envelope in the trash she shoved it in her bag.

After everything was put back the way it was, Jonelle headed for the door. She came to an abrupt stop when she heard voices.

Frantic, she searched for a place to hide. Her eyes settled on the back door used for patients to leave without being seen. She headed for it. The voices got louder. She opened the door, slipped through and careful not to close it all the way, slid into the narrow hallway. With her heart pounding hard, Jonelle put her ear against the crack in the door and listened.

Kelly's door clicked open. Unable to make out all the words, it sounded as though one was male, the other female. Jonelle held her breath. Someone rattled what sounded like the file cabinet. That was followed by a loud "Damn" and hushed whispers.

Another series of rattles later Jonelle heard the female say, "Just open the damn thing," followed by "it's not under there." Several loud bangs later the woman said, "finally."

Jonelle turned her head and peeked through the crack. A blond woman, her back to Jonelle, lifted the envelope from the desk drawer. All she saw of the man was his arm. The actions told her two things: one, the male wasn't Kelly since he'd have his own key, and two, they found what they were looking for. The woman passed the envelope to the man and slammed the desk drawer in anger.

Whoever it was didn't care if anyone found out that Kelly was burgled. Jonelle prayed they wouldn't leave by the back door. As the voices faded, she risked opening the door wider. The two had stopped in front of the main door.

A few moments later, without a word, they left Kelly's office.

Jonelle counted to one hundred and followed the narrow hallway around the other side and over to the bank of elevators and down to the lobby.

A stroll to the subway station gave her time to contemplate different possibilities, none of which got her any closer to why Susanna would connect to a homeless person like Luther. When she returned to the office on Monday, she'd call Finkleberg. She'd see what he had to say about meeting Kelly.

CHAPTER 27

She almost missed the man staring at her from across the street. Preoccupied with trying to figure out what all the information she'd seen in Kelly's office meant, Jonelle had passed the gray sedan without looking. As she stood in front of her building and inserted the key in the outside lock, a quick glance in the glass reflected the car with someone sitting with his arm draped over the driver's side door.

Jonelle turned around to get a better look. The male occupant wore dark glasses. She stared at him and he stared back. From where she stood, she couldn't tell if there was anyone in the passenger seat, but if those were the same two men she'd seen outside Polly Cole's house, she was sure someone else sat next to the driver. For a brief moment, she considered walking across the street to their car, to see what they would do. At the same time she moved in their direction, the building doors opened and neighbors Mathilda and Franklin Brobish stepped out.

"Well, hello dear," said Mathilda. "Are you coming in? Franklin, hold the door for Jonelle."

Jonelle turned toward her elderly neighbors. Before she could get any words out, a car engine started. She turned back around in time to see the vehicle take off down the street.

"Is that someone you know?" Franklin asked.

"No. I noticed the car as I walked up. Have either of you seen it before?"

They shook their heads in unison. "Is there a problem? If you want, I can keep an eye out for it." Over a year ago Mathilda had offered assistance when Jonelle needed to find her husband's missing body. Eyesight clear and hearing astute, Mathilda made it her business to know everyone's comings and goings, which could work to Jonelle's benefit.

"I even saw the man behind the wheel," Mathilda added, a touch of pride in her voice.

"You did? From here?" Franklin asked. His tone indicated he didn't quite believe his wife.

"Of course I did." Mathilda sniffed. "I've got my new glasses, remember."

All three stood on the sidewalk. Jonelle didn't want to get into a family disagreement. While the Brobishes had stayed married for forty years, the couple could get a bit prickly.

"Tell you what. If you happen to see the car again, come get me if I'm home or call me and recount what you've seen. That'll let me know if these guys warrant a closer look."

Mathilda touched Jonelle's arm, a gleam in her eye. "If I see them do you want me to ask them what they want?"

"No! Please don't. Let me know and I'll handle it." Jonelle hoped she hadn't opened a Pandora's Box.

"You're not in any trouble, are you dear?"

"Not at all." At least she hoped not. "It's just the curious part of me wanting to know everything about everybody out of the ordinary."

Franklin grinned. "Guess that's why you're our very own hotshot detective."

She eased by the couple and entered the building. "Don't know if I'd say 'hotshot', but thanks for the compliment." She waved goodbye and watched as they strolled hand-in-hand down the sidewalk on the second of their two daily walks. Jonelle felt confident that should the strangers appear in front of her home again, Mathilda would notice and report back.

Jonelle's hand paused above the door knob to her condo. The notes of a cello embraced the lobby with its deep, mellow sound as if giving the vestibule a warm bear hug. Upstairs neighbor Hamilton Yee was rehearsing again. Everyone loved it when he was in-between concerts. His music often helped settle Jonelle's nerves whenever she'd had a stressful day.

Jonelle checked her watch. It was too early to visit her other upstairs neighbor. Sheila MacIntosh worked nights and grabbed sleep when she could. Jonelle let herself into the condo. Nothing wrong with spending a quiet evening at home. Unless. She could always call Adrienne. No. She wasn't in the mood for her friend's high-energy attitude. What about Burt? She shook her head. She'd wait for him to invite her out. Besides, she'd probably have to tell him about the information she'd "found." He'd have a million questions and she wasn't ready for that.

When she discovered the rental car receipt, she thought it might've been tied to Sophia. What if instead, Kelly had ties to the men who were following her. Why? Jonelle shook her head. It didn't make sense. She walked into the kitchen and turned on the stove to preheat. She'd made a tuna noodle casserole and had frozen the leftovers. While she waited, she poured herself a generous glass of Chardonnay.

As she rummaged in the cupboard for the fish food, she knew there was no way the rental car company would give her information about a customer. The hotel receipt indicated a location known for its cheap rates and transient population. She'd pay a visit tomorrow. Jonelle sprinkled fish food in the aquarium. She hadn't even met Kelly when she noticed the men on her last night of surveillance. Who were they and how did they know where she lived?

CHAPTER 28

Armed with the .38 nestled comfortably at the bottom of her shoulder bag, Jonelle journeyed to the now familiar abandoned warehouse located on Baltimore's west side. Unease no longer nagged at her; she was used to the area and the building's inhabitants.

All the same, Jonelle scanned the area before she left her Jeep. Of the few sodium lights in the area, the one on the corner in front still worked. She approached the building. After skimming the area once more, she turned sideways, eased through the sagging chain link fence and headed for the gaping opening that would allow access inside. Before she entered, she inhaled deeply several times. Her claustrophobia usually kicked in once she entered the cavernous space.

Her hand grasped the penlight stashed in the bag. She shuffled forward. Her athletic shoes slid over piles of paper and crunched over … who knew what. A push of the button and a slim beam of light played out before her. With eyes aimed straight ahead, she walked forward several steps and veered to the left. She knew where she was going. Past trips had identified Luther's personal space.

She shouted a heads-up to the people she couldn't see, but knew were there. "Hello? It's me, Jonelle Sweet." She cocked her head and listened. "I'm here to see Luther. I know you all don't like me to come here, but I've got something very important to discuss with him. And also with Chester if he's around. Hello?"

She shivered against the cool night air that swept through the building. Jonelle wrapped the knee-length cardigan tight against her body and waited. Nothing. He had to be here; this was his home at night. When she first met him over a year ago, he and the rest of his crew had already claimed this space and the city left them alone. Jonelle felt many eyes upon her. In the past, it hadn't taken long for someone to draw near. This time was different.

An uneasiness gripped her. "I know somebody's here. You guys can see me so you know I'm alone. Come on. I've never done anything to betray your trust. Please."

Jonelle stood rooted to the spot and waited. After what seemed like several minutes, an uneven shuffling noise sounded on her left side. She relaxed and aimed her light at the ground toward the sound of the footsteps. Scuffed and worn work boots covered the figure's feet. Jonelle slowly worked the beam up past the dirty jeans, flannel shirt and heavy torn jacket.

"Don't you 'member what I tole you about that light?"

"I'm not going to aim it in your face, Luther. Why didn't you answer when I first called out? I thought maybe you'd left."

He cackled. "An' go where? Las' bus for Florida left yestiddy."

Jonelle ignored the comment. At least Luther's attitude was the same, which indicated things seemed as normal as they were going to get. "Is Chester around? I'd like to talk to the both of you." Although the light was pointed away from Luther's face, she saw him nod.

"Hey, Chester. Where you at? We got company." A loud cough in the distance was the reply. Luther let out an exasperated sigh. "Damn fool. Follow me." He led Jonelle deeper into the bowels of the building. That familiar tightness squeezed the middle of her chest. She breathed deeply.

How the man could walk with confidence in near darkness without running into anything, or anybody, amazed Jonelle. It was as if he'd been born blind and what little light there was, was superfluous. She sniffed the air and caught a whiff of smoke. At pinprick of light shone in the distance. The light grew as they walked closer.

Four men and a woman stood around a barrel with fire leaping from the top. "Chester. Ain't you hear me call you?"

One of the men stepped away from the others. "Yeah. But it's gettin' cold and I got to warm up before I hunker down." He peered at Jonelle. "She the one got somethin' to do with Susanna?"

It was hard to tell the ages of any of the homeless she'd met so far, but Jonelle pegged Chester's age at around fifty. Phil's description was spot on. Chester had dirty, shoulder-length gray hair and scraggly whiskers. She couldn't tell the color of his eyes in the dim light. He was as thin as Luther, but taller even with the slight stoop in the shoulders. A dirty bandage ringed his head.

The fire emitted enough light for her to see, so she flicked off the penlight. "How's your head?"

He touched the filthy dressing as if to reassure himself it was still there. "That why you here?"

One of the things she most admired about those who lived on the street was their no-nonsense attitude. "Partly. I'd like to find out what happened that night you were attacked. Luther told me some of it, but often people remember facts they didn't know they knew or thought unimportant at the time."

Although the idea didn't appeal to her, Jonelle looked around for someplace to sit.

As if reading her mind, Luther said, "We got some crates back here."

The three of them skirted prone bodies and ignored stares from the others. Another barrel of fire provided weak illumination as the two men cleared off wooden boxes against the concrete wall. They waited while Jonelle tested the container to make sure it would hold her weight. She'd have trouble getting them to take her seriously if the thing smashed to the floor when she sat down.

Satisfied she wouldn't take a tumble, Jonelle began her questioning. "First, Chester, could you please tell me what happened before, during and immediately after the attack."

Luther snorted but didn't say anything.

Chester stared at her, mouth open.

"You gotta give it to him in small bits," Luther said. "Chester, when didya first notice them guys?"

Great. I'm being schooled on how to do my job by a homeless person, Jonelle thought.

Chester looked from Luther to Jonelle. He cleared phlegm from his throat. Jonelle willed herself not to grimace at the noise.

"Well. Guess it was a few days before Suze"—his eyes darted in Luther's direction and just as quickly back again—"I mean *Susanna* was killed. Some shithead was talkin' 'bout how I knew where a lotta money was at that she had. But I don't know nuthin' 'bout no money, an I tole them so. The las' time was when we was all standin' around talkin' about how they arrested Luther and we knew he didn't have nuthin' to do with her gettin' killed." He emphasized those last words with a firm nod. "Then I went out to the places I usually go. They got me when I was comin' back. But not too close to here." He looked quickly at Luther who stared back through narrowed eyes.

"What did they look like?" Jonelle asked.

Chester stood and lowered his hand about two inches from the top of his head. "About this here tall, an' fatter than me." Jonelle thought grimly that she was fatter than Chester and needed more specifics.

"Do you mean solid fat? Like if you drew a line around their bodies, would they be pretty, um, square like? You know, as wide as they were tall?"

A gape-toothed grin covered Chester's face. "That's it. You nailed it right there on the head." He sat back on his crate and rested his body against the wall.

"Okay. Luther said you told him they looked Mexican but didn't sound Mexican. I'm not sure what that means."

"Me neither," Luther grumbled. Jonelle's look told him to keep quiet.

"Just describe everything about them."

Chester let out a frustrated sigh. "I don't know how to describe it better'n that. Long black, straight hair, brown skin … but not as dark as you an' Luther."

Luther snorted again.

Chester continued. "Kinda squinty eyes but not like Chinese. An' they didn't really have no accent. Most Mexicans I ever heard had an accent. These guys didn't."

Because somebody looked Mexican to Chester didn't mean they were. Chester's description caused a faint stirring in Jonelle. She wondered if what she thought was what Chester saw but decided he wouldn't know the difference.

"What did they say?"

"Both of 'em?"

Luther groaned. "Of course, you ole fool."

"Luther, please." Jonelle raised her hand in a gesture to ask him to stop interfering.

Chester touched his head. In the dim light Jonelle saw him grimace.

"This conversation will go no further than this place," Jonelle said, looking around. She thought about Burt and quickly decided that if Chester revealed anything of value, she'd have to tell the detective. What she wouldn't tell him was the name of the person who gave her the information.

Chester hesitated. Luther opened his mouth to speak and Jonelle silenced him with a shake of her head.

"They kept sayin' they knew she hung out somewhere 'round here," Chester said. His eyes darted in Luther's direction. "Said the bum she hung out with lived there."

"How'd they know that?" Jonelle asked.

"Ever'body knows Luther and knows his camp."

Anyone with access to the news knew the person who discovered the body was homeless, Jonelle thought to herself. She couldn't remember if the news reports gave Luther's name.

"What else did they say?"

"Kept goin' on an' on about where was the money at. Tole them I didn't know nuthin' about no damn money." Another glance at Luther. "An' I still don't neither."

"None of us do," Luther said with an edge in his voice.

Jonelle studied the two men. She wondered if Luther knew more than he was letting on about Susanna's money.

"Let's think about this. What I know is, Susanna stole money from her job in Michigan."

Luther and Chester's mouths dropped open. She directed her next question at Luther. "She never told you where she came from or what she did up there?"

He shook his head.

"She ever tell you how much money she had with her?"

Luther looked as if he'd been sucker punched. Another shake of the head. "Only that it was a lot. An' she didn't tell me she was no thief neither."

"So. If I came to you for help in hiding a lot of money, where would I do it, knowing it would be safe until I could be sure the coast was clear?"

Chester looked confused. Silence stretched on for several seconds.

Luther looked at Jonelle. "It's gotta be close by."

CHAPTER 29

After a fitful night's sleep, Jonelle woke early and drove back to the warehouse. She and Luther had agreed to meet during the day to search for Susanna's money. Jonelle knew that Luther had a special area for his stuff but found it hard to believe that hundreds of thousands of dollars could remain concealed so well that no one would find the hiding place.

She pulled up to the curb next to a pacing Luther. "Don't know why you wanna do this. The cops already been through here. Let's git this over with. I got places I gotta be at," he said to her through the open driver's side window.

Oh, no, Jonelle thought. That's not the way this is going to proceed.

"Listen Luther. I can understand it if we were only looking for where Susanna hid her personal items, but I'm talking a lot of money here." She left her Jeep and locked the doors. "Hiding that amount of money ..." she glanced at him. His face remained impassive. "To hide that amount of money could mean she hid it in stages. You said yourself that there were times she stayed by herself."

They walked to the building and stood outside the massive opening.

He nodded. "When she first come, she stayed pretty close. After a while, sometimes she'd come with me downtown and we'd split up. But there was other times ..." He stopped and looked up at the building. "Other times I left and she'd still be here."

"She give you any reason for staying behind?"

He shook his head. "Naw. I jus' figured she needed more time to get her stuff together."

"That's different from what everybody else did, right?"

"She wasn't like ever'body."

The yawning space didn't look as threatening during the day, but the sunlight filtering through the many broken windows highlighted the bleakness of Luther's living conditions. "Have you thought about maybe, I dunno, picking up some of this trash and throwing it away. Might make you feel better about coming here every night."

The scowl on Luther's face indicated what he thought about her suggestion.

"Take me to where she had her things," Jonelle said before Luther fired off a sarcastic remark. Jonelle knew the cops had confiscated the few items Susanna had stuffed in a black, plastic bag. She also knew that the few women "residents" had probably filched the rest.

"What else did the cops find when they searched this place?"

He shrugged. "Wasn't no money or else they'd still be swarmin' 'round here like ants over spilt sugar. She didn't have much in the way of clothes."

That didn't sound right. "I know when she left Michigan she had some belongings with her. I also know that when the police searched her room at the Lancelot Inn, all they found were a few items of clothing. So where's the rest of her stuff?" Jonelle pointed to a spot further inside the warehouse. "Let's have another look."

Luther led the way with his head down and hands shoved deep into his pockets. Neither one spoke as the homeless man preceded her deeper into the bowels of the place he called home. At the back wall, concrete stairs led to the second level. Jonelle paused.

"She stayed up there with you?"

"You implyin' somethin'?"

Jonelle ignored the question. "Who else stayed up here?"

"Nobody."

No one spoke until they emerged on the second level. Instead of one huge open space, this level looked as if several rooms occupied the area in the past. Luther limped past several doorways and stopped at what Jonelle counted as the fourth space. He entered and pointed to the spot where Susanna kept her belongings. All that remained were a few empty shopping bags and empty cracker and cookie boxes. Jonelle couldn't hide her disappointment.

"Ain't no way stuff's gonna hang around here without somebody takin' it," Luther said. "Especially clothes. I asked Connie an' Flo already if they took some 'a Suze's stuff and they said no. But they lie like all the rest. So who knows?" He shrugged.

With her hands on her hips, Jonelle circled the area. She stopped in front of Luther and put a hand over her mouth, face scrunched up in concentration. "Do you have anything of hers?"

He folded his arms across his chest and stared at the ground. "She didn't give me no money an' I already tole you I don't know where the money's at."

"That's not what I'm asking you and you know it. What do you have that once belonged to Susanna?"

Luther's nostrils flared. She held his gaze, noting the throbbing vein in his forehead. He turned on his heels and stomped over to the far corner. She skirted a few plastic crates and cardboard boxes to catch up to him.

He stopped at the wall. His hand reached in his back pocket and he pulled out a knife. A push of a button released a four inch blade. Jonelle gasped and stepped back. Her hand groped inside her bag before she realized her pistol was still locked in the Jeep's glove compartment.

"Relax. I need this to open somethin'." With his back to her, he stooped down and with the knife, chiseled around some of the concrete. A few moments later, he removed a brick and set it to one side. Jonelle watched as he glanced at her over his shoulder and put his hand in the opening. He pulled out a filthy cloth.

Dirty fingers opened the folds of the material. In the middle was one of those scrunchy hair things, a gold cross necklace and a pair of diamond stud earrings.

"Susanna's?"

He nodded.

Jonelle reached inside her bag and pulled out a penlight. "I'd like to see what else is in there."

Luther moved to one side without comment.

Jonelle shined the light in the narrow hole all the way back to what looked like another wall. Nothing. She couldn't hide her disappointment.

"I checked my other hidin' place and I swear to Jesus she didn't hide no cash." He squinted at Jonelle. "You think I'd still be livin' in this hell hole if I had a shit load 'a money?"

She studied Luther carefully. "I believe you. But if I don't see for myself, I'll always wonder. So let's just take another look. Please."

Deep lines formed between his eyebrows. He turned on his heel and hobbled over to the far corner. On the way he gathered up several old, plastic milk crates. "Grab some more 'a those," he said.

Jonelle did as he asked. He stacked several of them in a pyramid type fashion, under a rusted chain hanging from the ceiling. Next, he hobbled over to a stack of bags, reached in one and pulled out a metal rod with a hook on one end. "Hold this."

She did as instructed and watched in amazement as he climbed on the boxes and pulled on the chain which squeaked in protest as a ceiling panel slowly descended about six inches. "Gimme that thing."

She handed him the pole.

Luther inserted the pole in the opening, and wiggled it around. A satisfied look appeared on his face as he removed a small, dusty, red velvet bag. He handed her the pole and climbed down.

"What's that?"

He opened the bag and exposed a small metal box. He shoved a few items aside and picked up a tissue-wrapped parcel.

"Those las' few days she give this to me for safe keepin'. Said she was gonna sell them for the money … in case she needed more." Dirty fingers opened the paper. In the middle sat a gold band and a diamond and sapphire ring.

CHAPTER 30

On Monday morning, a frustrated Jonelle drove to the office in a fog. Not only had Luther refused to give her the ring he also told her he was going to hide it in a different place should she come back intent on searching on her own. Two different emotions swirled within. First, she knew that keeping a personal item of the victim's from the police might be construed as withholding evidence. Second, she also knew that she wouldn't turn him in. If Luther kept the jewelry because he wanted to pawn the ring for the money, he would have done so by now. The only reason for Luther to refuse to give her the ring was that he wanted it for sentimental reasons.

Jonelle trudged up the back stairs to the agency.

She opened the door to an empty reception area. A quick, "Hello? Rainey you here?" was met with Rainey's head peaking around the open door situated to the side of her desk.

"Just needed to refill the copier. You want something?" Rainey asked.

"Not really. Anybody else in?

"Hold on a sec." A few moments later she came and sat down at her desk. "Marvin had an early appointment and the guys are on assignment, so it's just us girls here right now." Rainey peered into Jonelle's face. "You okay? You don't look like your usual happy self."

Jonelle resisted the temptation to sit next to Rainey's desk and tell the receptionist everything that had happened. "I made a stop Saturday concerning my case and it didn't go well." She shifted her bag from one shoulder to the next. "It's something I'll have to work out on my own." She gave a weak smile and headed for her office. Halfway down, she turned around and came back.

"Did I get any calls on the office line?" Jonelle hoped that if Sophia somehow forgot or misplaced Jonelle's cell, she'd at least try the main number.

Rainey shook her head, setting in motion two yellow pencils dancing in her hair. "Afraid not, hon. You expecting something important?"

"I haven't been able to reach Sophia Reyes. If she calls, please let me know, no matter where I am or what I'm doing."

Rainey nodded, pencils bouncing. "Will do." She turned and began working on her computer.

After putting her bag away, Jonelle sat and pulled up her emails, hoping that one of the many she'd received would produce one from Sophia. None were from the victim's sister, but she perked up when she noticed an item from Winston Hackett, Rosemary Wilkins' attorney.

She tried calling him first, but the call went directly to voice mail. Jonelle read through the message twice. Hackett stated Rosemary had additional information about her relationship with Susanna. Rosemary wanted Jonelle to know more about what led up to Susanna's decision to take the money and run. Jonelle noted with a wry smile that Rosemary again stated it was all Susanna's idea to drag her into the whole mess. Hackett's message stated he was coming to the area to attend a two-day conference in Arlington, Virginia starting tomorrow and if she wanted to meet him, he'd tell her what additional information Rosemary revealed.

Jonelle's fingers flew over her keyboard so fast she had to keep going over words she misspelled. The gist of her reply was yes to a meeting, anytime and anywhere. In the meantime, she called Sophia's hotel again, not really expecting her to be there and she wasn't disappointed. Next, she called Kelly's office even though she'd been told he wouldn't be in until the next day. She left another message with the secretary to have him call.

The worst part of her job was the waiting. The urge to pace propelled her out of the chair. After the second pass around her office, a ping from the computer notified her of a new email. In it, Hackett stated he'd be available from around the one o'clock lunch break on either day until three, or if that wasn't possible, the seminar ended at six so he could meet sometime around seven p.m., on Tuesday. She responded that two or two thirty would work better on Tuesday and that she looked forward to it. Excited at the prospect of learning something new about Susanna, Jonelle grabbed her bag again and decided to stake out Sophia's hotel. If the woman was avoiding her she wanted to know why.

The possibility also existed that Sophia and Kelly were together. Almost as soon as the thought entered her mind, Jonelle dismissed it. Jonelle was certain Sophia was the blond she saw Friday afternoon, and the man wasn't Kelly. The only person she could think of was Finkleberg. If so, why steal the envelope?

CHAPTER 31

Jonelle sat in a large chair inside Sophia's Inner Harbor hotel, near the entrance. The area was semi-secluded and hidden by a long, low wooden partition, the top half of which contained several large, dracaena, philodendron and pothos plants. Surveillance work bored her; being ignored ticked her off.

Settled in, Jonelle waited. The only reasons she could think of that would answer the question of why Sophia didn't return her calls was that her client had something to hide. Jonelle shifted in her chair.

Two butt-numbing hours later, with no sign of Sophia, Jonelle had had enough waiting. And she was tired of beating around the bush. At a near run, she left the lobby of the hotel and retrieved her Jeep from the expensive underground lot. She didn't believe Kelly was out until Tuesday, so she decided to travel to DC to see for herself.

For the first time since she walked into Kelly's practice, the receptionist's smile faded as Jonelle strolled up to the desk. "I'm afraid the doctor doesn't have time to see you today. All his appointments are filled." The receptionist searched her computer.

"Why did you tell me that the doctor wouldn't be in until tomorrow?"

"He, um, he had to cancel his previous commitment so he could see a few more clients." She searched her computer. "The only time he has free is next week, at—"

"I'm not waiting until next week. He'll see me as soon as he's free with his current client." Jonelle stomped over and sat close to an elderly gentleman who slid over into another chair.

A worried expression clouded the secretary's face. She picked up the phone and spoke quietly. Fifteen minutes later Jonelle was told Kelly was free and to go on back.

"What's this about? I've been away and I don't really have time for you today," Kelly said as soon as she entered. His eyes looked at a space on the wall behind Jonelle.

"I'll make this as brief as possible. Where is Sophia Reyes?"

He sighed dramatically as his eyes looked up at the ceiling. "I told you before, I don't know."

"I think you're lying, doctor."

Kelly's eyes slowly settled on her face. "How dare you say that? You need to leave now." He started to rise from his chair.

"Oh, cut the dramatics please."

With shaking fingers Kelly reached up and straightened his already straight tie. His eyes wandered to his desk.

"What's the matter Doctor? You seem a bit, I don't know, out of sorts."

"Um. Well, it appears someone tried to break into my desk." He gave a nervous laugh.

"Have you contacted the police?"

He shook his head. "No. Nothing of any, uh, value was stolen."

Jonelle moved over and inspected the damage. "Wonder why someone would do this? You don't keep drugs or anything in there, do you?" Jonelle got perverse pleasure in watching the doctor squirm. Serves him right for holding back.

She returned to her seat. "Any of the other doctors burgled?"

Kelly paled and shook his head. "No," he said. "I asked everyone."

"So this"—she pointed to his desk—"is personal then."

"Since you put it that way I suppose it is," he mumbled. He looked as if any moment he'd have to excuse himself and run to the bathroom.

Jonelle wasn't about to let up. "Why do you suppose whoever did this, targeted you specifically?"

"Targeted?" Kelly blanched.

For the first time since they'd met, Jonelle believed that the stories about the man being the abused rather than the abuser were probably true. She kept prodding him.

"Sure. Looks like they were looking for something they knew only you had … and they wanted that something. What do you suppose it was?" She looked him in the eyes.

He shrugged.

"Did they get whatever it was you had in there? Come on, Doctor Kelly. Help me out here. If you had nothing to do with Susanna's death—"

"I didn't," he interrupted, voice raised. A thin line of sweat formed on his upper lip.

"Okay. Fine. I'd like to know everything that happened after Susanna called and said she wanted to stay with you for a while. You said no because of the relationship you said you were in, but is that true? I'm guessing that when she asked you for help, you gave it to her."

Sweat migrated from lip to forehead. He pulled his wedding photo closer to him.

"That's none of your business," he said. He lifted his eyes and shifted them to the side window. She didn't want to interrupt whatever it was he was thinking about, so she waited.

He nodded, as if coming to a conclusion. "I did see Susanna after her initial phone call. When I say I told her she couldn't stay with me, that's the truth. Imagine my surprise when after that phone conversation, she showed up here at the office a few days later."

Jonelle leaned forward in her chair. "Whoa. You're saying Susanna came here? What happened?" She rummaged through her bag, found notebook and pen and removed both.

Kelly's eyes widened. "Wait a minute. What are you doing?"

"Relax. I'm just taking a few notes for my use. I'm still trying to figure out why Susanna ended up with homeless people."

He stared at the pad and pen for a few moments. An exasperated sigh escaped from his lips. "Fine. Guess it doesn't matter much at this point."

Jonelle indicated for him to continue.

"So. When she realized she couldn't stay with me, she appeared at the office in disguise and insisted on at least meeting somewhere."

"What kind of disguise?"

"Typical Hollywood stuff. Laughable really. She had on a headscarf and dark glasses."

"Then what?"

"She said she had something to tell me. I agreed that we should walk over to the park off of K Street. I was more than a little nervous because by this time, I'd heard from Norm Finkleberg, and that really spooked me. My God. She'd stolen money from the town." He slapped his hand against his forehead. "They can't afford that." He stared at Jonelle. "What was she thinking?"

"Unfortunately, we can't ask her," Jonelle said. She immediately regretted the comment when she looked at the expression on Kelly's face. "Sorry." She motioned for him to continue.

"She told me she was staying at some two-bit hotel on Baltimore's west side. You know the type of area, right?"

Jonelle didn't answer.

"Anyway, it was surrounded by bars and pawnshops, those kinds of businesses. And if you went just a few blocks east, a bunch of rundown row houses. At the time I couldn't understand why she'd choose to stay in a place like that and then I figured it was because she didn't want anyone from Oldenberry to find out where she was."

Jonelle shook her head. Something wasn't right. "You knew what she'd done because Finkleberg told you. Did you let on where she was staying?"

"I … not exactly." Kelly looked sick.

Jonelle waited. When nothing was forthcoming, she said, "Please explain to me what *not exactly* means. Either you told Finkleberg where she was or you didn't."

He looked sharply at Jonelle. "I told him she was in Baltimore, but I didn't say exactly where."

Jonelle shook her head over and over.

"What else was I supposed to do? She committed a crime for crissakes." Kelly lowered his voice. "When we met at the hotel, I tried to get her to contact Finkleberg and return the money. I told her that if she gave the money back, maybe they wouldn't be too hard on her."

"Did she tell you why she took the money in the first place? She came from a wealthy family and was making a decent salary. I considered that maybe she had some kind of addiction, but no one has indicated anything liked that." Jonelle studied Kelly's face which remained passive, but she thought she saw something flicker in his eyes. When he didn't say anything, she continued.

"Other possibilities were she had a personal vendetta or wanted some kind of sick thrill. To say to the town 'screw it.' So, I'd like to ask you. Did she say why she took the money?"

Kelly kept his mouth shut.

Jonelle leaned forward in her chair and pointed a finger at him. Her patience with his wishy-washy attitude was wearing thin. "You said you tried to get her to return the money. So don't tell me you didn't ask the question."

The doctor swiveled in his chair, all the while avoiding Jonelle's eyes. "Fine. I did ask. But I swear the only response she gave was that she'd tell me everything later if I promised not to tell Finkleberg where to find her. Susanna told me she needed to think some things through first."

"Did she tell you where the money was?" Luther said she'd sometimes go places on her own.

Kelly picked up a pen and held it between his fingers. Jonelle saw him wince as his eyes landed on the burglarized desk drawer. "I swear to God she didn't tell me where the money was hidden. What she did say was that it was in a place where no one would think to look. That's all. I swear."

He stood and checked his watch. "I have a client coming soon. I'm afraid you have to leave."

To Jonelle's ears it didn't sound as if Kelly was sorry to see her go. "One other thing," she added. She ignored the sound of a groan coming from his lips.

"A detective friend of mine stated that Finkleberg is coming to the area for an interview. Did you know that?"

Kelly's face remained impassive.

"I've been told I could have a few words with him, and just to be completely honest with you, I plan to go over what you and I discussed. Just so you know."

He swallowed hard. "Fine."

Jonelle turned to go. She stopped at the door and faced Kelly. "Also, I haven't been able to locate Sophia. I've left several messages and I even went to her hotel but no luck. She hasn't checked out so I wonder if you'd heard from her."

Kelly paled and shook his head.

Jonelle's eyes narrowed. "If … I mean *when* … you do, tell her it's important I speak to her." Jonelle needed to tighten her grip on Kelly. She left his office with a curt, "I'll be in touch again, Doctor."

The whole family was messed up, she thought as she waited for the elevator to take her to the lobby. A wealthy woman stole money she didn't need, and called her ex to ask to stay with him. Jonelle exited the building. Kelly claimed he rejected the request. "But he still kept her picture close," Jonelle mumbled to herself. She ignored stares from passersby as she expressed some of those thoughts out loud and continued going over the case in her mind. Susanna took a room in a sleazebag hotel, met Luther and alternated living with him on the street and in the hotel room. After her death, no one found the stolen 330,000 dollars.

And where was Sophia?

CHAPTER 32

Jonelle wandered over to one of DC's many little parks and sat on a bench. She wondered if Sophia knew more about Susanna's possible involvement in the embezzlement than she let on. One of the things Jonelle hated was being taken for a fool. She went over the few established facts and still couldn't resolve why Susanna's twin would be interested in rental car and hotel receipts? And who was the man with her?

While she contemplated her next move, Kelly emerged on the opposite side of the street, head down and fast walking over to the Farragut subway station. On impulse, she followed. He seemed so intent on where he was going he barely noticed the people milling around him, much less Jonelle looming behind. He rode the escalators on the Red line side heading toward Union Station. The crush of people hurrying to get home hid her as she stood at the end of the subway car, eyes laser focused on the bald spot on the back of his head. When the doors opened at Union Station, Kelly rushed off.

Jonelle fought her way through the crowded car. Once on the platform she didn't see him. She turned in a circle. Where was Kelly? She swore under her breath. There he was! He stood midway on the up escalator. Grateful that the people knew the rules, with the riders standing on the right, while the walkers scurried up the left side, Jonelle spotted Kelly as he headed for the MARC station's Penn Line platform. Where the hell was he going? Jonelle rushed over to the window and with one eye on his back, purchased a MARC ticket.

She'd learned from Chester that he'd seen Susanna, or at least he thought it was Susanna, entering the Lancelot Inn. If that's where Kelly was headed she couldn't understand why. Unless he thought the money was still there and Sophia went looking for it. Jonelle's pulse raced as she allowed several commuters to board in front of her, all the while keeping tabs on Kelly.

Kelly left the train at the West Baltimore station with Jonelle close behind. At the corner of Baltimore and Charles streets, he paused and looked left and right as if confused on where he should go. Jonelle slipped behind a bus kiosk. A quick glance to the left and in the distance, posted high on a pole, Jonelle read "Lancelot Inn" and "Vacancy." She smiled to herself, proud she was able to predict Kelly's actions. The smile quickly faded as Kelly crossed the street and instead of walking in the direction of the Lancelot, he turned right. With Jonelle several paces behind, he walked a few blocks to where another man stood, pacing back and forth in front of what looked like a small bar. From her vantage point she watched Kelly approach the man with a slight build and thinning hair, dressed in gray slacks and navy blazer. A sharp intake of breath followed as she realized the pacing man was Finkleberg.

The two men entered the bar. She hung back and waited a few minutes for either one to come back out. Maybe they planned to go to the hotel together. Tired of playing yet another waiting game, Jonelle crossed the street.

A few feet before the bar, she heard a *swoosh* as something covered her head, plunging her into darkness. She tried to scream but couldn't open her mouth or her eyes. Her nose lay flat against her face. Her breathing became labored. She tried kicking her legs behind her and once heard a yell as her heel connected with flesh. She raised both arms over her head and tried to grab the face of her attacker, to no avail. Rough hands pulled her backwards, and she lost her balance, falling to her knees with the attacker's weight on her back.

Afraid he'd crush her ribs, she was relieved when coarse hands pulled her up. Warm, rank breath huffed on the back of her neck. Her feet scraped the pavement and she was filled with dread when she realized she was being dragged down the sidewalk. Whoever had hold of her possessed enormous strength. The overwhelming urge to breathe coupled with the thought of being hauled down a blind alley kick-started her adrenaline into overdrive.

Her fingers clawed behind her and this time her nails connected with skin and she dug deep. After a loud "dammit" the grip tightened around her even more. All she could do was twist and turn, hoping to dislodge the viselike hold around her neck and shoulders. Breathing became more difficult. She felt lightheaded and willed herself not to faint.

Where the hell were all the people? It was still daylight. After what seemed like an eternity of fighting an increasingly losing battle, sounds penetrated the cover over her head. Seconds later, searing pain erupted from the side of her head, and as she slid to the ground, darkness followed.

Annoyed at something hitting her face again and again, Jonelle moaned and tried to wave the irritation away. She opened her eyes and stared up at two fuzzy shapes looking down at her. She blinked several times dislodging the fog behind her eyes. Two women gazed down at her. They asked if she was all right and should they call the police. She performed a mental evaluation of her condition and decided she felt fine. Or so she thought. As she attempted to rise, dizziness seized her and she sat back down on the pavement until the feeling passed. Her head hurt like hell.

"You don't look so good," said the woman in a blue-flowered dress. "You want me to call nine eleven?"

"No. Really. I feel better. Just stood up a little too fast." The women looked at each other and nodded. Each took an arm and helped Jonelle to her feet. A slight wave of nausea came and just as quickly passed. That was followed by a quick intake of breath as she realized someone had mugged her. "My bag. Did he get my bag?"

"I got it right here," said the other woman in gray sweat pants and white crew neck sweater. "We saw the whole thing. Bastard dragged you down the street and when we started hollerin', he slugged you and took off. Didn't see him even try to take your purse. Why you suppose he didn't?" That last question was addressed to the other woman with her, who shrugged.

"Looked to me like he had somethin' else on his mind." She peered closely at Jonelle. "You piss somebody off lately?"

Jonelle believed she was pissing off a whole lot of *somebodies* lately. Her breathing returned to normal and her head felt more like a small rubber ball, hitting against her skull instead of a hammer. She glanced back to the bar several feet down. Jonelle had to find out why Kelly and Finkleberg went inside and she couldn't do it standing in one spot. She took a few tentative steps in that direction. "I gotta get in there," she said more to herself than to her two helpers.

"You sure you wanna do that now?" asked the youngest of the two. "You don't look so good to me."

The truth was, Jonelle did feel a little woozy, but she'd hate herself if she didn't at least look inside the place on the off chance the two men were still in there. "I need to find someone and I believe he's inside." A look passed between the two women.

"Tell you what," said the older woman, "how about we make sure you get to where you're going without you gettin' hit again. After that we gotta go."

Jonelle nodded her gratitude and instantly regretted stirring up the pounding in her head.

With her saviors close on her heels, she staggered up to the bar's entrance. Her hand shook as she reached for the handle. She pulled and nothing happened. Either it was heavier than she anticipated or the bump on the head was interfering with her movement. She inhaled and willed more strength into her right hand and pulled again. This time the door opened and she stepped inside the dark room and stood next to the door as her eyes adjusted.

The dark coolness did wonders to improve the way she felt and she took several deep breaths. To their credit, both of her escorts remained at her side. A bar stood on the left and Jonelle counted two men and a woman sitting on high stools. No one paid her any mind. Of the five tables situated on the right side three men occupied one and two women sat at another. All patrons were black. Where were Kelly and Finkleberg?

Jonelle walked up to the bar where a heavyset man on the other side gave her a wary look. Before she opened her mouth, he pointed to her head. "What happened to you? We ain't got no phone in here for you to use to call the cops."

Jonelle touched her head and withdrew sticky fingers tinged with blood.

"I'm not calling the cops. Two white men came in here a few minutes ago. Did you see them?"

The bartender shrugged. "People come. People go."

Jonelle didn't feel like playing games. Her damn head hurt. "How many white people come and go?" She spread her arm around the room. "I'm gonna take a wild guess and say not many."

The man closest to her left arm answered. "Both of 'em came in, sat down, talked some and left out the back jus' afore you come in."

The bartender glared at him. "When you gonna learn to keep your damn mouth shut, huh?" He looked Jonelle in the eye. "We don't want no trouble."

"I'm not giving you any. Had you seen either man before?"

After a slight hesitation, the bartender shook his head.

"Me neither," said the man at the bar and was rewarded with another dirty look.

Jonelle took a few steps forward. "Where's the back door?"

"What you wanna know that for?" the bartender asked.

"Places like this only have one way in and out. Unless …" She headed for the back where an open area revealed two doors, one with a legless figure in a cutout dress, and the other without a dress and no head.

Jonelle opened the door to the men's room and recoiled at the stink. She took in the one urinal and one stall. She covered her mouth and pinched her nose as her eyes swept the tiny, filthy space. Not one window in sight.

The women's room was just as dirty and again, windowless.

"You done?" the bartender asked as he stood near her elbow.

"Almost. If you don't have a back door for customers, I'm assuming you let them use the service entrance. Since when do barkeeps let their customers go out that way?"

She stared at him until he turned away.

He slipped back behind the bar without speaking, picked up a cloth and proceeded to half-heartedly wipe down the bar's surface.

"Aw, why don'cha tell the lady them guys paid you to use the back, huh? I gots a feelin' that unless you tell her what she wanna know, she ain't movin' from here. Am I right?"

Jonelle threw the man a weak smile.

The bartender sighed. “I’m tellin’ you this so’s you get the hell outta my bar. A hunnerd dollars, okay? They gimme a hunnerd dollars to use my back door. Now go on outta here.”

The tight space and the dark atmosphere, combined with her two escorts staying close, triggered Jonelle’s claustrophobia and she had to leave soon or else someone would have to call emergency services. “Thanks for your help,” she said with an edge to her voice and headed for the entrance. Her two guardian angels followed.

“Wait a minute,” said the woman in blue. “Maybe you oughta wash some ‘a that blood off first.”

“Don’t believe he’d appreciate my going back in there. Besides, I don’t think I can hold my breath that long.” Jonelle rummaged through her bag and pulled out a wet wipe. She swiped her head several times and looked at her newfound friends with raised eyebrows.

“That’s better,” said blue dress. “What you think, Angela? She okay now?”

Angela stepped away from Jonelle. “I kinda agree, Vernel-la. I think you’re okay to get home, Miss.”

“Please call me Jonelle.”

“Okay, Jonelle. You live far?”

Jonelle told them MARC’s Penn station was her destina-tion, and assured them she could walk that far.

Jonelle glanced over in the direction of the hotel. As long as she was so close, maybe someone else besides the maids might give her information. Especially for some extra dough.

“I need to check something at that hotel over there first,” she said.

Both women frowned. Vernella shook her head. “I think you should head on home Jonelle. You look a little shaky to me.” She looked over at Angela and received a nod in confirmation.

"I appreciate your concern, but I'm fine. Really. I need to ask a few questions of the desk clerk and then I'm heading home."

Vernella peered at Jonelle. "You a cop? 'Cause if not, you should be. Never met nobody who got mugged before wanna hang around and ask a lotta questions." The two women turned to leave.

"Speaking of questions." Did someone groan? "Almost forgot the most important one. Did you two get a good look at who grabbed and hit me?"

Angela answered. "White guy. Dark hair, kinda long and straight. Looks like he works out a lot. You not doing drugs are you?" Her eyes searched Jonelle up and down.

"No. Can you tell me more about him? What was he wearing? Did he say anything?" Jonelle looked at both women in turn.

"He was wearin' jeans and a long-sleeved dark green sweatshirt. The shirt had some kinda writin' on it in white." Vernella crinkled her eyes in concentration. "What did that writin' say? Hmm? Angela, did you see it?"

Angela shook her head.

Vernella's eyes brightened. "I got it. On the front was written somethin' weird like 'Mouse Country.'"

Angela laughed. "'Mouse Country'? That don't make no sense. Mice don't have no country."

CHAPTER 33

Jonelle's two good Samaritans escorted her to a corner drugstore where she purchased painkillers and a bottle of water. Outside the store she downed a few tablets and assured the women once she questioned the employees inside the Lancelot hotel, she'd walk back to MARC's Penn line station for the journey back to DC to retrieve her Jeep.

Angela put a hand on Jonelle's arm as all three women stood in front of the hotel. "You sure you wanna go in there? Don't look on the up and up to me. What you think, Vernella?"

"Anybody else I'd say no, but this one here,"—she pointed to Jonelle—"can handle herself. Ain't that right?"

Before Jonelle answered, Angela piped up. "No offense Jonelle, but you didn't do so good before."

An embarrassed Jonelle agreed. "I plan on paying more attention to people around me from now on." *You're beginning to sound like a broken record,* Jonelle thought. *Might not be so lucky next time.* "The guy who jumped me sounds like someone I've seen before."

"Say what?" both women said in unison.

"Yeah. I don't think he's coming back. You guys were awesome scaring him off like that. I can't thank you enough."

"You can thank us by taking our phone numbers and calling if you need help." Angela and Vernella recited the information and watched Jonelle program everything into her phone. All three hugged each other and after a quick wave,

Jonelle entered the lobby of the Lancelot and walked up to the desk.

Behind the bullet proof partition an elderly Asian man looked her up and down. “No vacancy,” he said.

“Then you’d better change your damn sign.” She was so not in the mood. “Besides, I’m not looking for a room. I need to ask you a few questions.”

“No answers,” he said. A lopsided smile exposed several missing teeth.

Jonelle’s hand reached inside her bag. The clerk’s eyes widened and he pushed away from the counter. “Relax. All I want to do is show you a picture and if you recognize her, tell me what you remember.”

“We don’t give—”

“Yeah, right. Whatever.” She pressed two twenties and a ten in front of the glass.

He pointed to the slot below.

Jonelle shook her head. “Nope. You give me information first.”

“How I know you not gonna stiff me?”

Jonelle slid the ten under the glass. “This is a deposit.” She held Susanna’s picture up for him to see. “Well? Do you remember seeing her?”

He waved his hand dismissively. “Oh, her. Cops already ask about her. Told ‘em everything. No big deal.”

Jonelle ignored the comment. “Did you ever see her with anyone else? An average looking white guy, slender build, glasses?”

“Nope always by herself. Also told cops bag she had, she took when she left first time.”

“What bag?”

He shrugged.

Jonelle suppressed a groan. “Okay. What do you mean ‘the first time’?”

"I mean she leave once with bag, then come back. Without bag."

Damn. "What was she like?"

"Like everybody else. No big deal."

Jonelle waved the remaining twenties in his face. "Try again."

"Okay, okay." He scrunched his face in concentration. To Jonelle it looked as though it was part of some perverse act but she decided to wait him out. His face relaxed. "This my opinion. No big deal. When she first come, she was different, you know? Not like most, uh, visitors we get. She look, well, clean is best way to say it. Even though most who come here don't look dirty, also don't look clean. Understand?"

Jonelle nodded. She knew exactly what he meant.

"And, she always speak. Say hello. Say goodbye. Say thanks. Until last time. Last time she seem upset. Kept looking around like she never saw this place before. Not so polite. Hardly spoke."

Jonelle tried to tamp down the feeling of excitement. "So, she seemed the same, but different. Is that what you're saying?"

He nodded.

Jonelle dug into her bag and retrieved the picture of Susanna and Sophia together. She showed it to him. His eyes widened and his mouth gaped open.

"Two? Makes lotta sense now."

"Besides the attitude change, did you notice anything else different from the way she acted the first time she stayed here?"

He indicated with his fingers he wanted more money and she obliged by slipping the rest under the glass.

"I notice lot about her, because she good-looking, see? Last time she still good-looking, but more, um, harder. Get it?"

Jonelle frowned. "Do you mean scared? Did she look scared?

"Not only scared. More, um … like this." He opened and closed his fist several times.

A puzzled Jonelle had trouble figuring out what he meant. "Strong?"

He shook his head all the while opening and closing his hand faster.

She got it. "Determined?"

He grinned. "Right!"

"What else?"

"For somebody without much money she had a lotta change of clothes. Some really nice, some kinda shabby." Jonelle wondered what happened to the clothes and figured the police probably took control of Susanna's possessions.

Susanna must have made a huge impression on the man that he could remember so much. Based on information from Luther and Finkleberg, Susanna had probably stayed at the hotel after being rejected by Kelly. So why hook up with Luther on the street?

The walk back to the station took less than thirty minutes, even walking slow so as not to aggravate her headache. She considered leaving the Jeep in DC until the next day but didn't want to be without her vehicle. The anger she felt for getting ambushed, was assuaged by what the hotel clerk revealed. No wonder Luther said Susanna disappeared for periods of time. But why keep coming back to the street? Jonelle figured it had to do with keeping tabs on the money. Woman was probably frantic someone would find it and everything she'd done would've been in vain.

After retrieving her Jeep from DC, Jonelle decided to stop and see Burt. She'd deal with Kelly later. Did he know she was following him? Why were Kelly and Finkleberg meeting close to the place where Susanna had stayed?

Upon entering the police station Jonelle received a visitor's badge without comment. She signed the book and wrote down Burt's name and location. A weak smile and nod later to the desk sergeant, Jonelle made her way down the familiar hallway.

Burt waited by the open door to the division. His eyes widened when he saw her. "Whoa. You look a little … what's the word? Frazzled." His body blocked the open door as he leaned in and studied her face. "You okay?"

"I'm fine. Mind if I go in?"

He moved to one side. "Of course. Sorry."

Jonelle followed him toward the back to his cubicle. He motioned for her to sit.

"So. What happened?"

Jonelle frowned. "How do you know anything happened?"

Burt pointed to her shirt. "You've got dirt all up and down your blouse, and if I'm not mistaken, that's a scrape on your left cheek and a bump above your eyebrow."

She touched her face and smiled weakly. "You got me." Jonelle gave him a brief rundown of what happened when she tried to enter the bar, omitting some details. On the way over, she'd decided to mention Kelly's name. If the doctor was involved in something dicey, a little help from the police wouldn't hurt.

Burt scribbled some notes. "You positive the man you saw Kelly with was Finkleberg? That's something else I'll ask him about when we talk. He and this doctor are friends, right?"

Jonelle came to attention. "You're interviewing Finkleberg?" Her eyes scanned the room. "Now?"

Burt shook his head. "He's not here now. He's coming in later, and before you ask, no I can't allow you to sit in."

A scowl creased Jonelle's face. "I need to ask him a few more questions. I'll bet anything he knows who mugged me."

"Then you'll have to find some other way. Sorry."

Burt's face indicated he wasn't all that disappointed she wouldn't question Finkleberg at the same time he did. "Tell you what," Burt said. "I'll ask him to give you a call when I'm through with him. How about that?"

"Hmm. Okay." Jonelle's mind raced. What might be even better is if she just happened to run into him as he was leaving his appointment with Burt. "So, what time is he due here? Just so I can get some kind of idea of when to expect his call."

Burt's round, dark eyes narrowed. "If I tell you, do you promise not to talk to him before I do?"

Jonelle shrugged. "I don't even know where he's staying, so how could I possibly see him before his appointment with you? Honestly, Burt. I think you're getting paranoid." She rose quickly. "Well, gotta go. When you talk to Finkleberg, let him know that *I* know he went into that bar with Kelly and that I have every intention of finding out why he went there. And ask him about Sophia. I still haven't been able to reach her."

CHAPTER 34

Across from the police station, a narrow stand of trees separated the building from a small strip mall with a donut shop, nail salon, pizza carryout and urgent care clinic. She drove over to the line of stores and parked closest to the road facing the department, with the hope of catching Finkleberg before he entered the Northern District station. If that didn't work, she'd intercept him when he left.

She opened the glove compartment, nudged the gun aside and removed mini binoculars, and settled down to wait. Time crept by and still no sign of Finkleberg. The aroma from the pizza place wafted through her open window, a reminder that she hadn't eaten since breakfast. Not wanting to risk going inside the carryout and missing Finkleberg, Jonelle used her phone and dialed the number printed on the eatery's window. After ordering a small cheese pizza and diet soda, she waited for Finkleberg to appear.

Fifteen minutes later with no sign of the commissioner, Jonelle rushed over and retrieved her order. The time spent away from observing the station was a scant five minutes so she felt sure she hadn't missed his arrival. It'd take him that long to find a spot in the crowded parking lot.

Time crept by and still no sign of Finkleberg. She shifted in her seat. Maybe she shouldn't have consumed the entire large soda. After a quick glance at her surroundings, her eyes settled on a combination gas station and mini mart. There was probably a restroom she could use.

Decision made, Jonelle opened the Jeep's door but instead of leaving her vehicle, she stopped. A slight man with stooped shoulders hurried toward the police department's entrance. With binoculars in hand, she zoomed in on a worried-looking Finkleberg. Too late to stop him. Now that she knew for sure he was keeping his interview with Burt, it was only a matter of time before she could confront him about his meeting with Kelly.

A little over an hour later, Finkleberg emerged, sucking on a pipe and walking more slowly this time. Eyes trained on the commissioner as he trudged back to his vehicle, Jonelle was disappointed when, instead of getting behind the wheel of a gray sedan, he entered a white SUV. She put the Jeep in gear, intent on following wherever he led. A quick trip down interstate 95 and Finkleberg exited in her part of the woods. She stayed close as he drove into the lot of a Hampton Hotel.

Not wanting to go through the front desk, Jonelle decided on the direct approach. When he exited his vehicle, she was right behind him. "Hey, Mister Finkleberg," she called out. He stopped and turned at the mention of his name.

"What're … how did you get here?"

"Same way you did. By automobile." She didn't care that she was exhibiting a fair amount of snark. The bump on her head reminded her that she didn't like being manhandled, neither figuratively nor literally.

"Are you following me?"

"Sure am," Jonelle answered. "I've got a few questions I need to ask." At that time of day, the parking lot was fairly crowded. Several people turned to stare at the thin white man and tall black woman. "We can either do it right here, or perhaps inside the hotel would be better. Your choice."

Finkleberg shook his head. He held the mahogany pipe in one hand, the smoky-sweet aroma floating in front of her face. He opened his mouth as if to say something. Jonelle held his gaze until he shrugged and looked away. "Guess inside would be better." He turned and headed toward the hotel's double doors.

He angrily knocked the pipe's contents on top of a sand-filled metal container. Once inside the lobby, Finkleberg turned right and stomped toward the main level's sports bar. Jonelle didn't bother to hurry; she had no intention of letting him get away from her. Although Finkleberg didn't acknowledge her presence, she planned on staying and talking to him for however long it took.

Finkleberg snatched a table farthest from the entrance to the bar. Without waiting for permission, Jonelle sat across from him, next to a large window. A waitress dressed in black slacks and white blouse with a small red apron draped around her waist, came and took their order. Lager for him, white wine for her. While they waited, Finkleberg looked everywhere around the room, except at Jonelle. She wondered if he really expected her to disappear and decided to get right to the point.

"In case you're curious about how I found you, I was waiting for you to leave the police department."

He gaped at her. "What? Why?"

"The detective you had an appointment with is a friend of mine. We're working on Susanna's case together."

"You two are in collusion? How dare he tell you about me."

Jonelle waved a hand in the air. "Save it. Unless I'm mistaken, this is the first time he's interviewed you, so I knew more than he did. He's not a priest for crissakes. I'm a licensed private investigator with a vested interest in this case. Sophia Reyes hired me, remember?"

Finkleberg's nostrils flared as he stared at Jonelle. The two didn't say a word while the waitress placed drinks before them. Jonelle took a tiny sip and waited as he slurped beer and wiped the foam from his mouth with the back of his hand. Lovely.

"Look," she said. "Detective Burton isn't going to reveal the specifics of what you talked about and frankly, I don't care about that. What I do care about is, what were you doing meeting Doctor Kelly in west Baltimore?"

Finkleberg choked on his drink. He got himself under control and studied Jonelle. "How long have you been following me?"

"Not you necessarily. But I did suspect the good doctor hadn't been completely honest with me, so it was him on my radar. You were just the extra tidbit that came along. You didn't answer my question. What were you two doing in that part of town? A bit low rent for the both of you I would've thought."

Finkleberg's eyes darted around the bar, settled back on Jonelle, then resumed its flitting around the dimly lit room. "Barry and I are friends," he said, after several seconds. "I just wanted to … uh … catch up on a few old times."

Jonelle hooted. She lowered her voice as a few occupants at other tables turned and stared. "Catch up? You had to go all the way to the low rent district to do that? Give me a break. There are far nicer places closer to where he works." She leaned back in her chair. "Did you happen to mention your 'catching up' with Kelly to Detective Burton?" Jonelle paused, waiting for an answer that never came. "I didn't think so."

"It's none of your damn business, anyway," Finkleberg said through clenched teeth.

"Oh, but it is. It's my business if I caught somebody watching me and it's my damn business if that somebody, or some*bodies*, attacked me as I started to follow you into that bar."

He stared openmouthed.

"Your goon didn't tell you what happened?"

Finkleberg shook his head. "I don't know what you're talking about," he said in a soft voice.

Jonelle eyed the person across from her. For a brief moment she almost believed him. Still, there was something off about the man. "I think you do. The only connection with me and this mess with Susanna I can come up with is the money. I believe that for some reason you seem to think I know where Susanna hid the cash. Well, I don't."

His hands shook as he picked up the half empty beer mug. Jonelle waited while he consumed the rest of the liquid. This time, he wiped his mouth with a napkin and then used it to remove the sweat from his brow. "I'm here of my own free will. I won't sit here and be accused of …" He shuddered. "I want the money back. That's all. I don't know who killed Susanna or why."

"You've got to believe that her death is connected to the money she stole. Has to be. Otherwise, why kill her? A random mugger wouldn't take the time to do what he did to her."

Finkleberg lowered his head down so far that it almost touched the table's surface. "I don't know," he muttered. "This is getting out of hand. This is not …"

When he didn't finish the thought, Jonelle nudged him a little.

"Okay. Let's start from the beginning, shall we? Susanna and Rosemary stole the money and took off. Rosemary headed for the Canadian border and Susanna came down here. She called Kelly. He says he didn't know anything about what she'd done, yet he admits he talked to you about that same time." Jonelle tapped the table until Finkleberg's head came up. "Did you tell Kelly what she'd done?"

Finkleberg nodded.

Finally, Jonelle thought. "And Kelly told you she wanted to stay with him. Right?"

"He said he told her no. He didn't want to get involved." His hands wrapped around the empty glass.

The waitress came and asked if he wanted a refill. Finkleberg nodded.

"Did either you or Kelly know where she was staying?"

A scowl came across his face. "We had no idea."

Jonelle wasn't buying it. "Somebody knew. Otherwise why did she end up living on the street … at least part of the time. Even that didn't keep her safe." Jonelle remembered a question that had nagged at her since she first became involved in the case. She waited while the waitress set Finkleberg's drink down and walked away.

"Why embezzle the money in the first place? She came from a wealthy family. Her mother told me the only heirs to the family's estate were the two girls. I assume the county paid her a decent salary. So why take a lousy 350,000 dollars? I can see maybe thirty million, but not that paltry sum."

Finkleberg's complexion took on an unhealthy sheen. Behind his glasses his eyes blinked several times in rapid succession. Jonelle hoped the poor man wouldn't keel over before she had finished asking her questions. "I'll ask again. Why do you think she took the money in the first place?"

He cleared his throat several times and took another swig of beer. That small action seemed to give him a short burst of confidence. This time he met Jonelle's gaze. "I honestly don't know. I've thought about it but can't figure it out." He sat up straighter. "That's why I was meeting Barry. I wanted to discuss it with him. See what he had to say about this whole mess. He was adamant about not meeting anywhere near where he worked. He, uh, knew the area. Said one of his clients lived around there."

Jonelle examined the man fidgeting in his seat. All her senses screamed that he was lying. Kudos to him for that quick excuse, but she didn't buy it.

"You mentioned the impending audit. For that small amount of money, couldn't she have talked her way out of any wrongdoing?"

He shrugged. "She set up a bogus bank account. They could've easily traced it back to her."

"Or not. She seemed like a smart person who could've lied her way through any suspicion. What about drugs? Is it possible she was hiding a drug habit and needed the money?"

"I don't know anything about drugs," Finkleberg said.

Jonelle racked her brain. "Was she covering up for someone else?" she asked, more as a result of grasping at straws than anything else. Finkleberg turned his head and stared out the window. Jonelle thought she might be on to something. More often than not, twins stood up for each other. While Sophia's physical appearance indicated she married well, Jonelle also knew there wasn't any information on Mr. Reyes in Sophia's file. She had to find Sophia.

The break in conversation allowed Finkleberg to catch the waitress' attention. She gave him the check and he paid for the drinks. He started to stand but Jonelle's voice stopped him. "I have to ask you about Sophia."

His brow furrowed. "Sophia? I thought you were interested in Susanna."

"The two are intertwined in this whole mess. Plus, I haven't been able to reach her and Kelly claims he hasn't seen her either. I'm wondering if you know where she is." She carefully studied Finkleberg's face. The blank expression indicated he had regained his composure.

"I have no idea where Sophia is," he said, getting up from his chair. "Since I've given my statement to the police about the embezzlement, they have all my information should they find the money. All I have to do is pack my few things for the last flight out of here this evening."

With Finkleberg on his way back to Michigan and Sophia missing, Jonelle wasn't feeling too confident in her ability to discover more about Susanna.

"Have you ever been to Kelly's office? When he wasn't there?"

Finkleberg hesitated. He turned, curled his lip in a nasty snarl and stomped out.

She couldn't stop Finkleberg from walking out of the bar; right now there was nothing else she could get out of the man.

For several minutes after he'd gone, Jonelle sat in the chair, staring out the window. She hadn't felt this useless in a very long time. The case was in danger of stagnating and she didn't like it one bit. She exhaled a long burst of air and frustration and decided she needed fresh insights. For that, she'd call Adrienne and run by what she'd found out about everything so far. Her best friend could be overwhelming sometimes but also enlightening at others.

Jonelle left Finkleberg's hotel and headed for her Jeep. As she settled behind the wheel, the *Hawaii Five-O* theme rang in her purse. She glanced at the phone's display. Detective T. Burton's name appeared. She sighed and considered not answering but changed her mind. He might be calling to give her information about Finkleberg's interview.

After her hello, she listened in stunned silence as Burt announced that the body of Sophia Reyes was discovered in an alley near the Lancelot Inn.

CHAPTER 35

"I cannot believe this. What the hell's going on?" Jonelle threw her bag on Burt's desk. She was angry. Angry at herself, angry at Finkleberg for his evasiveness and angry at Kelly for what she perceived was his lack of honesty. She glared at the detective before taking the seat across from him.

Burt raised his hands in an effort to ward off the outrage coming from Jonelle's mouth. "I need you to calm down," he said. "You didn't have to come all the way back here. I could've met you at your office."

"Yeah. Well, I'm here now. Are you going to give me any information or not? After all, the woman was my client." Tears welled in the back of Jonelle's eyes. The emotion shocked her. She didn't know Sophia that well, so how to explain the feeling? Was it empathy? Or maybe frustration at being thwarted at every turn the moment she felt she was getting close to the answers she sought. Jonelle willed the tears to stay put. Even so, she felt like running outside, and standing in the middle of the street, screaming her freaking head off. No amount of odd behavior or evasiveness should have warranted the woman's death. Jonelle took several deep breaths.

"Better now?" Burt asked.

"What happened?" she managed.

"Okay. Just the facts ma'am, right?" Burt's smile faded as Jonelle's lips pursed in a tight, straight line. "Right." He cleared his throat. "The department received a call of a woman's body lying in an alley between a liquor store and a discount electronics store. The location is near the Lancelot Inn which is a—"

"I know what it is," Jonelle interrupted.

Burt continued without acknowledging Jonelle's words. "The caller admitted he'd gone back there to take a leak and noticed a pair of legs sticking out from behind two large metal bins. He said he thought maybe somebody had thrown out a mannequin since there's a clothing store a few doors down. Guy decided to grab it and play a joke on his friends.

"When he got closer, he noticed the blood, backed out of there almost at a run and called us. Claimed he didn't see anything but blood before dialing nine eleven."

"You believe him?"

"No reason not to. His friends were in the bar and can verify he'd arrived with them and they'd been there for at least two hours. The M. E. says the body hadn't been there long. The blood was fresh, her skin barely cold to the touch and no rigor."

"Nobody heard or saw anything?"

"As of right now, no. But the investigation's at the beginning stages so that may change."

Jonelle stood and paced the length of Burt's cubicle. She grasped her gold necklace and worked the charms through her fingers.

Burt's eyes followed her movements.

Before completing the fifth circuit, Jonelle stopped, stood still and took several deep breaths.

With one hand Burt indicated the guest chair. Jonelle sat.

In a calm, quiet voice, Burt said, "She was found with her throat cut. The preliminary exam indicated it was similar to her sister's. Her clothes weren't disturbed, so it doesn't look like a sexual assault, at least not now. She still had her purse and a wallet with a couple hundred dollars and two credit cards.

Leaving the money tells me they want to send a message. What that message is and who it's meant for is a mystery."

"Was she wearing a ring?" Jonelle remembered the first time she met Sophia, the woman's fingers were bare. Sophia had told her she didn't want to risk wearing a ring in the area, yet she was found with money and credit cards on her person.

"Her hands were bare. Why?"

"Married women wear rings."

For a few moments Jonelle didn't speak. She looked up at the ceiling and willed that the moisture again pooling in her eyes, wouldn't spill down her cheek. Jonelle blinked rapidly several times.

"You don't look so good. Can I get you anything to drink? Water? Coffee?"

Jonelle shook her head. She wondered how she'd be able to lift herself off the chair and out of the building to get to her car.

The phone on Burt's desk rang. "Hold on a sec."

Jonelle stared off into the distance. Burt's loud "what the hell?" brought her attention back to him. He looked at Jonelle. His already round eyes opened even wider. "I don't fu … uh, don't believe it. Check the file again on Susanna. Make sure the composition is the same."

She leaned forward as he slammed down the phone. "What? What's going on?"

"Nobody noticed before because of all the blood, but once they cleaned it off, they noticed that like Susanna, Sophia's face had been painted."

"What the hell's going on Burt?"

"Damned if I know."

"This isn't just about the money any more, is it?"

He shook his head. "If it ever was. I gotta get Finkleberg back here." He grabbed his phone, made several calls, the gist of which Jonelle surmised was meant to prevent Finkleberg from leaving Maryland and heading back to Michigan. "Guy had all the right answers earlier," Burt said after he placed the last call. "This changes everything."

Jonelle leaned her elbow on the desk. "You think he had something to do with Sophia's death?"

"He comes to town and there's another dead body? You know as well as I do that cops don't like coincidences."

"What about Kelly?"

"What about him?" Burt two-finger typed on his keyboard, paused and read information on the screen.

Jonelle waited a few beats before she repeated her question. "Have you considered Kelly as a possible suspect?"

The lines between Burt's brows indicated he was distracted at this latest news. She persisted. There was something off about Kelly and she wanted Burt to know.

"I think Kelly, and maybe Finkleberg are the reason I got mugged," she said, the words tumbling out. "They didn't see me, but whoever attacked me stopped me long enough for the two to escape out the back way."

Burt pointed his index finger at her. "I'm not gonna lecture you about keeping out of police business 'cause you don't listen anyway." He turned back to his computer and after a few clicks started typing. "Okay, I noted what you just said. Got any other news for me?"

"Pull up a map of west Baltimore," she said. He complied without question. She came around and stood behind him. Jonelle recited the address of the bar. "Add the locations where Susanna and Sophia were found as well, plus the Lancelot's address," Jonelle insisted. That done, Burt and Jonelle stared at the result. Everything lay within a three-block radius.

"Two murders within walking distance," she said.

"Bastard wouldn't even have to waste a gallon of gas," Burt added, spitting out the words as if trying to get a horrible taste out of his mouth.

Jonelle waited for the unusual reaction from the laidback detective to pass. As she watched the muscles in his face start to relax, she brought up Kelly again. "I don't pretend to know what's going on, Burt, but I think Kelly is the key. The guy comes off as mister milquetoast, professional man, but he's a little too passive-aggressive, if you know what I mean."

The corners of Burt's mouth turned up. Not quite a smile, but almost.

"Thinking back, when I was in Michigan and asked about his and Susanna's relationship, some said he was the abuser. At the time, only Finkleberg claimed Kelly was abused. I think Kelly is key to this mess."

"You think he did Susanna and now Sophia?"

"I don't think he killed the sisters himself, but I'll bet anything he knows a helluva lot more than he lets on. Get him away from his cushy K street office. Bring his narrow ass down here and really let him have it."

This time Burt's smile spread across his face. "'Narrow ass?'"

"You know what I mean." Jonelle's phone pinged with an incoming text message. She looked at it and covered her forehead with her free hand. "Damn. I almost forgot." Her fingers typed a reply. "I've got Rosemary Wilkins' lawyer ready to meet me."

"Who?"

Jonelle explained. "This could work out. When I talked to Rosemary, I felt she knew more. The fact that he has something else to tell me could help link up what's going on."

Burt shook his head. "Stay mum about Sophia's death. It hasn't hit the news yet."

She stood to go. "Don't worry. This whole thing smelled from day one. Rosemary might shed more light on why a well-off daughter of one of the town's most prominent families, with an important job, no less, stole such a piddling amount of money."

CHAPTER 36

Jonelle found Winston Hackett sitting alone at a table in the main restaurant looking at several sheets of paper and nursing a cup of coffee. He looked up as she approached his table. "Have a seat." He gathered up the papers and put them in his briefcase.

Jonelle took the chair opposite the attorney. "Looks like you could use a cup of coffee," he said.

She smiled. "That bad, huh? Fact is, this case is not going well. It's … far more complicated than I originally thought it would be. I'm hoping you have news that might help clear up some outstanding questions I have."

Hackett ordered a refill for himself and coffee for Jonelle. She waved off his suggestion of something to eat and waited for him to begin.

He didn't speak until he'd poured cream in his coffee and Jonelle had taken a sip of hers. "When you left that day, I could tell something was bothering Rosemary, even though she told you pretty much the same thing she testified to in court." His eyes looked into Jonelle's. "Your expression told me that you thought Rosemary was holding back."

Very perceptive, counselor, she thought.

"I didn't push her. Rosemary can't take much stress. She tends to clam up if she feels any kind of pressure whatsoever. Which is why her involvement in this was so puzzling. I think the judge felt the same—she was a puppy being led around by someone smarter and savvier than herself." He shrugged. "She thought that since Susanna knew the ins and outs of that office, they could take the money without anyone noticing for a long time."

"Typical, isn't it?" Jonelle asked, without expecting Hackett to answer. "What do they say? The jails are full of so-called smart people who thought they could beat the system."

Hackett chuckled. "Keeps guys like me in business."

Jonelle put her cup down and leaned toward Hackett. "I'm bothered by the relatively small amount of money they took. Why not take more?"

"I got the impression they wanted to and, based on what Rosemary said, that they got spooked when they heard the auditors were coming."

"That doesn't sound right," Jonelle said, shaking her head. "See, everyone I've talked to told me how smart Susanna was. I'm pretty sure she could've made some excuse about the money … at least for a while. They'd done audits in the past and gotten a clean bill of health. Finkleberg said he had no indication that anything was wrong." Finkleberg's name nearly stuck in Jonelle's throat.

Hackett picked up on her reaction. "That's the reason why I wanted to speak to you. Two days after her talk with you, Rosemary called to say she wanted to see me again. Normally, I only go out to the prison once a month, but she was so insistent, I decided to meet with her." He looked down and played with the knife sitting on the table. "What I'm about to tell you is pure speculation on her part, but she wants you to know this. If you tell anyone else what I'm about to say, please stress that Rosemary has no irrefutable truth."

"Does this have anything to do with Sophia Quinley Reyes at all?"

He frowned. "No. Why?"

"She's … my client, so I have to be sure." She had no intention on backing out of her promise to Burt not to tell anyone about Sophia's death.

"I see. Rosemary didn't mention the sister at all."

"Good." Jonelle indicated for him to continue.

"Rosemary stated that based on what she called 'hints' from Susanna, Finkleberg knew what they were doing and had no objection."

Jonelle tried to remain calm. "How much can you tell me?"

Hackett's fingers tapped against the side of his cup. "Rosemary stated that when Susanna first asked if she wanted to make a little extra money, and then explained what she wanted to do, Rosemary got scared. Not only for herself but for her son. She'd heard what happened to people who stole from the government, that they always went to prison.

"Susanna convinced Rosemary that they weren't alone in the scheme. That the only person with the authority to blow the whistle on them was aware of the plan."

The waitress approached and left the check. Hackett smiled up at her and waited until she left.

"Did Rosemary actually say it was Finkleberg?" Jonelle couldn't believe what she was hearing.

"No. Rosemary didn't mention him by name because Susanna wasn't specific. Only that they had nothing to worry about because the person at the top—those were Rosemary's words—knew what was going on."

Jonelle sat back in her chair. "Wow."

"My thoughts exactly. The main thing I really wanted you to know was that Rosemary admitted the plan was thwarted when Susanna called and told her they had to leave right away."

"Why?"

"According to Rosemary, Susanna had argued with him and he had gotten angry they were taking too long to steal the money. Seems he wanted it done quickly so they could hide as much as they could and thereby cover up as much as they had to." Hackett paused.

Jonelle seized the opportunity to put forth an idea. "You know, I've wondered why they only took a little over three hundred thousand. Sounds like Finkleberg—,"

Hackett cleared his throat.

"Or *whoever,* wanted more and the two fell out for some reason."

Hackett was shaking his head before Jonelle had finished. "Now, I want to make clear Rosemary didn't specifically say the other person was Finkleberg." The lawyer's pale eyes looked at Jonelle. "I debated with myself on whether to mention something Rosemary did say about Finkleberg and Susanna." He hesitated. "This is probably office gossip, but …"

"What?"

"There were whispers that the two were having an affair. That doesn't mean he was involved in the embezzlement."

Jonelle tried to contain her excitement. "Who else could it be? He ran that place. And if they were romantically involved, this adds a whole new dimension to what went on." Jonelle fiddled with her necklace. The urge to stand and pace almost overwhelmed her, but she remained seated. "What I can't figure out is why have her killed? What good would that do?"

The lawyer's eyes never left Jonelle. "I agree it's a helluva leap from stealing to murder. I can't work that bit out. Assuming of course, it really *was* Finkleberg."

"I'll admit it's a stretch, but how much do we know about him anyway? Usually it's greed that leads people to crime and maybe Finkleberg is financially strapped. If he was cheating on his wife, he may have felt he couldn't afford a divorce unless he had money that the missus didn't know about."

Hackett shrugged. "That's possible. Rosemary said that while she was a nervous wreck when they decided to leave and not tell the other person, she said Susanna was almost giddy about what they had done. Like it was some kind of prank she was playing. Some joke, huh?"

"Got that right."

"Another thing," Hackett said.

Jonelle's eyebrows shot up.

"Don't know how important this bit is, but …" The lawyer paused so long Jonelle started to wonder if he lost his train of thought.

"Rosemary's primary concern has always been for her son. She only mentioned what I'm about to tell you because she hasn't heard from the baby's father in a while. Don't know if I told you, but she and the father aren't married."

Jonelle didn't care. She nodded encouragement to keep Hackett talking.

"So. A few months after she started in the commissioner's office, Finkleberg asked her if she knew anyone who could do odd jobs for him. Drive him around, act as bodyguards when he went somewhere. I know," Hackett said, waving his hands in a dismissive gesture, "why bodyguards in a place as small as that? Don't know. To cut to the chase, she suggested the father of her child and a few of his relatives for the job. He hired all three."

"Not sure I see the connection," Jonelle said.

The lawyer leaned back in his seat. "Rosemary said the other two watched everyone's comings and goings, and it made her nervous."

"He used them every day?"

Hackett nodded. "Rosemary said they also got paid for doing personal jobs for him around his house. She knows because she saw the bills."

Oh boy.

"Her impression was that Finkleberg asked them to keep an eye on her and Susanna."

"That include her baby's daddy?"

A smile creased Hackett's face. "To his credit, her boyfriend was the one who mostly ran errands. Rosemary was happy he was making money because she was having trouble getting child support out of him."

Hackett signed the check and reached down to pick up his briefcase. He glanced at his watch. "If I don't leave now, I'll miss the next panel."

He stood to leave and Jonelle stood with him.

"For my own curiosity, what do these men look like?"

She walked next to Hackett as he headed for the exit.

He turned toward her. "Native American. Dark hair, worn a little too long for my taste. Thick builds. Dark skin. That part of Michigan has a large Chippewa population."

"What're their names?"

"Yazzie. The last names of all three are Yazzie."

CHAPTER 37

"Let's see," Adrienne said, a glass of red wine poised between French-tipped fingers. "You start off with a dead woman who hid a boat load of money no one can find, an ex-husband who may or may not be so 'ex' and a nerdy, high-ranking government guy who's probably hiding something. Now you got another dead lady who's the twin of the first one." She pointed at Jonelle. "You got yourself a heck of a mess, girlfriend."

Jonelle sighed and stared into her own wineglass. "Don't I know it," she said. "And, unless the name Yazzie is as common up there as Smith or Jones is around here, the strange Native American woman I met in Michigan is related to the father of Rosemary's child."

Adrienne had dropped by on her way home from work and settled herself into the plush armchair. Jonelle's best friend was dressed in what was conservative for her: black leather skirt, red cowl-necked cashmere sweater and short black leather boots with five-inch heels. Jonelle tried stilettoes once. She still got a twinge in her lower back every time she relived the experience.

"So, what're you gonna do about it?"

"First thing I need to do is steer Burt in the right direction. At first I figured I couldn't betray anything to do with Sophia's case, but with her dead, all bets are off. Problem is, even though he's a friend—"

"Can't believe you two are still at the friend stage after all this time," Adrienne interrupted with a smile.

"Our friendship is still professional and I want to keep it that way, especially when it involves us working on the same case," Jonelle said, her back resting against the couch cushion. She swallowed the remaining liquid. "Sometimes I get the feeling he still doesn't take me seriously enough and I don't plan on waiting for him to realize I know what I'm doing. At this point, I don't have a problem with sharing everything I've found out, but I can't wait for him to act on it."

"Why not?" Adrienne asked. "Your client can't object."

"Because one of Finkleberg's thugs attacked me once, and he might try again."

"You a hundred percent sure they're connected with this guy?"

"They have to be. They sound like the group he hired to protect him and do his odd jobs. I just wonder if one of those jobs included murdering two people."

"Hmm." Adrienne reached over and poured more wine into her glass from the bottle sitting on the coffee table. "So, how're you gonna get this Finkleburke—"

"Finkle*berg*."

"Whatever. How're you gonna get him to fess up?"

Jonelle rubbed the cup of the empty wineglass back and forth between her hands. "Not sure. Guy's a little nervous and that's always a good thing—means he could make a mistake. But he's also smart. Smarter than he looks. My gut tells me he'll play along at being Mister Nice Guy, while his goons do the dirty work. They've staked out the condo once. I have to figure out how I can keep them on me until Burt can act."

Adrienne sat up straight and set her glass on the coffee table. Her face creased in a worried frown. "Whoa. Those guys know where you live? You better call the cops. Or at the very least, tell Marvin. He'll know what to do."

Jonelle took a deep, impatient breath. "Why do you always keep telling me to check with Marvin? You're as bad as Burt. I can handle this."

"You still packin' heat?"

Jonelle rolled her eyes to the ceiling. "Yes, I still have my gun, loaded and ready if I need it."

Several moments of silence hung in the air. Mention of the gun brought home that this was no longer a case of why Susanna Quinley ended up on the street. She knew the answer. Where else could a person hide in plain view? The homeless were the unseen. For most people it was almost an art form to pass by them every day as though they didn't exist. Several days without bathing, dirty hair, no makeup, dressed in old clothes and Susanna would blend right in. As far as keeping the hotel room, that was probably because she had to hide the money and that seemed like the safest place. Who'd expect someone carrying that amount of cash would stay in a hotel like that? So where was it? The cops had searched the Lancelot more than once.

She got up from the sofa and headed to her office.

"Where're you going?"

"Be back in a sec. I wrote down my conversation with a lawyer earlier today. I want to check on something."

Jonelle rummaged through the desk drawer in the spare bedroom she'd converted into an office. Inside were several notebooks. While she owned a laptop as well as a desktop, she found that writing down notes in longhand helped her think. She found the spiral-bound book she was looking for and returned to the living room to find Adrienne munching from a box of cheese crackers.

Jonelle pointed to the box. "Why didn't you pour some in a bowl? I might've wanted a few to nibble on."

"So go get a bowl, then," Adrienne said, hand deep inside the carton. "What you got there?"

Before she answered the question, Jonelle stepped into the kitchen, retrieved a small bowl, poured out a generous amount and returned the box to Adrienne. "Put it back when you're done."

"Oh, don't get pissy," Adrienne said with a grin. She pointed to the pad in Jonelle's hand, eyebrows raised.

"These are the notes I made after I talked to Winston Hackett, the lawyer who represented Rosemary, Susanna's accomplice. When I talked to her she appeared honest enough but I got the feeling she wasn't telling me everything. And I was right." Jonelle flipped through several pages. "She initially said no one else was involved. Now I find out someone high up knew about the embezzlement. I think that person is Finkleberg. He could help Susanna hide the theft while they accumulated a lot more money. Something happened that led Susanna to take what they had so far and leave before Finkleberg was ready and without his prior knowledge."

"What happened?"

"Not sure. Office rumors hinted at an affair. Maybe Susanna started making demands and threatened to tell his wife. He could've called her bluff, so she took off."

"Hmm." Adrienne crunched several crackers. "Did the wife know about the embezzlement?"

"I don't know. I doubt it. Too many people already knew what was going on."

"Didn't you say something about an audit? That could've done it."

Jonelle shook her head. "I thought so at first, but no. Who besides Susanna as treasurer would be concerned about someone going through the books? The commissioner? That was Finkleberg."

"Ah. So the two people who would've been alerted were the two who were already involved. Clever."

"And no one would've been the wiser until large sums of money turned up missing. And maybe not even then. I mean, who would've ratted them out?" Jonelle stood and began pacing. "I don't know why Finkleberg wanted her dead, though. The only plausible reason I can come up with is blackmail. She threatened to expose him, unless …"

"Unless what?"

Jonelle flopped back down on the sofa. "I don't know. She couldn't expose him without implicating herself. Damn. This whole mess makes my head hurt."

"People have been known to kill to protect their affairs and to avoid a messy divorce," Adrienne said. "Those psycho-nuts always think they can get away with it."

"True. Then he should've killed his wife. Not Susanna."

"Right. Now *I'm* starting to get a headache."

Jonelle reached over and poured herself another glass of wine. "I wonder if … let's assume they did have an affair. Suppose the wife found out and blamed Susanna, got pissed and hired a hit man."

"What does this guy Finkle*whatsit* look like? Is he a hottie?"

Jonelle's pulse raced; she was on to something. "No, but neither is Susanna's ex-husband. In fact, now that I really think about it, Kelly and Finkleberg kinda resemble each other. A lot of people get involved with the same type of person over and over. I like this theory … a lot."

Adrienne closed the box of crackers. "Where you gonna find a hit man in an itty-bitty town like that?"

"Doesn't matter how big the place is, people will do all kinds of things for money. Rosemary said Finkleberg hired her baby's daddy and other Chippewa family members as his chauffeur, bodyguards and to do odd jobs. His missus could've paid one of them."

"So, you think the wife's involved?"

Jonelle leaned forward, elbows on knees, head in her hands. "No. Doesn't make sense. She wouldn't send someone all the way down here. She'd be glad the woman was gone. Damn."

"What about Rosemary?"

"I can't see her engineering something like this. True, she was upset about Susanna leaving her to take the blame for everything. And, she was distraught about being stiffed on the money. So …" Jonelle shot up. "Maybe, just maybe the baby-daddy took matters into his own hands. That's a possibility. And the Yazzies would've found out where Susanna was because they hung around Finkleberg all day."

With wine glass raised in the air, Adrienne saluted Jonelle. "There you go."

Jonelle flipped through her notes on Sophia and scanned the pages. "Here's something else," she said, her brows furrowed. "I knew I had the twins' tattoos correct."

"What tattoos?"

"Burt said the autopsy on Susanna showed a red rose tattoo on her shoulder. Yet I wrote right here,"—she tapped the page—"that Sophia said *her* tattoo was a rose."

Adrienne uncrossed her legs and leaned forward. "What do you think that means?"

"There are two possible reasons. One, Sophia lied about it for some reason I can't fathom, or … she was telling the truth and she's not who she says she is, or was."

CHAPTER 38

After her conversation with Adrienne, Jonelle called Burt's phone and was disappointed when it went to voice mail. The differences in the tattoos was important and she wondered if the person she talked to was actually Susanna and that the other twin, Sophia, actually died first. Why would the twins reverse identities? And why not just admit to being Susanna instead of Sophia? Maybe, despite Luther's devotion to her, Susanna didn't completely trust him. Now that she thought about it, "Sophia's" questions about the man could have been a fishing expedition—a ploy to find out exactly how much Jonelle knew.

A quick call to the agency advised Rainey she wouldn't be in, with the excuse that she had some field work to do. Afterwards, Jonelle pulled on jeans, cross trainers, beige turtleneck and an oversized, brown wool, crewneck sweater. She checked to make sure the pistol had a full magazine and instead of tucking the weapon in her purse, strapped on a black leather holster between the two sweaters.

Jonelle pulled up the address of the hotel found on the documents in Kelly's office and plugged the address into her GPS system.

Adrenaline coursed through her veins. This wasn't the first time Jonelle felt exhilarated at the thought of finding herself in a dangerous situation. She didn't know whether or not to be concerned.

If her assumption was right this was where the men stayed and one of them had already attacked her once. Goosebumps erupted on her arms. She tried Burt's phone again and got the same result. This time, her message told him where she would be and why and also left information on the car the two men drove. After a slight pause, she suggested he mention the Yazzie name to Finkleberg. She knew Burt wouldn't like being told how to handle the situation and frankly, she didn't care.

After arriving at their hotel—a scant five miles from the Lancelot, Jonelle noticed—she drove at a snail's pace, up and down the parking lot. Near the entrance, on the north side of the building, she spotted the gray sedan and passed it by, noting there weren't many cars in this section. For the first time she regretted having her Jeep and wondered if maybe the agency could acquire a less distinctive company car. Jonelle aimed her vehicle toward the front of the building again, and as far away from the sedan as possible while still keeping the car in view. Pistol loaded and secured next to her body, Jonelle settled in to wait for her targets to come out.

She didn't have to wait long. A heavyset, brown-skinned man with long, straight black hair left the hotel via the front entrance. He stood under the green awning and lit a cigarette. Soon after, another man emerged who looked almost identical to the first one. She understood how everyone who'd seen the men referred to them as Mexican.

One of the men turned and looked in her direction. Jonelle slid down in the seat, her eyes peeking through the steering wheel. Although some distance away, she saw him cock his head as his eyes zoned in on her Jeep. Damn. The first one turned his head and said something to the other, who also looked in her direction. They left the portico and the taller of the two headed in her direction. Jonelle unsnapped the holster and removed her gun. She slid further down in her seat so that her eyes were level with the dashboard. The tall man kept coming.

About twenty feet away from Jonelle's car, the other man called out, "Leave it. We gotta git goin'." The man stopped. Before he walked back to his companion, he looked right at Jonelle and smiled.

Although it took all the nerve she could muster, Jonelle sat up and tried to smile back, but the muscles in her face wouldn't work.

After the second Yazzie returned to his brother, they both got in the car without another look in her direction. With her cover blown, Jonelle could either give up her plan to follow or go ahead and see where the situation led. She chose the second option.

The gray sedan exited the front of the hotel and turned right. Jonelle waited until two cars pulled in front of her before taking the same route. Since they knew she was behind them, Jonelle wondered if they'd take her on a wild goose chase. Only one way to find out. After ten minutes of tailing the sedan, Jonelle's phone sounded. With one hand she scrounged through her bag, found her phone and glanced at the screen.

"Burt. Thank goodness it's you. I've got myself in a bit of a … uh … situation."

She listened as Burt asked her to join him at the station. Finkleberg had returned and had agreed to cooperate.

"I'm not surprised," Jonelle said. She told him about the two men and what she knew up to that point was the connection to the twins. "At first I thought they were Finkleberg's 'muscle' but now I'm not so sure. Rosemary Wilkins' lawyer gave me vital information about the embezzlement, which takes this whole mess in a different direction."

As the gray sedan pulled into the parking lot of a Walmart, Jonelle ditched the idea of tailing them any further. The interview with Finkleberg presented more possibilities to get answers to what was going on.

A scant forty minutes later, Jonelle entered the detective's division. She'd given Burt her promise that she'd be a silent witness to Finkleberg's interrogation. He'd grudgingly given her special permission since her client was murdered and might have information to help solve the case. If Finkleberg asked for a lawyer, she'd have to leave.

Once inside the small, windowless, gray-walled, room, Jonelle felt her chest tighten. For a brief moment she didn't have to worry about keeping her mouth shut, her claustrophobia would do it for her.

Finkleberg was already seated at the small metal desk, with Burt opposite. Before Jonelle sat next to Burt she made a request. "Mind if I keep the door open a little?" Burt nodded.

Jonelle sat and studied Finkleberg. A fine sheen of sweat glazed his brow. His skin had the pasty look of someone suffering from a bad case of the flu. A box of tissues sat in the middle of the table, yet he didn't touch them. Jonelle hoped he didn't keel over before they had a chance to ask their questions.

"You okay?"

Finkleberg managed a slow nod.

Jonelle turned to Burt. "Think we can get him something to drink? I'd like a bottle of water myself."

"It's on the way," Burt said. No sooner had the words left his mouth, than a quick knock on the partially opened door allowed another detective to enter with three bottles of water, which he placed in the middle of the table without comment. Both Finkleberg and Jonelle reached for a bottle.

"Okay," Burt said. "Let's get started." He cleared his throat. "The victim, known as Sophia Quinley Reyes, was found in the alley near the Lancelot Inn and about three blocks from the location where her sister, Susanna, was murdered. This was less than five miles from the warehouse where

Susanna stayed on occasion." He shot a sharp look at Jonelle. She stared back without comment.

He continued. "Mrs. Reyes was killed in the same manner; her throat cut, her face painted white, with black around the eyes and mouth. "

A strangled cry emerged from Finkleberg's throat. Gone was the arrogant individual she'd talked to earlier.

"Mr. Finkleberg, you're in Maryland because of your knowledge about why Susanna Quinley left her job in Michigan. You stated that she had embezzled money from the county and you wanted to know what we'd done to find and return the money to Michigan. Is that correct?"

He nodded.

"And you've been informed that the money hasn't been recovered. Is that correct?"

"Yes."

"Has anyone contacted you as to the whereabouts of the missing money?"

"No."

"You sure about that?" Jonelle asked, eliciting a frown from Burt.

Finkleberg glared at Jonelle without speaking.

"Do you have any idea who might have killed Susanna Quinley?" Burt asked.

Finkleberg inhaled deeply and sipped water before answering. "No. And I have no idea who killed Sophia either." He put his head in his hand. "This is getting out of control. I don't know what the hell is going on."

Jonelle pulled out her notes from her Hackett interview. "Do you know who Robert, Sherman and Alex Yazzie are?"

Burt shot her an angry look, which she ignored.

"Well?"

"Jonelle. I thought I asked you to ..."

She turned toward Burt. "I know. But I might have some information that could help you, if you'd just let me get it out. Okay? You can tell me to leave, but at least hear what I have to say." She focused back on Finkleberg. "Do you know the men?"

"I know them. Oldenberry is a small community. Everybody knows everybody. Secrets are hard to keep."

"Someone told me you hired them as bodyguards and to do, um, odd jobs."

"I bet I know who that someone is. So what?"

No way was Jonelle going to admit she'd burgled Kelly's office. "I came across their names again because two men in a gray sedan were watching me. I discovered the car was a rental, so after some, um, investigating I determined that they were the ones who leased the car. What I don't know is why they were following me."

Burt shifted in the seat next to her. She was afraid to meet his eyes. He knew better than she did that rental companies don't give out that information.

Lines appeared on Finkleberg's brow. "How would I know the answer to that?"

"Because when I followed you and Kelly to that bar in west Baltimore, I was grabbed from behind, dragged down the street and hit on the head. A couple of ladies stopped him and the man they described reminded me of one of the two who shadowed me." She pointed at Finkleberg. "Did you know they were here?"

Burt held up his hand. "Don't answer that, Mr. Finkleberg. I called you in to provide a basic status report and to see if you could shed any light on why the second twin was killed. This is going in a direction vastly different from the one I had anticipated. Your appearance here is entirely voluntary. If you want to leave, you can. I have nothing to charge you with … at this point."

Finkleberg blanched. "Charge me? Do you plan on arresting me?"

"Not unless I have to. So I'd appreciate it if you'd cooperate since you knew both victims."

No one spoke for several seconds. A few times Finkleberg stood as if ready to leave, but changed his mind.

Burt glared at Jonelle. "You might have told me what was going on instead of having me find out here." He waved his arms around the cramped interview room.

Jonelle bristled. "The reason I didn't was because—"

"I'm not finished," Burt interrupted, his voice rising to a level she hadn't heard before. "If I didn't know you as well as I do and if I didn't respect your skills as a PI, you'd be out of here so fast everybody'd get wind burn."

After a few moments of uncomfortable silence, a somewhat chastened Jonelle asked, "So, I can stay?"

"For now."

Finkleberg's head had swiveled from one to the other as the exchange played out. His gaze settled back on Jonelle.

"To continue," she said, with a sideways glance at Burt, "why are they here?"

"I don't know. You might want to ask Barry that question."

Burt piped up. "Did they know you were coming here?"

After a slight hesitation, Finkleberg nodded. "I swear to God I told them I could handle everything myself."

"Why'd they come? What's in it for them?" Jonelle asked.

Finkleberg ignored the question, clutched his water bottle and drank.

"Was Kelly aware you were coming to Maryland?" Burt asked.

"Sure. He's a friend. I thought maybe I could stay with him, you know, save money on the hotel. But, he said no. Some friend, huh?"

"Is money an issue with you?" Jonelle asked.

A red flush crept up Finkleberg's neck. "This isn't about me."

Jonelle thought otherwise.

"What reason did he give for you not staying with him?" From the tone of Burt's voice, she could tell he wasn't happy with the turn of events.

"Said he didn't have the space and that considering all that went on with Susanna, it was probably best I didn't stay with him. Might look funny." Finkleberg snorted.

Jonelle decided to present information Rosemary's lawyer told her as rumor rather than fact. "Susanna hinted to Rosemary, that the embezzlement wouldn't be discovered because—let me make sure I say this right—someone high up was involved so their crime would be invisible. Rosemary assumed you were that person."

Finkleberg started to rise.

"Sit down please," Burt said.

"I think I'd like a lawyer," Finkleberg said. He started sweating again.

"You're not under arrest," Burt said.

"In that case, I'm leaving."

Burt held up his hand. "Wouldn't you like to clear up a few things? I'd hate to have to consider you a person of interest in both murders."

"What?" Finkleberg sounded as if he got something huge stuck in his throat. He fell back into his seat. "I might have done some things I shouldn't have, but I'm no murderer."

"Well, someone is, and at this point the logical person is you," Jonelle said. "I can see why you'd want Susanna dead—she knew you were involved in the embezzlement. Rosemary also said the original idea was to take a lot more than they ended up with, but that you and Susanna had an argument about your affair and Susanna decided to split with what they had already. That about right?"

Rosemary didn't specifically name Finkleberg, but the man sitting across from her didn't know that.

Jonelle didn't think it was possible for Finkleberg to get any whiter than he was, but he paled even more. She glanced over at Burt. She didn't want the man to die on them. He really didn't look well. Burt must have read her mind.

"Do you need a break?"

Finkleberg leaned his elbows on the desk and placed his head in his hands. "I can't believe this is happening."

Silence in the air took on an almost physical presence.

Jonelle interrupted the stillness that permeated the small room. "What about Sophia?"

Finkleberg raised his head.

"Were the two of you in contact with each other after Susanna took the money and ran?"

Finkleberg remained tight-lipped.

Burt smacked his hand on the desk. Finkleberg and Jonelle jumped at the sound.

"Normally I'm a patient man. But I'm looking at two murders here and I don't like it one bit. Things will go a whole lot easier for you if you're upfront with me. Were you and Sophia Reyes in contact with one another?"

For a moment Jonelle had the sick feeling that Finkleberg would clam up and insist that Burt either charge him with a crime or he walked. Fortunately, like most people, he was intimidated by the authority inherent in the law. The look on his face told Jonelle that he weighed the trouble he was in with how to come out of the mess unscathed.

"Okay." He slumped back in his chair. "Yes, I knew Sophia was here because she told me she'd kept in contact with Susanna. Susanna didn't just screw me, she also screwed her sister. The fact is, we all were supposed to benefit from the, uh, scheme. The plan was to embezzle about twenty-two million total—about ten million each for me and Susanna. Susanna had promised to give Sophia some of her take to help ease her sister's financial burden. Two million for Rosemary and everyone would leave the country. Susanna was always vindictive; she couldn't put her personal animosity aside and just go through with the plan. She wanted more. She wanted me to leave my wife so the two of us could share our cut and I couldn't do that."

Jonelle didn't believe they had planned to give Rosemary two million dollars. She let it go. "Did your wife know what was going on?"

"No," he said, a little too loudly.

If it wasn't for the fact that there were two dead women, Jonelle would almost feel sorry for the man.

"Rosemary's boyfriend also worked for you. Maybe the brothers were pissed because she has a young child and you guys stiffed her on the money and left her to take the blame for everything."

"Listen," Finkleberg said in a stronger voice. "Nobody was supposed to die. Ever. You have to believe me when I say I don't know why the twins were killed. I didn't do it. If the Yazzie brothers were involved they either did it on their own or somebody else paid them."

"What other reason would they have to kill the sisters?" Burt asked.

"I have no idea. To my knowledge they'd never killed anyone before."

Jonelle fingered the gold necklace. "Did you offer them some of the money to keep quiet about the embezzlement?"

A large, frustrated sigh escaped Finkleberg. "Yes. I had to. They drove me to the bank several times. More times than I needed for personal business. Plus, Susanna and I felt it safer to use the Limo when we, uh, met. It seemed more private, more secure."

"So, when Susanna split, they got nothing, right?" Burt asked.

Finkleberg nodded.

"Seems like they're eliminating everyone involved in this."

Jonelle agreed. She held Finkleberg's gaze. "They can't get to Rosemary; she's in prison. Looks like you're the only one left."

Finkleberg's eyes watered behind his glasses.

"Not exactly," Burt reminded Jonelle. "There's still Kelly." Burt stood. "Stay here the both of you. I need to make a phone call."

The door clicked as Burt left. Jonelle had no intention of waiting for him to return to pursue her own ideas about the case. "You got yourself into one helluva mess, Norman."

To her great satisfaction, he nodded. "I don't know how this got out of hand."

"Do you have any idea where Susanna stashed the money?"

Finkleberg shook his head.

"The police looked all over that hotel room in Baltimore. The manager said Susanna had him lock up a leather satchel in his office, but it's not there." Jonelle stood as tightness developed in her chest. "Sorry, but I've gotta open the door a crack." Afterwards, she stuck her head out and took several deep breaths.

"Touch of claustrophobia," she said and decided to go for broke. "I think those two goons spooked Susanna and she took the money and hid it somewhere. They don't know where it is either, which is why I suspect they followed me. Were you with Sophia when she took an envelope out of Kelly's desk?"

"What … how?" He looked incredulous.

Jonelle had to take advantage of the fact Burt was out of the room. With him in charge, she couldn't be as free to ask what she wanted without implicating herself. Plus, she was getting sick and tired of Finkleberg dancing around the truth.

"I'm asking the questions right now. Well?" Jonelle put all the authority in her voice she could muster. Bottom line: if Finkleberg clammed up there wasn't a thing she could do about it. She tried not to show her relief as he answered her question.

"Sophia was spooked when she noticed the Yazzie brothers also following her. She accused me of hiring them to tail her, but I convinced her I didn't. Since it wasn't me, the only other person involved had to be Kelly so she wanted to search his office. Everything was locked up but Sophia knew he kept a spare key under the pen and pencil holder—except it wasn't there. So we had to uh, force the drawer open."

"How did she know about a key?"

Finkleberg raised his hand. "I swear I don't know. We found an envelope with a few documents and left with it. That's all."

Jonelle believed him on that point. She tried a different tack. "Was Sophia here before Susanna was killed?"

"Yes."

"Were you and Sophia in contact that entire time?"

Finkleberg swallowed hard. "Yes … and no."

"What does that mean?"

"Susanna called a few times. Mostly to taunt me, I think. On each call I tried to convince her to return the money. She screwed us all when she split early. Sophia was supposed to convince her to come clean, but she failed. So, Sophia said she'd try and find out where the money was and let me know. No harm, no foul."

"Except for the fact someone slit Susanna's throat."

"I almost lost it when you called and told me."

Jonelle had trouble believing him. "You mean to say that Sophia didn't call you right away? I've been told that the two were seen together just before Susanna's murder."

He shook his head over and over. "Your phone call was the first I'd heard about her death."

"Did you speak to Sophia afterwards?"

He sat back in his chair. He looked as if the weight he'd been carrying around was slowly dissipating. "Oh, yeah. We were both freaked. Sophia even more so."

"Can't blame her considering it was her sister."

"Yeah. But … she seemed different somehow."

"What do you mean?"

"More scared than angry. Not as self-assured as before. Sophia was always the ring leader. The one Susanna looked to, to plan things. Now she was acting, I don't know, lost I guess is the best word. You know?"

"Go on."

"We talked after she hired you. And she said something peculiar." He paused.

Jonelle gestured for him to get on with it. Any moment now Burt would reappear.

"Well, she said she needed help in recovering the money. As I said, she felt she was being followed and was getting nervous."

Jonelle honed in on the remark. "Hold on. She said *recovering*, not *finding*"

"It didn't hit me until later," Finkleberg said with a nod. "We were so focused trying to figure out what Kelly knew that I completely forgot about what she'd said."

Jonelle opened her mouth to ask another question but stopped as Burt entered. He had a frown on his dark, round face. "I tried calling Kelly but couldn't reach him."

"You try his home? Oh, sorry, I'm sure you did." Burt's expression warned Jonelle he was in no mood to be second-guessed.

"After I tried his cell I called his office. The people there are worried. They haven't seen him in a few days and aren't able to reach him. I dispatched a few uniforms to check out his place. I've got a bad feeling about this."

CHAPTER 39

Fear brought out the worst in people. And based on everything Finkleberg had revealed, those involved had an acute case of the nerves. Jonelle also knew there was no need for her to pursue anything since her client was dead. The advance Sophia had paid covered the expense of traveling to Michigan and the several hours of work up to her death. Case closed? Not exactly. If anything, Jonelle was more determined than ever to find out what was going on.

She'd already withstood Burt's wrath when she gave him information on what she knew about the two men. Finkleberg mentioned their prior arrests in the Upper Peninsula and Burt had left to issue a BOLO—be on the lookout—for the Yazzie brothers. When he returned, she told him she had a plan for enticing the men to reveal themselves. Since they were on to her, she knew they wouldn't be too far away. The idea of using herself as bait to tempt the men into action was met with strong disapproval from the detective.

"Uh-uh. No way. If these two are our killers, you're risking your life. I can't let you do that."

"Hear me out. You know I can handle myself, and I won't take unnecessary risks. All I want to do is lure these guys out in the open. How about it?"

Burt rubbed his head. "It's that word *unnecessary* that I'm worried about. What I'm gonna do is pay them a visit at their hotel. See if I can get a sense of where they're coming from.

Think I'll mention the fact I know they've been following you. See what kinda reaction I get."

Finkleberg, who'd watched the entire exchange, piped up. "I vote for letting her try. Those guys are street smart. They're used to dealing with the cops, so you're not gonna get much out of them. I don't want to end up like the Quinley twins."

Burt shot him a look which forced Finkleberg to slump back in his chair. "We're doing it my way."

All the way home, Jonelle had kept one eye on her rear view mirror, wondering if she'd see the familiar gray sedan somewhere behind. Every time a gray car of any type came into view, Jonelle tensed. If she didn't relax, Burt's assessment of the situation and her involvement in it would prove him right to be concerned. Jonelle didn't want that to happen. While he tried, and failed, to get her to promise not to do anything until he could gather enough police resources, it became obvious to her that the two men were operating on their own. What was the trigger which led them to kill both women?

The fact that Burt couldn't reach Kelly worried Jonelle. The man didn't appear able to control two seasoned felons. With these murderous goings-on taking place all around her, Jonelle felt a desperate need to sort everything out. Something nagged at her just beyond her grasp and she knew she had to pull it in before it slipped away.

Jonelle drew up in front of her building. Before she slid the Jeep into her assigned spot, she scanned the area. No sign of the men or the gray sedan. She locked and engaged the Jeep's alarm before rushing to the entrance. Once inside she didn't even stop to check the mail. No time. Adrienne should've left the university by now, unless she'd been delayed. A quick call followed by a promise to stop by in thirty minutes made her feel better.

She had little in her refrigerator to offer her skinny, yet somehow always hungry friend. A jar of creamy peanut butter and wheat crackers, a frozen pizza and a container of hummus with sesame seed breadsticks were all she had to suggest as a snack. She did however have every slot in her wine rack filled.

A little over half an hour later the buzzer sounded on the outside door of the building's security system. Normally she'd just press the release since she expected Adrienne. This time, she poked her head outside her unit and walked to the spot where she could see outside the glass doors. Adrienne stood with one hand on the door handle and the other around a large plastic bag. Jonelle walked over and opened the door. She looked up and down the street.

"Why didn't you buzz me in?" Adrienne asked.

"Wanted to make sure it was you, first."

Adrienne followed Jonelle, and stopped outside the condo. "Isn't that why you have an intercom? It's not broke, is it?" She cocked her head. "Hey. How come I don't hear music?"

"Hamilton's away."

"Darn."

"The intercom works. Just needed to check on something outside. What's in the bag?"

"Knowing your 'empty cupboard' syndrome, I decided to stop and pick up Chinese. Hunan shrimp for you and shrimp with garlic sauce for me."

"Egg rolls?"

"Of course. Wouldn't be Chinese food without them."

Idle chit-chat prevailed while Jonelle dished out the food and poured glasses of white wine. Never one to beat around the bush more than necessary, Jonelle plunged right in to the dilemma she faced. "Do you remember the case I've been working on? Sophia Reyes, twin of the murdered Susanna Quinley?"

Adrienne nodded, mouth full of food. "Hmm."

"And about Sophia's murder, right?"

Adrienne nodded.

"At first, I thought the county commissioner was involved, especially after Susanna's accomplice told her lawyer that the plan was originally to steal a helluva lot more than just the 300,000, and that their tracks were covered by someone higher up. The only higher up above Susanna was Finkleberg."

"He's the commish, right?"

"Yep. He came down here at Burt's request to help with trying to figure out what might've happened to the missing money. And I think he was the one with Sophia who searched Kelly's office."

Adrienne stopped chewing. "And you know this, how?"

Her best friend knew her better than anyone, except her uncle. "Kelly's main office area was already open, so technically I didn't really break in."

The look on Adrienne's face indicated she didn't buy the explanation.

Jonelle continued. "Anyway, once I got one of the desk drawers open"—Adrienne sighed dramatically, which Jonelle ignored—"there was an envelope with car rental and hotel receipts. The car rental papers showed the sedan that had been following me as well as the name of a hotel. I know the Yazzie brothers drove that car and stayed at that hotel."

The entire time Jonelle talked, Adrienne had sipped wine without comment.

"Everyone suspects Susanna originally hid the money in the hotel's office," Jonelle said.

"Why not put the money in the hotel's safe?"

"The place is kinda shabby. All the manager could offer was to lock it inside. Imagine all that money sitting in a flimsy, locked closet."

Adrienne waved her chopsticks at Jonelle. "Continue."

"This is where it gets hairy. Only two people were supposed to be involved. Finkleberg and Susanna. Susanna wanted help from Rosemary who, as a single mother and for a share of the money, was more than willing to keep her mouth shut when she noticed her boss funneling cash into different accounts. Though, to be honest, I think a person could've waved money in front of Rosemary's face and she wouldn't put two and two together."

"Elevator gets stuck a few floors from the top?"

"That about sums it up. So, now we've got three people who know about the embezzlement. To make matters worse, Susanna and Finkleberg got into a major argument having to do with their affair, and I find out one of the men hired by him to do quote, odd jobs, is Rosemary's baby-daddy."

A sly grin crept slowly across Adrienne's face. "I love it. 'Rosemary's baby.'"

Jonelle rolled her eyes. "Anyway, they wanted to embezzle several million, but after the fall out, Susanna got pissed, took what they'd accumulated so far and she and Rosemary split."

"And good ole Rosemary ended up in jail. And the baby-daddy is pissed."

Jonelle nodded. She took a few bites and drank wine before continuing. "My guess is Susanna noticed the men, got scared and called Kelly. He claims he knew nothing about the embezzlement, but I don't believe him, and Finkleberg said as much. Claimed when he called Kelly and told him what Susanna had done, Kelly admitted he'd heard from her."

"So now, we've got, what, four people involved in this?"

"Five. I'm convinced Susanna told Sophia."

Adrienne reached over, grabbed the wine bottle and filled her glass. "Talk about amateurs. Why not send out a bulletin for crissakes?"

"Exactly." Jonelle played with her necklace. "See, I think Kelly tried to help Susanna as a way to get back into her life. Guy still loved her."

"Ahh. Okay. So the two bad guys did all this killing for Rosemary? Seems a bit extreme."

"Problem was you had all these people circling each other and nobody really talking to anybody else. Rosemary didn't know where Susanna was, so she couldn't have sent the Yazzie brothers down here. My guess is when Kelly told Finkleberg he'd heard from Susanna Finkleberg sent the brothers here to get the money back. But, in order for that to happen Susanna had to tell them where she hid the cash. I'm guessing she wouldn't … or couldn't. So, when Kelly heard Susanna was killed, he got nervous."

Adrienne wiped her mouth on a napkin, and held it to her lips, suppressing a burp. "Tell me something. If your client's dead, why are you involved in this mess? I'll just bet Burt isn't too happy."

Jonelle grimaced. "I don't really care if Burt is happy or not. I want to find out why Susanna and Sophia were killed. And here's another thing. The community up there is really small and close-knit. It didn't take long for the bulletin to go out about me and what I was doing there."

"No offense, but you couldn't exactly blend in with the natives. Am I right?"

Jonelle ignored the dig. "My point is, once the plan opened to more than the two having knowledge about it, all bets were off. We find Kelly, everything falls into place."

"So, where is he?"

"Don't know. He's not at his office or at home. He could've left the area. Or … damn!" Jonelle bolted upright.

"What?"

"I think I know where he is."

CHAPTER 40

The next day, Jonelle rejected Adrienne's pleas to wait until she got off work so that she could go with her.

"Okay, fine. But no matter what," Adrienne had said, "you call and let me know what's going on, or I'm calling the cavalry."

Jonelle had dismissed the idea that Kelly would go back to the hotel where Susanna stayed because he couldn't risk running into the Yazzie brothers. In spite of everything that had transpired, Jonelle still had problems believing that Kelly was the force behind Susanna's death. Not only that, why kill Sophia? She had to find the missing doctor. The location was obvious once she thought about it. Susanna hid in plain sight, so why not her ex?

Driving on DC streets always made Jonelle nervous. The city was one of those places that practically insisted all persons not familiar with the area had best take public transportation unless one had a death wish. Jonelle didn't want to waste time trying to figure out what mode of transportation she needed to get to the marina in the southwest quadrant of the city, so she plugged in the address on her GPS and hoped for the best.

Almost an hour later, after swearing at the myriad of no left turn signs in the city, she arrived at the marina only to be faced with a large notice outside the open-air parking lot that stated a permit was required. Damn.

She took a deep breath, plastered the best smile she could muster and approached the kiosk. A bored looking middle-aged white man looked up from the small screen perched on his counter.

"Help you?" he asked in a voice that hoped she'd say no.

"Yes, please. I'm here to see Doctor Barrington Kelly. I need to—"

"You need a permit to park here," he said, interrupting her. He pointed to the sign.

Jonelle forced herself to remain calm. "I know that … sir. Doctor Kelly called with an urgent request to see me as soon as possible. He might not have had time to let you know. The truth is, he sounded a bit, um, frantic. I'm sure you have visitor's parking." She looked around and noticed a few spots to the left of the security hut that confirmed the statement. She smiled at the man again.

He rolled his eyes while simultaneously pulling out a clipboard. "Name?"

"Mind if I reach in my purse to show you my ID?"

The man shrugged.

She pulled out her PI shield and showed it to him. A slight widening of his eyes indicated she'd finally gotten his complete attention. Jonelle recited her name, cellphone and PI shield numbers. He cocked his head over to the side, indicating where she should park her vehicle.

"Thanks," she said, happy he didn't put up any further resistance. He grunted his reply and went back to watching his screen.

With that barrier removed, Jonelle walked down the path from the lot to the marina and faced a large, octagonal building with a blue roof. Printed below the front window was the word "Security" in red and below that, "Dockmaster." Directly behind, a chain link fence fanned from both sides of the structure and wrapped all the way around as far as she could see. Jonelle sighed. This place had more layers of protection than the Baltimore airport. She inched closer to the fence. While she knew Kelly's boat existed, Jonelle had no idea if this was the correct marina, nor what he named the vessel. The reference about the existence of the craft was so casual, she didn't ask for any details. Now she could kick herself as she gazed out on all the many vessels bobbing in the water.

A loud, rhythmic *wop, wop* of blades sounded above her head. She squinted at the large olive green helicopter. Definitely not a traffic copter. Then she remembered the Pentagon lay a few miles south.

Not wanting to initiate a game of twenty questions, she skirted the building and ambled over to the first gate in the fence like she belonged. She walked up and read the sign that entrance required a special card to slide in the security slot. Shoot. She explored the mechanism for some kind of button to push. Surely there were times when owners misplaced their cards. Ahh, there it was. Jonelle pressed the button and waited. Footsteps sounded behind her. She turned and watched a portly gentleman in blue work clothes and with billowing white hair stride in her direction.

"Noticed you when you passed by," he said. "You could've stopped by the office instead of standing out here. Would've saved us both a little time."

"Sorry," Jonelle said sheepishly. "I didn't think. Dr. Kelly asked me to deliver several forms to him, but he forgot to tell me how to get in here."

The man nodded without saying a word. Gray eyes never wavered from Jonelle's face.

"Fact is, he's a client of mine." The man's eyes narrowed at the word *client*.

"Mind if I reach inside my bag? That's where I keep my private investigator's shield."

Again, the wordless nod.

Jonelle dug into her purse and after showing him her ID, came up with a manila folder that she'd intended to leave in her office. "He needs to sign these ASAP and since I didn't want the papers delivered by a courier, here I am. But, uh, I forgot the boat's name." Jonelle's face felt hot. She'd need to practice how to lie if she was ever going to get any good. "I think the name was something like *Suzy Q* or …"

"You mean *Oh Susanna* I think."

Thank goodness for helpful, trusting people, she thought.

"That sounds right. Is it okay if I go on in and deliver the information? It's important I give it to him personally." That last statement was intended to cover her in case Mister Helpful offered to deliver it himself.

He studied her a bit more before responding. "Now you're standing at A dock." He pointed to the right. "I think the craft is down there near the T—not sure of the exact slip number—on H dock. But you can't get on the dock without a key card. Sorry. Maybe you can give him a call to come meet you?"

Oh damn. "The T? What's that?"

He gave her a lopsided grin. "It's what we call the spaces at the end of each dock. He's lucky. Those're easy to get in and out of. If we were on hard ground, where he's located would be considered prime real estate."

"So. If this is A that means I have to walk all the way down there?" Jonelle pointed in the distance. Good thing she was wearing her cross trainers. "Thanks. I'll walk closer down and call him." She turned to go. And maybe I'll slip in behind another helpful citizen, she thought.

Jonelle strolled in the direction pointed out to her by the dockmaster, and found she didn't mind the walk at all. The cloudless blue sky had just a touch of chill in the air, a faint hint of more to come. At several intervals a sign announced the piers in each section. She stopped and faced a sign that included the H pier. She nudged the gate a little, in case one of the boaters forgot to engage the latch and was disappointed to find she couldn't get in. Jonelle pulled out her phone in the hope that maybe Kelly would answer her call.

After letting the number ring several times she got his voicemail and left another urgent message. The man had to be here. Where else could he go? She turned around hoping against hope that someone would come her way. Her wish was answered but it wasn't the one she wanted A security guard headed straight for her.

Uh-oh. From the purposeful way he strode as he came closer, Jonelle knew the delivery ruse wouldn't work, so she'd try a little bit of truth and a little bit of … not so much truth.

"Hi," she said, before he spoke. "I'm on my way to see Dr. Barrington Kelly. Would you happen to know if he's aboard the *Oh Susanna*?" It worked. The frown on his face relaxed. Still, the man looked as if he took his job seriously.

"Is he expecting you ma'am?"

"I'm a private investigator working for his sister-in-law. Mind if I reach in my bag to show you my badge?"

He nodded.

Jonelle pulled out her leather case. His hazel eyes widened as he studied the badge. She'd definitely have to thank Marvin and give him feedback on the badge's effect. There was no name on the man's dark green shirt, and as she studied him, she figured he was only about ten years older than her own thirty-two.

"Looks okay. I'll go ahead and let you in, but please remind Dr. Kelly again that we need to know when he's expecting visitors. That way, we won't have to detain you."

Again? "I understand."

The guard disengaged the lock and opened the gate. "Just touch the red button on the other side to get out," he said.

Jonelle thanked him and went off in search of Kelly's boat. A few minutes later she found the dock. She stepped on the pier and pulled back. She tested one foot and then the other. The pier's movement unnerved her a little so she stopped and waited for her legs to settle underneath her. Confident now, she eased down the long floating walkway. Jonelle knew very little about boats. Intrigued at the many different sizes and styles, she was amazed that the few closest to the dock actually resembled the type of house a person could buy on dry land. She ambled down toward the two boats moored at the end.

CHAPTER 41

Now for the hard part. By all accounts Kelly appeared afraid of something. When fear took hold and became the overriding force, rational people often became irrational. Jonelle knew she could defend herself, but at what cost? Surprise wasn't her friend in this case.

The *Oh Susanna* rocked gently on the water in front of her. Next to the boat was a set of wooden steps painted blue. Jonelle took a deep breath and climbed aboard. Once again, the sway unnerved her and she gripped the steering wheel to settle herself. "Doctor Kelly? It's Jonelle Sweet. I have some bad news to tell you about Sophia. Hello?"

She looked around. Except for the guard she'd encountered earlier, no one else was out and about. Jonelle remembered something she'd seen on television. "Uh. Permission to come aboard." Once the words left her mouth, she felt ridiculous; she was already on board. No response from inside. Rather than stand outside and draw attention to herself, Jonelle took a leap of faith, opened the door in front of her and entered the cabin.

A mug of what looked like black coffee sat on a teak table with sage green placemats. Jonelle picked up the cup and noticed how cold it felt. She sniffed. Stale coffee aroma and something sharp assaulted her nose. Jonelle stared at a closed door at the opposite end.

"Dr. Kelly? I'm alone, Doctor. I need to talk to you. Finkleberg is talking to the police about the twins' deaths and they want to help you." At least she hoped that was Burt's plan. She rapped hard against the door. "I don't believe you had anything to do with the murder of either twin, so, if you want protection, you need to tell me what you know."

Jonelle heard movement from the other side. She stepped a few feet away so as not to intimidate him and also to give her space to retreat if necessary. "I need to ask you a few more questions," she called out, "since I haven't been able to reach you at your office or on the phone."

A muffled voice came through the door. "How'd you find me?"

Jonelle sighed. "Look, Doctor. This'll go a whole lot easier without this door between us."

"It's open."

Jonelle reached inside her bag and felt for the pistol. She took a deep breath and opened the door to find Kelly sitting on a large bed in a teak-covered room with a drink in his hand. "Meet my good friend Johnny," he said, raising the glass in the air. He giggled. She smelled the liquor before she noticed the half empty bottle on the nightstand.

A few feet away, a silver-plated revolver lay next to the bottle.

Uh-oh. Jonelle tried not to show how alarmed she was, but Kelly's eyes followed her gaze on the gun.

"It's all been too much, too much," he said in an eerily calm voice.

"How about we sit out front? If you want, I'll make you a cup of coffee if you show me where everything is, in the uh, galley I think it's called." Jonelle inched closer to the weapon.

Kelly picked up the weapon. "Nope. You need to stay where you are."

She stopped. "Fine. But let's sit out front. There's more space so we'd both be more comfortable." Jonelle's hand curved around the grip of her pistol. She'd achieved the rank of sharpshooter and would use those skills if necessary, although in the doctor's inebriated state, she didn't think he could hit her even at this close range.

The sides of Kelly's mouth curled up. "Don't worry. If anybody's blood paints these walls, it'll be mine."

"Please?" She gestured to the main cabin.

He grunted. As he attempted to stand, the glass fell from his hand. Instead of retrieving it, he grabbed the liquor bottle and pulled himself up. He swayed several times and after sidling past her, gestured with the pistol for her to sit across from him at the table.

"Please don't wave that thing at me."

"Oops. Sorry. Where's my manners?" he giggled again. After a few beats, he placed the gun in the center of the table and poured himself a generous amount of whiskey in the coffee cup. Two swallows later, bloodshot eyes squinted at Jonelle. "How'd you find me anyway? Not many people know about my girl here."

Jonelle decided that if she needed Kelly to be honest with her, she'd come clean on a few things. "I saw the picture on your desk and since this is the closest marina to your office, I decided to take a chance. It didn't take much for me to figure out the name." She held his gaze. "Looks like you're in a bit of trouble."

"Doesn't matter anymore." He sipped more alcohol. In the short time she'd been there he'd drained and refilled his glass. She had no idea when he started drinking, but the man didn't look good. Time to get as much out of him as she could before he passed out.

"What's your relationship with the Yazzie's?"

Kelly gagged. He put his hand over his mouth and Jonelle sat back. She was afraid he was about to spurt brown liquid, and whatever else, on top of her. Instead, he shook his head over and over.

"I ... don't know what you're talking about," he gasped.

"Sure you do. I discovered them following me and put two and two together. Well?"

A weak smile played over his lips. "You broke into my office, didn't you?" His bloodshot eyes held hers.

"I wasn't the only one." He winced at that remark.

"Sometimes you gotta dig through a lot of muck before you get to the clean surface below. I've seen those guys from a distance and I know from personal experience what they're capable of. I'm starting to believe they are the prime suspects in Susanna's and Sophia's deaths. And they're still here, which tells me they aren't finished. What I can't figure out is why." She pointed to Kelly. "That's where you come in."

Jonelle waited while Kelly poured more liquor.

"Listen. I'm not leaving here until you answer my questions. The police are not happy they've got two murders on their hands and since Finkleberg is cooperating, you're next on their agenda. Might help your case if you're more forthcoming."

He reached forward and touched the gun.

Jonelle's stomach clenched. She relaxed a bit as he left the weapon where it was on the table and sat back.

"Susanna should've stuck with the plan. Instead, she included that dipshit Rosemary and started diddling Finkleberg." He smirked. "'Course she always did like dominating people."

"How was the plan supposed to work?" Jonelle already knew part of it from Finkleberg but she wanted to hear Kelly's version.

"Simple. She set up a few bank accounts under bogus names. Oldenberry is small and she'd gotten the reputation of someone who was smart and extremely good at her job. No one questioned her, especially when they noted Norm had signed off on everything. She was supposed to start siphoning off funds as they came in and making deposits into the accounts."

"What about audits?"

"Who's gonna look too closely when she's the treasurer and has the backing of the commissioner? No one. Gravy train was simple and only involved those two. Problem started when she felt sorry for sad sack Rosemary and her bastard kid and decided she wanted to *help*." He snorted. "All her life, she'd only thought about herself, now all of a sudden, she felt compassion for someone else. Go figure."

"Finkleberg said jealousy also played a part. He said Susanna wanted him to leave his wife and he refused. That's why she took off before she got all the money."

Kelly stood and nearly toppled over. "Whoops," he said. "Gotta go take a pee." He staggered off somewhere behind her. Jonelle resisted the impulse to follow. She moved his gun closer to her in case he tried reaching for it again. A few moments later he reappeared.

"You got any more coffee?" she asked, hoping he'd take the hint. "I'd like a cup if you don't mind."

He slumped down in his seat. "Naw. Tried drinking the rest of it this morning. Haven't had time for any shopping. So, yeah I agree with Norm. She wanted to show him he couldn't screw around with her without consequences."

"That's dumb." What the hell was wrong with these people? "Why leave with a few hundred thousand just because some guy wouldn't leave his wife?"

"Because that's how she was. She didn't need the money. It was the thrill of seeing if she could get away with it and then proving she was in control if you made her mad."

Kelly's eyes clouded over. "Except she didn't get away with anything. Death is a helluva way to prove a point."

"Were you involved from the beginning?"

"Not the planning. She called when Norm rejected her and said she wanted us to get back together and the money would be a good start."

"Did you believe her?"

"Of course I did. Loved her from the moment I saw her at school, right up until …" His eyes watered.

"Did you hire the Yazzie boys?"

Kelly grimaced. "That was Finkleberg's stupid idea. All of a sudden he needed protection or some such nonsense. Maybe he figured he could help Rosemary's kid if he hired the father. Hell if I know. Again, too many people knew too much." He hesitated.

Jonelle waited.

After a few moments of looking all around the cabin as if seeing it for the first time, Kelly continued.

"They were supposed to come down here, grab Susanna and the money and drag her back to Michigan. I was their contact because I knew that Susanna was staying at the Lancelot. No one expected them to go rogue and take matters into their own hands."

"How do you know they did?" Jonelle agreed that of all the players connected to this case, the two seemed the most likely perpetrators.

"Because they put the squeeze on us. Said they wanted two-thirds of what Susanna had already stolen. Two-thirds! I told them no way. I offered a five thousand dollar finder's fee—no more."

"Did you pay them?"

Kelly looked down into his empty glass. "I contacted Susanna and she refused, so Sophia agreed to take them the money late one evening. When we heard about the condition of … the body, I knew they were involved. They had to make a statement. That's why they not only cut her throat but they painted her face. Some kind of pagan BS, but we got the message, loud and clear. Finkleberg and I tried to reason with them, but they weren't having it. This time they demanded *all* of the money.

"We believed they thought they'd killed Susanna so we tried telling them we had no idea where Susanna had hidden the cash. They gave us a week to find out. When that didn't happen, they went after …." His eyes watered.

Kelly slumped forward and leaned his head on his arms. His body shook as he sobbed.

While Jonelle waited for the man to compose himself, she looked around the salon for a box of tissues. Finding none, she dug in her purse and pulled out a small packet. She placed it on the table next to him.

A few moments later, he lifted his head, wiped his eyes and nose with a tissue.

In spite of everything, she felt a heavy sadness for the man. He'd dabbled into something he didn't have the stomach for and got himself into a mess he saw no way out of. All the same, two people were dead because of what they'd done. Jonelle remembered the code found on the body.

"Why didn't she give up the money?"

"She assumed they thought she was dead and the stolen money was gone with her."

"Do you know where the money is?"

He shook his head.

"Do you think they killed the twin they thought was Sophia because she knew where it was and refused to tell them?"

Kelly looked at the almost empty whiskey bottle and grimaced. He slid the glass away from him with distaste. "When I refused to help Susanna that first time, she contacted Sophia. Once again, she added another person to this mess. What I know for certain is that neither Norm nor myself have any idea where the money is."

CHAPTER 42

The tattoo mix-up now made sense.

Kelly focused on a spot behind Jonelle's shoulder. "I tried getting her to reveal the hiding place. Even thought she'd crack when we, uh, got intimate one evening."

Jonelle was surprised at the amount of disgust she felt. "Go on. Tell me everything you know about them switching roles."

Kelly gulped more liquor. A loud burp, followed by a sigh escaped his lips. "When Sophia came here to help, Susanna's idea was to go to a local bank and open an account for the three hundred thousand. By this time she knew the area 'cause she'd been going back and forth between the hotel and that bum she was staying with sometimes. She dressed up in Sophia's expensive clothes for obvious reasons and planned on using my address.

"Sophia agreed to pretend she was Susanna so her little … friend wouldn't worry and go looking for her. Susanna thought she'd go to different banks. Spread the money around. The code to where the money was hidden was pinned to Sophia's clothes for safe keeping so that Susanna could start applying for bank access and Sophia could retrieve the cash the next day. She never got the chance."

"Is the money hidden somewhere close to the warehouse?"

"Yes."

"And she didn't tell you where? Not even after what happened to her sister?" Jonelle sat staring open-mouthed at Kelly.

"She said she'd get it herself when she felt it was safe."

"And you're telling me that the first person killed was actually Sophia? Damn. And the woman who hired me was Susanna? Why?" Jonelle's head was spinning.

"Because everyone thought she was dead. Susanna figured she would use you to go and retrieve the money."

Jonelle didn't like being played. "So, why didn't she just tell me where the damn money was? Why go through this … this sick game?"

"How could she explain what she knew at this point? She was the bereaved sister, not someone who was a part of an elaborate scheme. Besides, Sophia's death freaked her out since she knew it was supposed to be her. Seems the bum spoke highly of you and your, uh, skills. She said she'd wait a while and if you couldn't figure it out, she'd throw a few hints."

Several supposedly smart people decided to play games with the devil and two ended up dead. "Why didn't Sophia … I mean Susanna … tell the brothers where the money was and end this dangerous, and deadly, game?"

"I don't know. I paid all their bills down here, you'd think they'd be happy and leave."

Jonelle gasped at the utter stupidity of that statement.

Kelly continued as though he hadn't noticed. "She probably got greedy and thought she could talk her way out of this mess." He reached for the bottle. Jonelle slid it from his grasp.

"Oh no. You've had enough. You're coming with me to the police station. This has to stop now." Kelly believed that the money was somewhere in or around the warehouse. Jonelle felt certain that if Luther had found it, he'd tell her. Or would he?

"I gotta get out of here," Kelly said. "They won't hesitate to kill me if they find out where I'm staying."

"If you're so damn worried about that, why the hell didn't you sail on out of here?" His woe is me attitude grated on her nerves.

"Because I don't have enough money for gas, that's why." His hoarse laughter turned into hiccups.

A noise from outside prevented her from shouting at the man. She walked up on deck to check out the commotion. At the opposite end of the dock two men were struggling with the security guard she'd met earlier.

CHAPTER 43

Jonelle rushed to the salon. "Is there another way out of this place?"

Kelly seemed not to have noticed all the noise going on outside. "Told you I don't have money for gas."

An angry Jonelle grabbed his shoulder. "I'm not suggesting we sail to the Bahamas, I want to know if you have enough to at least get us to the middle of the basin." After that, she had no clue as to what she'd do next.

He looked up. "Why?"

"Because all hell is about to break loose if you don't. The Yazzie's are outside and I don't think they came for coffee."

The mention of the name "Yazzie" sobered Kelly as if he'd consumed a dozen cups of coffee and the effects had kicked in. "Where? Where?"

Jonelle grabbed the front of his shirt. "We don't have time to chat. You need to move this thing now. That's the only chance we have to come out of this alive until the cops get here." She didn't mention her weapon. While she was an expert marksman, the only time she had to shoot someone the experience made her physically ill. And she wasn't looking forward to reliving the feeling all over again.

At the same time Kelly's hand touched the door to the salon, they heard a loud *crack!* Instead of running to the back bedroom to hide, the noise propelled him to the front. He tripped up the two stairs before he settled behind the wheel.

Jonelle saw his hand shake as he turned the ignition. Nothing happened.

"Hurry up." She yanked the pistol from her bag. One of the brothers ran down the pier and bumped into one of Kelly's neighbors who had left his berth. Both struggled for a while until Yazzie threw the person to the ground.

Another turn of the key and this time the engine caught.

"Untie the bow and stern lines from the cleats," Kelly shouted. However impaired he was from his alcohol consumption earlier, he appeared in control. His eyes focused and both hands gripped the wheel.

Jonelle instinctively unwound the ropes.

"Hurry so I can get this damn thing outta here."

Jonelle moved as fast as she could. Once the last rope was removed from the cleat she hopped back on board and breathed a sigh of relief as Kelly expertly steered the craft away from the dock.

Another loud *crack!* Followed by the sound of splintered wood as the bullet hit the cabin.

"Is he shooting at us?" Kelly asked, panic rising in his voice.

"Just drive—"

"You don't drive, you—"

"I don't give a damn what it's called." Was he arguing with her? "Drive, steer, aim, who gives a damn. *Move* this thing as far as you can, as fast as you can." Jonelle lifted her weapon, aimed at a spot over the shooting man's head and fired. She smiled as he ducked and ran back, two slips farther away. Emboldened, she fired again, this time aiming for a spot to the outside of his left foot. Bits of concrete dust rose as she hit the pier. "Bulls-eye." The Yazzie boy ran back down to where the other one was rushing to meet him. He stared and pointed. Apparently they didn't count on the black lady being armed and such a good shot.

Once again Jonelle hadn't noticed she'd been followed. I should've paid more attention, she thought, as she realized the brothers had tailed her without her noticing. That was the only way she could think of as to how they found Kelly.

The loud report of gunfire brought more attention to the pier. Several heads popped up and almost as quickly ducked down again. She fired several shots above her head in rapid sucession.

"What're you doing?" Kelly asked, his voice rising in alarm.

Adrienne's words came to Jonelle in a flash. "I want your neighbors to know this isn't a case of fireworks or backfiring of some sort, so I'm calling for the cavalry," she said, a slight smile playing on her lips.

CHAPTER 44

Impressed the men had not turned and hightailed it out of there while gunshots rang in the air, Jonelle inhaled sharply as they jumped into a small yellow dinghy tied to the dock. She kept her gun at the ready. Come on, she thought. Where the hell were the cops when you needed them?

The strain of a motor that wouldn't catch eased Jonelle's concern somewhat. After several attempts the small engine finally caught.

"Damn." Jonelle peered over at Kelly who had the determined look of a man whose life was about to dramatically change. While she had no doubt he could pilot his boat, she wasn't sure about his shooting skills nor too thrilled about having to find out. Kelly aimed his launch across the channel toward a strip of land surrounded by trees. In front of the trees was a white fence of some kind.

"What's that over there," she asked, pointing across the water.

"East Potomac Park," he said. "We can make it that far, but that's about all."

Kelly guided his launch as far away from the marina as he could and still keep what was going on at the pier in sight. A few seconds later, the sound of a small engine sputtered and died out.

Was it possible they caught a break? Several coughs of the dinghy filled Jonelle with hope.

"The Carmichaels kept meaning to get the motor fixed. Thank God they never got 'round to it," Kelly said.

Jonelle had no intention of getting stranded in the middle of a body of water that she knew she couldn't swim. She placed another 911 call and was told help was on the way.

If the situation wasn't so serious it would be comical as the Yazzie boys bobbed along in a bright yellow rubber dinghy. They gestured wildly as one of the two fought with the motor. As long as they kept their distance, Jonelle believed they could ride the danger out until help arrived.

About the same time those thoughts occurred to her, the roar of the motor revved and the dinghy moved.

"Can you get close enough to the shore so we can jump off and make a run for it?"

Kelly stared at Jonelle open-mouthed.

"Are you kidding? I could damage this thing. I can't afford to fix it or buy another one," he said. "Besides, I don't know if I can jump that far and not end up in the water. And frankly," he added, looking her up and down, "if I can't make it, I'm pretty sure you can't either."

Jonelle ignored the comment. The dinghy wasn't making good progress toward them. "Wonder what's going on?"

Kelly grunted. "I'm surprised they got it started."

"Surprised or not, they haven't given up," Jonelle said, as the image in the distance grew.

Next to her, Kelly grumbled something indistinguishable.

"What did you say?"

"I said, this thing's almost on empty."

The dinghy got closer.

So did the bank on the other side. Jonelle's heart sank when she saw what Kelly meant about not being able to get near enough to shore so that they could safely leave the boat.

More shots rang out from the brothers. One shot whizzed to the left of the bow. Too close. What would happen if a shot pierced the engine?

Only one thing for her to do. "That dinghy's made of rubber, right?" she asked.

"Yes. But if you're thinking of doing what I think you are, I'm telling you now, I don't want to pay for—"

Another shot rang out that zipped past Kelly's head. "Shit! Never mind. Shoot that thing out of the water. Go on. Do it."

Jonelle crouched next to *Oh Susanna*'s railing, took aim and fired three shots in rapid succession.

"Bulls-eye," she said with satisfaction. The small craft's forward movement abruptly ceased.

As soon as the word left her mouth, she heard the faint pulsating sound of sirens in the distance.

Kelly heard them too. "About damn time."

"How many ways can the cops get in and out of this place?" she asked.

"From the road?"

She nodded.

"Just the one. The same way you got in."

"Good." She stole a glance at Kelly, his hands still glued on the steering wheel, piloting the boat toward the park. "Um, I think you can stop now and save gas. I don't wanna get stranded out here. Unless it takes more gas to restart the engine."

"Right." He looked at the gauge. "I think we've got enough to get back."

The indecision in his voice unnerved her. She glanced around and noticed two orange life vests. Never comfortable with her rudimentary swimming skills, she contemplated putting one on, just in case.

"What're those guys doing to that dinghy?" Kelly asked.

The sound of sirens grew louder.

Jonelle frowned. "They've turned around. Looks like they're trying to make it back to the dock. Guess the fact that they've got a leak is making them nervous. Yep. That's what they're doing."

Several cops had arrived and were running down the pier.

"They've made it back to the pier and are heading right into the cop's hands. Oh wait, now I see them jumping on a boat. Uh-oh. Oh damn." She turned toward Kelly. "Do you happen to know if the occupants of the boat next to yours are on board?"

He nodded. "That's the *Two Old Fogies.* They were aboard earlier when I fixed a cup of coffee. Not sure if they're still on board though. I've been too preoccupied trying to figure out how I made such a mess out of my life."

She hoped no one was there watching in alarm as the brothers disappeared inside.

Jonelle's phone rang. A quick glance at the screen announced that Burt was on the other line.

His deep voice sounded before she said hello. "Where the hell're you?"

Jonelle explained the situation as fast as she could and was relieved the detective didn't interrupt. She advised Burt she'd seen the men go on board the *Two Old Fogies* and had no idea whether or not it was occupied. His worry that they might have a hostage situation on their hands mirrored hers.

"It's possible the boat's vacant since there was a lot of, um, noise earlier and I didn't see anyone come out to investigate."

The *Oh Susanna* floated with the current toward the opposite end of the marina. To Jonelle's great relief no other launch followed. At least not for now.

Kelly piped up. "Could be they were too scared to come out. People don't shoot off guns around here." He glanced sideways at Jonelle, who resisted the impulse to point out a pot calling the kettle black moment.

Jonelle managed to convince Burt that she and Kelly were fine and swore she heard him smile though the phone when she explained they were sitting in the middle of the Washington Channel and were in danger of running out of fuel.

Not wanting to surprise Burt any more than she had already, Jonelle advised him she was armed and had fired several warning shots at the brothers. "Please tell me you returned fire and didn't initiate the gunplay."

Jonelle held her anger in check. "Listen, Burt," she said, her voice tight. "I know better than to shoot unless I have to, knowing there are innocent citizens about. So, yes, I was trying to keep myself and Kelly out of harm's way until the cops showed up. Why else," she added, her voice rising, "would I be sitting on a boat with very little fuel floating who knows where. And stop telling me to calm down." She clicked off.

"Do you think that was wise?" Kelly asked. He crossed his arms tight around his chest.

"Keep your hands on the wheel," Jonelle said, pointing.

"It'll drift without me steering."

Rapid movement on the dock announced the arrival of more law enforcement. Yet, no one moved toward the craft the Yazzie's boarded. Puzzled, Jonelle asked Kelly if he had any binoculars.

"No," he said. "What's going on?"

Jonelle fingered her necklace. Something was off.

Kelly studied Jonelle's face. He turned toward the marina and followed her gaze.

"I don't like that it's quiet. Why aren't the Yazzie boys doing anything? They lived surrounded by water, so I assume they know about boats. How come they're just sitting there? I don't like it."

CHAPTER 45

Several minutes went by with no movement on the dock, nor on or around the *Two Old Fogies*. Jonelle was getting antsy at the lack of action, and Kelly's constant, "What's going on?" every couple minutes didn't help either. There wasn't enough room to pace without bumping into Kelly so she worked the necklace back and forth through her fingers. Although she hadn't checked with Burt since she hung up on him, she believed the police were in contact with the brothers.

"Think maybe you should call your friend the detective and see what's going on?" Kelly asked as if he read her mind.

"DC isn't his jurisdiction. I'm guessing he's got to coordinate with the local police." She glanced at Kelly. "I'm thinking the Coast Guard too. Who handles crime in these places?" Jonelle wasn't embarrassed to admit she had no idea.

Kelly shrugged. "We don't have crime here. Those security guys are pretty effective. Besides, most lowlifes don't have a clue on how to handle themselves around all this water."

Not knowing what was going on was driving her nuts. Jonelle pressed Burt's contact button and the call went right to voice mail. Not sure whether that was a good or bad sign, Jonelle merely told Kelly, "His line's engaged."

"So what do we do?"

"We … hold on." Jonelle squinted. Sure enough, two dark clad figures emerged from inside with guns pointed … and with a body held in front as a shield.

"Uh-Oh," Kelly said. "Jack Carmichael's got a bad heart."

One Yazzie stood behind the other with the hostage. While Jonelle couldn't hear anything, the police pulled back farther down the pier, their weapons still drawn. The three stumbled back inside.

"Damn. Looks like they're trying to escape."

She pointed back to the saloon. "That gun you had back there. Are you a good enough shot to back me up if needed?"

Kelly blanched. "I, uh, don't know. I just bought the thing a week ago. All I really know how to do is load it. I've never fired it before."

Great, just great. "I hope you're a quick learner. You have to do exactly as I say, when I say it. Understand?"

Kelly nodded.

The motor on the *Two Old Fogies* kicked to life. She turned away from Kelly and watched in horror as the boat left the pier aimed toward Kelly's vessel. Coast Guard or no, Jonelle couldn't sit still and wait to be rescued.

The cruiser closed the distance.

Jonelle found two coolers and piled them one on top of the other on the starboard side to provide more cover. While it helped it wasn't enough. "You got anything else I can use for cover?"

Kelly left and returned with two thick seat cushions. Jonelle placed those on top of the coolers. "I suggest you get below, Doctor."

"What're you doing?"

"Trying to save both our butts." Jonelle crouched, opened a small space between the barriers and waited.

"Hold on a sec," Kelly said behind her.

Inside the saloon items scraped across the floor and something smashed to the ground.

"Here, use this." Jonelle risked a quick glance. Kelly had a deck chair in his hands. "If you sit down, it'll be less stress on your knees."

"Thanks." Jonelle took up her position and waited. The *Two Old Fogies* slowed; the motor cut off.

"What the hell're they doing now?" she muttered.

Kelly followed her gaze. "Ah, now I get it." Kelly smiled.

"What's so funny?" Jonelle peered at Kelly who'd kneeled down beside her.

"Why'd they stop?"

"They've realized, probably from Jack, that they don't have easy access to open waters."

"Is that right?" All Jonelle could see between the two land areas was nothing but water.

"This basin narrows as it enters the Potomac River, then you've gotta go into the Chesapeake Bay."

"So, that means they're sitting ducks. Not to mention that they'll probably face kidnapping charges on top of everything else. That gets the Feds involved." Jonelle raised her weapon.

"What're you going to do?"

"If they decide to risk it I'll remind the boys that I'm not playing. I suggest you take cover."

Silence.

The *Oh Susanna* floated between the marina and park. She knew that if the Yazzie's aimed the Carmichael's craft toward the strip of land the most direct way, they'd pass by her. Would they abandon ship? Jonelle thought not. On the other hand, if they headed back toward the marina, cops waited on the dock.

And more cops approaching from the east as indicated by the appearance of two red-hulled response boats heading fast in their direction, the words *Coast Guard* printed in white. Mounted on the bow and stern of each vessel, two automatic weapons sat at the ready, their operators clad in red vests.

Someone used a bullhorn.

"This is the United States Coast Guard. Lay down your weapons and raise your hands above your head."

CHAPTER 46

The Yazzie brothers released their hostage and placed their hands above their heads. The Coast Guard boarded the *Two Old Fogies* and took control. For all the horror the two men had perpetuated in the past several days, their surrender seemed anti-climactic.

Jonelle sat in the Coast Guard office as the investigators tried to sort everything out. At every step of the way she complied to their requests for information without question and felt heartened when Kelly did the same. Right now, the authorities had to figure out the mess of the kidnapping and stolen property. She quickly explained the reason she fired her weapon was in self-defense not only for herself but also for protecting Kelly. To add credence to her story, Kelly's boat contained several bullet holes from the Yazzie weapons.

Although most of the agents ignored her after she'd given her formal statement, Jonelle overheard several snippets of conversation. The DC police and several federal agents were studying the floating crime scene and Burt and the law enforcement contingent from Maryland had arrived and were relaying information about the twins' murders. Kelly had sobered up and gave the shorthand version of why he thought the brothers were after him. The brothers were charged by the Coast Guard and the DC police and released to the Maryland homicide division to face the more serious multiple murder charges.

Kelly was arrested for withholding information in a murder investigation. Jonelle almost felt sorry for him when, hands cuffed behind his back, his eyes pleaded with her as he was taken away. In spite of everything, if he didn't have a criminal lawyer, she'd recommend a few.

For her part, Jonelle was admonished for acting without waiting for law enforcement and released into Burt's custody which pissed her off. At least Burt assured her he'd fight against her being charged with any crime.

"Thanks, I owe you one," she grudgingly said.

"Your IOU's are adding up," he replied, as they were escorted back to the marina after the interrogation. The sun sat low on the horizon and in the dim light she glanced at the empty slip where the *Oh Susanna* had been moored. Towed away as evidence, Jonelle felt Kelly wouldn't be too heartbroken if he never saw the craft again.

"Yeah, I know. That's why I'm grateful. Really."

Burt thanked the Coast Guard for the lift back to the marina.

Jonelle and Burt walked along the dock in silence. A few boats had lights inside where the live-a-boards were settling in for the night after that day's excitement. She wondered what kind of person would choose to live where there was always movement under your feet. She shuddered.

"Cold?" Burt asked.

Jonelle shook her head. She turned and grinned at him. "If you think for one minute I'm going to let you take your coat off and put it over my delicate shoulders, you've got another think coming." She winked at him to show she was just kidding.

He laughed. "Right. Forgot who I was dealing with for a minute.

Except for a few police cruisers and Burt's unmarked, there weren't many cars in the visitor's lot at that time of night.

Jonelle's Jeep sat all by itself under a sodium light. She strolled over and stood next to her vehicle. She turned to Burt before she let herself into the driver's seat. "My stupid mistake. I should've assumed that once I caught them following me the first time, they wouldn't let up. I didn't pay any attention when I came here. I was so focused on confronting Kelly, I let my guard down. Dumb. Just dumb."

Burt placed his hand on Jonelle's arm. It felt warm and dry on her cool skin. "Don't beat yourself up about it. Kelly's alive because of you. Don't forget that."

In more ways than one, she thought, remembering the pistol lying in the middle of the table and how drunk and depressed he was.

"After all that went on today, Kelly still doesn't know where Susanna hid the money. Maybe we'll never find it."

Burt stretched his arms above his head, cracking a few bones in the process. "I find it hard to believe that someone who wasn't all that familiar with the area around here could hide money so well it couldn't be found. It's got to be somewhere so obvious we can't see it."

Jonelle removed her cellphone and pulled up the information on the note. She squinted at it for a few moments. "What if . . ."

"What?"

"She had to hide the money fast, right?"

Burt nodded.

"You told me the cops thoroughly searched the hotel, plus she didn't have time to open a bank account and I went through the hiding places at the warehouse with Luther. But." Jonelle stopped.

"But what?"

In the waning light, she smiled at Burt. "I searched all through the warehouse. What if the money is somewhere on the *outside*?"

Burt shook his head. "I'm not following you."

"Yes, you are," she said, unlocking her Jeep. "You're following me to the warehouse."

"Now?"

"Let's go before someone else figures out what I just did."

Jonelle's Jeep and Burt's unmarked sedan pulled up in front of Luther's warehouse—that's how she thought of it these days. A few of the homeless, on their way through the gap in the fence, stopped and stared when they saw Burt.

"Don't worry," Jonelle called out. "He's not here to bother you."

Burt grunted his objection but stayed quiet.

Jonelle dug in her bag for her cellphone again. "You got your flashlight?"

"Yeah."

"Okay. Check out the codes. Now look around and tell me what you see."

"I'm tired and it's getting too late to play games."

"Humor me. Do as I say. Please."

Burt walked closer to the warehouse and shined his light around the outside. "I see a helluva lot of trash—mostly bottles, cardboard boxes, metal barrels, five rusted out old cars, stacks of old tires and some rickety old grocery carts." He faced Jonelle. "That what you wanted to hear, Sherlock?"

Jonelle ignored the comment and studied the note that held the code found on the first twin's body. "There are four letters here. *WH* printed together, then a *V* and an *M*." She could barely contain her excitement. She picked her way over to the third of five rusted out old vehicles, and pointed to an ancient van. "Look at this. *WH* could mean white, and *V* might stand for Volkswagen. And check this out." She motioned for him to shine his light on the rusted license plate. "*M* probably stands for Maryland, 'cause the only other white car with a plate has DC tags. The numbers are the actual plate numbers. See?"

"I'll be damn," Burt said, his voice tinged with awe.

Jonelle moved to look inside.

"Don't! I'm calling forensics out here."

She motioned for him to shine the light on what was left of the interior. "What's the harm in looking? Might save them some time."

Burt hesitated.

Jonelle turned and glared at him. "Oh for goodness sakes! Hand that thing to me will you? I'm not gonna spoil your scene. Look at all this damn rust. No way I'm going to tear through here and risk getting a cut. Can't remember when I had my last tetanus shot."

Burt handed over his police-issue flashlight. "If I catch any flak for this I'm gonna say you overpowered me and took matters into your own hands."

"Whatever. How big was that satchel?"

Burt told her.

"Well then it's safe to say it's gotta be in a place at least that size. My guess is it's probably under one of these seats." Jonelle lifted her leg as if to go inside.

"Absolutely not," Burt said, grabbing her arm and pulling Jonelle back.

She jerked away. "I'm not going to touch it, I just wanna see if it's here. Won't you feel a right fool if you call them all the way out here and they find nothing?"

"I'm willing to take that risk."

Jonelle sensed Burt's patience with her was wearing thin. She noticed a metal pole on the ground, grabbed it, hurried over to the van and began poking under the two remaining bench seats. Nothing. The other seats had long since disappeared. Was this too obvious for someone as devious as Susanna?

A quick look at where the engine resided revealed nothing but a few loose wires.

Burt spoke into his cellphone and gave the warehouse location.

Frustrated, Jonelle prodded all over the vehicle. She knew in her gut that was what the codes represented. Where the hell was the money?

Jonelle leaned against the passenger side door panel. Though cockeyed and resting on one hinge the structure felt secure under her weight. She tapped the side over and over in frustration. Deep in thought she tried to place herself in Susanna's shoes as she continued tapping. And stopped. She tapped again and this time Burt heard it too.

"Sounds different right there," he said, pointing to the lower quadrant. The excitement in his voice matched her feelings. Before he could say anything else, Jonelle cautiously probed with her fingers around the edge and felt a narrow opening. She forced the tips of her fingers inside and pulled. Instead of meeting with resistence, the outside panel gave way a little. She aimed the light into the crack and smiled.

CHAPTER 47

Jonelle paced the area while the crime scene techs set up their lights and removed the brown satchel. Except for several bite marks where rats had tried to make their way inside, the contents were deemed intact. Inside the bag, money and another note with a similar code lay taped against an inside flap. Using the same logic as before unearthed more money hidden in the wheel well of an old green Pontiac and encased in a black plastic bag. This time however, several tears in the bag disclosed some of the bills were shredded. No other notes were found.

"Check the rest of the vehicles in case she split up more cash without leaving a code," Burt instructed the techs. "We need to make sure in case a good bit of the money was used to make more rat's nests."

"Why on earth did she wrap the money in plastic? She had to know rodents would chew through the package."

"She probably figured she'd get to it all before that happened," Burt said.

"I guess." Jonelle glanced over at the warehouse and caught Luther standing there, arms crossed tightly in front of his chest. This was the second time she'd brought the police to his home and she couldn't blame him for being angry with her.

"Look, Burt," Jonelle said. "I hope you're not planning to bring Luther down to the station again. If he'd known where the money was, he would've taken it by now."

"Agreed. But I might need to ask him more questions."

Jonelle touched Burt's arm and stared into his eyes. "The person who stayed here initially for all those months was Susanna. It was only in the few days leading up to the first murder that the sisters changed identities to allow Susanna to try and stash the money someplace safe. He told me she sometimes hung around after everyone else had left. I'm betting that on those occasions, she hid the money. Sophia had the codes of the first hiding place pinned to her dress so she could retrieve the money when Susanna was ready."

"We'll leave him alone. For now anyway."

"I'm going over there to talk to him."

Luther stood in front of his ragtag group of followers like a general ready to lead the charge against the enemy. She hoped he didn't consider her a threat, and that he understood that she truly did care for him.

"Hi, Luther," she said, stopping a few feet in front of him. Somewhere in the distance she heard the word, *traitor*, and a few other comments attesting to what those assembled thought about her and her latest intrusion on their patch.

"I wish I'd never know'd you," he spat out.

Somewhat taken aback by the force of his words, Jonelle swallowed her disappointment and plunged ahead with what she wanted to say.

"I don't blame you for being mad as hell at what's going on here." She swept her arm around all the activity and lights.

"Burt, the lead detective over there, has all the information he needs about what happened to the twins and the money. He's promised not to bother you anymore unless it's absolutely necessary."

Jonelle inhaled. "As it happens, Sophia was murdered in the same fashion as, uh, Susanna." No need to go into any details about the identity switching at this point. Still, sometime in the future, when he wasn't as angry with her as he was now, the man had a right to know everything that went on almost on his doorstep. He had a relationship with Susanna, and also for a brief moment, whether he knew it or not, with Sophia.

"I know I'm not your favorite person at the moment."

Several more rude noises greeted that comment.

"I get that," Jonelle said. "But before you completely dismiss me out of your life, I want to tell you everything I know about Susanna's last moments."

A slight softening of his posture was the only sign Jonelle received that indicated Luther was listening to her. "How about this. Meet me at the Inner Harbor sometime tomorrow, say around lunch time. My treat. How about it?"

Luther sniffed. "I got things to do t'morrow."

Jonelle waited a few beats. "I'll be there, around one o'clock in front of the Disney store, whatever you decide." With that she turned and walked back to where Burt stood at a distance, watching.

"I really don't understand your connection to him," Burt said as she stood by his side.

"It's complicated."

In spite of Burt's insistence that he reward her by taking her out for a meal, she begged off, insisting she was too tired. Even though she heard the disappointment in his voice, she was too exhausted to care. As they strolled side by side back to their respective vehicles, Burt kicked a cardboard box out of his way. And something inside made a noise.

Jonelle stopped and cocked her head. "What's that?"

"Rats, probably. Let's get outta here. Those suckers seem to grow larger in the dark."

The noise sounded again. "No. Doesn't sound like a rat."

Taking advantage of the still lit area, Jonelle approached the box and looked inside. A small calico kitten stared back up at her. "Poor thing," Jonelle said.

"Leave it. Its mama is probably around here somewhere. She'll be back for it."

"I guess." Jonelle walked on a few steps. The kitten cried again.

"I can't. I can't leave it here." She went back and stared into the dilapidated box. "There's been too much death lately for my taste and this kitten's chances of surviving out here alone are slim to none."

Before she slipped her hand around the tiny body, she said, "Listen, cat. I don't want to leave you here so I'm giving you a short test. I'm gonna pick you up and if you scratch me, you're facing life out here on your own. Got it?"

"Are you talking to a cat?" Burt asked, his voice full of humor.

Jonelle ignored him, reached inside and picked up the kitten. Instead of scratching her hand, the tiny ball of fur started purring. "Okay," she said, stroking the small body. "You passed this first test."

Burt laughed. "I never figured you for a cat lady."

Jonelle rolled her eyes at him and walked the rest of the way to her car, kitten snug against her chest. "The least I can do is take her to a shelter tomorrow."

"You want I should give a quick look around, see if there are any more. A bona fide cat lady can't have just one, you know."

"Oh shut up." Jonelle grabbed a cardigan from the Jeep's back seat, molded it into a nest and settled the kitten on the passenger seat. She blocked off the side next to the door with her tote bag.

She waved goodbye to Burt, who walked off, shaking his head.

Jonelle looked down at her furry companion, curled into a tight ball. "Life sucks sometimes, did you know that kitty?

Awful what human beings do to one another." She touched the tiny body again.

On the way to her condo she stopped at the pet store for supplies, taking the store clerk's advice to purchase a few cans of kitty formula and a small dropper in case the kitten didn't know how to lap up the mixture. Returning to her car, there was a momentary sense of panic when she didn't see it, followed by immense relief when she found the small body burrowed under the sweater. Surprised at the magnitude of her feelings when she thought she'd lost it, Jonelle used her cell phone to call the vet's office to get the times they'd be open and headed home.

Poor thing's going to need a checkup.

Acknowledgments

To Editor Amy Harke-Moore, thank you for helping me shape the story. A special thank you goes to all my fellow Dream-weaversINK writers. Your invaluable critiques kept the story headed in the right direction.

About The Author

R. Lanier Clemons is an award winning author and active member of Sisters In Crime, International Thriller Writers and the Maryland Writer's Association. She lives in Maryland with her cat, Lucy and buckskin Connemara/Thoroughbred cross Glendale's Ramsey.

Made in the USA
Middletown, DE
24 January 2017